Prologue

Just outside the entrance to the Block Island Academy, a very old and large oak tree stands in the middle of an open field. The tree has a gnarled gray trunk that supports several tremendous limbs holding up a canopy of branches. The tree also sprouts two massive limbs that curl down from on high in parallel arches that touch the ground as if the oak were kneeling in prayer.

The Block Island Oak is thought to be more than five hundred years old. It is renowned as one of the oldest trees in all of New England. Tourists visiting Block Island often make the trip up to the school for a quick view of it. Arborists on occasion come to study the tree and to marvel at its age. For the residents of the island, however, and for the students and faculty of the BIA, the tree holds a more hallowed position. It is like a member of their community, part of the island's uniqueness, part of what makes it special. The locals look upon their ancient tree as one might look upon a wise village elder who has seen much of the passing world. Their tree has stood tall and steady for them for as long as anyone can remember. Stories abound of childhood games amidst its limbs, of love-struck entreaties beneath its canopy, and of sleepy summer afternoons beneath its massive trunk. Such stories have been passed on from father to son, from mother to daughter, throughout the generations of island residents. For them, the tree is a permanent link to their past, and an enduring bridge to their future.

They say that when Ramses II ascended to the position of Pharaoh of Egypt, the Great Pyramids of Giza were already a thousand years old. Such permanence, unknown to modern society, alters how men think of their place in the world. Egyptians of that time, in viewing the pyramids, must have felt a strong sense of continuity with their ancestors. So too do the residents of Block Island view their ancient oak, for it inspires in them an uncommon sense that time, for all the ticking of the clock, does not pass away.

Chapter 1

Block Island – One Year Ago

The boy's disappearance could not be explained. That was Prester's problem, or soon would be. Nothing quite like it had ever happened on Block Island before.

Oh, there had been the occasional disappearance over the years: the 1973 drowning off Sandy Point, the 1998 kayaking accident near Old Harbor. But those bodies had washed ashore within a few days, and those summer disappearances concerned themselves with the ocean, the tides, and the undercurrent. They were the natural price of living on an island, the compensation exacted by the cresting waves that separated this place from the world. Those losses, while sad, had been understandable and acceptable the way death is when it comes logically, legitimately, in a manner to be expected. The boy's disappearance, however, would neither be understandable nor acceptable to the eight hundred or so permanent and hardy winter residents of the island. The boy would quite simply vanish.

The day of the disappearance, December 21st, began as December days often do on the island. Prester Charles John, lifelong resident of the island and Assistant Principal of the prestigious Block Island Academy High School, had seen many such days. A gentle, windless snow had thrown a thick white blanket across the island during the night. As dawn approached, however, the tall capping grasses of the sand dunes began to sway in a freshening breeze.

At precisely eight o'clock that morning, as was his habit, Prester John stepped from his immaculate home on Water Street. He pulled tight the brass doorknob on his front door to close, but not lock, the house. He checked his watch against the distant tolling of the Chapel Street Church bell. He then started up the High Street hill for the quarter mile walk to the BIA campus. These were the facts to which he would testify at the inquest.

Tall and athletic, Prester dressed in a white and blue button-down Oxford shirt, solid yellow silk tie, and gray tweed jacket with gray wool pants. Against the weather, he wore a heavy black overcoat with matching hat, gloves and galoshes.

The wind was approaching gale force by the time he reached the level terrain of the campus grounds. Ferry service would no doubt shut down with this bluster, he thought, delaying the holiday departures of his students. Leaning in against the tempest, he pressed on like a slow-motion running back across a snow-covered gridiron. With one hand he held tight to the brim of his hat to prevent it from taking flight. With the other, he clutched a brown leather valise. In the valise were the precious boxed heirlooms that he would use for class that day.

Prester vaulted up the three steps onto the portico of BIA's main administrative building. Shaking the snow from his galoshes, he entered through double doors directly beneath the stone tablet engraved with the school motto. The words were in Latin, *"Debemus Invicem Adiuvent"* – We must help one another. Upon entering, he was immediately confronted by two uniformed police officers in the company of the Principal of the Academy, Aldus Beem.

"He's done it again," Beem said.

"Good morning, officers," Prester said. "Aldus, what's going on?"

Beem was a rotund man of short stature and timid disposition whose countenance constantly brought to mind lemons. "You need to speak with him, Prester," the Principal said.

"Who?" Prester asked, though he was all but certain of the answer.

"Kirk Renzo, of course."

"What did he do?" Prester asked.

"What else?" Beem said, and then stepped back in deference to one of the officers.

"Sir, the boy was picked up last night for disorderly conduct," the officer said.

"Fighting again?" Prester asked.

"Yes, sir, over that same girl apparently."

"Annie Sage," Beem said.

"Was anyone hurt?" Prester asked.

"No, sir," the policeman said. "He was lucky. He's too small to be getting into fights every weekend. He could have gotten his nose broken again, or worse."

"This is the second weekend in a row for Mr. Renzo," Beem said. "You need to talk to him again."

"We've told Principal Beem that if this keeps happening we'll have to press formal charges."

"I understand. Where is he?"

"In my office," Beem answered. "I didn't know where else to put him. Where should I have put him?"

"That's fine," Prester said. "I'll go speak with him." With that, Prester set out toward the Principal's office at the far end of the hall. Beem trailed along behind.

The role of school disciplinarian had fallen by default to Prester John as Assistant Principal. It was generally acknowledged by the BIA administrative board that Prester had the superior bedside manner, and Principal Beem did not dispute the point. If nothing else, Beem understood the need for delicacy in dealing with the privileged children of the wealthy elite.

As Prester started into the Principal's office, two sophomore girls were trading gossip just outside the office door.

"Good morning ladies," Prester said.

"Hello, Mr. John," they responded in unison, smiling brightly. Both girls would later testify at the inquest. One would claim to have observed Prester holding a blood soaked rag.

Entering the room, Prester released the self-closing door as he set his valise on a table. He had forgotten that the door was in need of adjustment, and it slammed shut behind him. Prester's shoulders flinched at the noise. His eyes closed, and he felt momentarily dizzy.

Shaking his head, he looked around the room at the banal collection of duck hunting paintings adorning the walls. Then he saw Kirk Renzo sitting on the floor in the corner of the room. At 16 years old, Kirk was slim to the point of being skinny. He was also three or four inches shorter than most of his classmates. His eyes, however, blazed with passion, and he wore his desperation like a birthmark across his face.

"It would appear we're back where we started," Prester said, and then suddenly had the feeling that he had done all this before.

"Guess so," Kirk muttered as he stood up.

"Are you all right?" Prester asked with genuine concern.

Kirk touched his hands to his face, nose and lips.

"I'm still all in one piece, I guess," he said.

Just then, Principal Beem poked his head into the office.

"One more thing," he said. "Perhaps we ought not bother the senior Mr. Renzo with this unless it is absolutely necessary. Understood?" Prester and Kirk just stared at him. "Good, good. Then I'll leave you two alone. Um, try not to let the door slam when you leave, will you? I'm getting it fixed next week. Oh, and be careful of the Queen Anne." With that, he slipped back out of the room, easing the door closed as he went.

"Like nothin' ever happened," Kirk pointed out.

"He never changes, does he," Prester agreed.

"Good old Balanced Beem," Kirk said.

"So, what did happen?"

"I don't know," Kirk said. "But we're here now."

"So we are. I think maybe you and I should sit and talk about this before we do anything else."

"Let me get my feet on the ground first," Kirk responded, now deep into his own thoughts as to what he would tell his father. He lowered himself down onto the armrest of a chair. Suddenly, the chair cracked and collapsed from under him, throwing him against the edge of the coffee table.

"Aaah!" Kirk yelped.

"Ouch!" Prester said. "Are you all right?"

"Yeah, yeah," Kirk said as his nose began to bleed. Prester handed Kirk a handkerchief.

"Unbelievable," Prester said, suppressing a laugh. "After everything that's happened, to be done in by a Queen Anne chair." Prester pushed a second handkerchief into Kirk's hand, taking back blood soaked one.

Suddenly, a teenage girl pushed open the door to the Principal's office.

"Oh, I'm sorry," she said. "I was told that Principal Beem wanted to see me."

"He's not here just now," Prester said.

"Oh, okay." Her eyes focused on the bloody handkerchief in Prester's hand. "Well, bye," she said, ducking back out and closing the door behind her. A moment later, a mechanical bell sounded announcing the impending commencement of the first period. Prester looked at his troubled student.

"I guess I'd better get to class," Kirk said, rising again to his feet.

"Class, of course. But we should discuss what happened."

"Sure thing, Mr. J," Kirk said. "We'll discuss it later. But right now, I'm kinda anxious to get back, believe it or not."

"I don't know what to believe," Prester said. "Go. I'll see you in class."

Kirk wiped his nose with his forearm, nodded his agreement, and strode from the room.

After Kirk was gone, Prester thought a moment. He then looked at his valise. Crossing to it, he opened it and removed a mahogany box that he gingerly laid upon the table. Carved in high relief on the top of the wooden box was a man in a flowing robe wielding a sword while another man lay dead at his feet. Prester lifted the lid with anticipation. There they were, both of them.

Chapter 2

Florence, Italy - Sunday, April 26, 1478.

L orenzo de' Medici set out from his palace dressed in his finest
garments and sword. It was a short walk to the Santa Maria del
Fiore cathedral, better known in Florence simply as the Duomo. They
called him "Il Magnifico." Only twenty-nine years old, he had already
been the chief banker, unofficial ruler and first citizen of Florence for
nearly a decade. Accompanying him was his guest, the young Cardinal
Raffaello Riario, grandnephew of the reining Pope Sixtus IV. A newly-
minted cardinal at the tender age of seventeen, Riario had been dispatched by his granduncle to visit Florence. His assignment had been
to ensure that Lorenzo and his younger brother Giuliano would attend
the High Mass scheduled for that day. A gentle and pious soul, Cardinal
Riario was a man truly devoted to God. On this crisp and sunny spring
morning, however, he had no idea that he was a pawn in a wide-ranging
conspiracy. A plan had been forged to change the power structure of
Florence and the fortunes of Europe.

As Lorenzo and Cardinal Riario strolled through the streets,
Brunelleschi's ingenious octagonal dome came into view.

"It is indeed a wonder to behold," said the young Cardinal.

"The largest dome in the world, larger even than Rome's Pantheon,"
Lorenzo said. "We Florentines are very proud of it."

"It is only fitting," Riario smiled. "I fear, however, that those assembled beneath it may be growing impatient for our arrival."

"They will wait for us, your excellency," Lorenzo assured him.

"And where is your brother this fine morning?" Riario asked. "Is he feeling any better?"

"I was informed that Giuliano slept well, and left the house early to take the cool morning air. He will meet us at the cathedral directly."

"Good, good. I was concerned for him when he missed the banquet. I have been praying for his good health."

"Your Grace is very thoughtful to be concerned with such matters."

"Not at all, Lorenzo. I pray for you as well. Florence is all the better for your leadership, and what is more, your people love you."

"You are too kind, your Grace. But I think it is my little brother Giuliano whom the people truly love. I simply keep the books."

The two young men laughed together, each cognizant of the other's growing power and influence, but each genuinely appreciative of their newly forged friendship.

On the streets of Florence that morning, amidst the tumult of citizenry going about their Sunday routine, a number of strangers were evident. Thirty crossbowmen congregated in the square adjacent to Santa Maria Novella. Nearby, in front of the Santa Croce church, another fifty mounted soldiers were assembled. Those who thought about it at all likely assumed that these collected soldiers were bodyguards for Archbishop Salviati of Pisa. Or perhaps they were assembled in the service of Cardinal Della Rovere of Genoa. Both would be in attendance at the High Mass, but the soldiers were not there for their protection. To the contrary, they had been assembled, organized and paid for by a small group of powerful men, rivals of Lorenzo de' Medici. They had been instructed to lay in wait until needed for the final stages of the coup.

Meanwhile, a short ride beyond the stone walls of the municipal perimeter, another aspect of the conspiracy was taking shape. Two armies were advancing upon the city at the behest of an additional member of the conspiracy, Federigo da Montelfeltro, Duke of Urbino. Their arrival was to be timed for maximum effectiveness. All phases of the plan were now in motion. For the conspirators, the die had been cast.

Lorenzo looked around for his brother as he and Cardinal Riario approached the cathedral. Near the Baptistry of St. John, Lorenzo saw his faithful childhood friend, Angelo Poliziano, standing with Giuliano.

"Good morning," Poliziano said as he grasped Lorenzo's hand.

"A very good morning indeed, my old friend," Lorenzo said in reply, and then turned to Giuliano. "And how fair you, dear brother?"

"Ah, my stomach betrays me still, and continues to sap my strength," he said, placing his hand on his belly.

"We must call for the doctor, Giuliano. You worry me."

"Rest is what I need, dear brother. After the service, I shall return home and take to my bed."

Just then, two middle-aged men approached from across the square, arms outstretched in an apparent show of affection. As they did so, Lorenzo spoke an aside to Cardinal Riario.

"Beware the facade of false friendships."

"Truly?" the Cardinal asked. "Who are they?"

"Miscreants both," Lorenzo whispered.

"Ah, my good and dear friends," Francesco de' Pazzi shouted as he and his confederate, Bernardo Bandini, approached. "Lorenzo, Giuliano, how pleasant to see you both." With that, Francesco uncharacteristically threw his arms around Giuliano and pulled him close, holding him a bit too long before letting go.

"To what do we owe this unexpected fellowship?" Giuliano inquired.

"I had heard you were not well, dear Giuliano. Naturally, I am overjoyed to see you up and about," Francesco grinned.

Francesco turned next to Lorenzo and similarly engulfed him in a momentary embrace.

"I have not been ill," Lorenzo pointed out as Francesco released him.

"Ah, Lorenzo, how could I embrace one brother and not the other?" Francesco said before nodding a general acknowledgment toward Cardinal Riario.

"Your Grace," Lorenzo said with a slight bow, "this is Francesco de' Pazzi and his associate Bandini."

"Good day, Gentlemen," Riario said.

"Let us hope so, Father," Francesco responded.

"Perhaps we should go in," the Cardinal added, motioning the group forward. As the group began to migrate toward the cathedral entrance, Bernardo Bandini stepped ahead.

"Lorenzo," he said. "I see you wear your sword. Do you fear the devil in the house of God?"

"God will protect me from the devil, Bandini," Lorenzo said. "My sword is reserved for my mortal adversaries."

With that, the brothers Lorenzo and Giuliano, along with Cardinal Riario, entered the cathedral to the general accolades of the assembled parishioners. Francesco de' Pazzi and Bernardo Bandini, meanwhile, lagged behind and were soon joined by two other men. Huddling just outside the cathedral doors, the four men exchanged brief furtive whispers.

"Do you have them?" Francesco asked of the two men who had just approached.

One of the men, a priest named Stefano da Bagnone, nodded and pulled back his frock slightly. Tucked into his sash was a bejeweled dagger with a black Turk's-head knot handgrip. The other man, Antonio da Volterre, wearing a charcoal hat and yellow cloak, likewise drew back his cape to reveal a second, identical dagger. The twin knives were each inlaid with a small ruby in the pommel of the handle, and each bore on their stock the twin dolphin crest of the Pazzi clan.

"Where is Montesecco?" Volterre asked, referring to a co-conspirator, the nobleman Count Giovan Battista Montesecco.

"Our friend has developed a chicken liver," Francesco spat with disgust.

"But he was to dispatch Giuliano."

"Give me the dagger," Francesco said. "I shall dispatch Giuliano myself while Bandini protects my flank. You two shall deliver the blow to Lorenzo, but only at the signal and not a moment before."

Antonio da Volterre nodded and slipped his sparkling dagger to Francesco. Within his cloak, Volterre kept several other less ornamental knives for himself.

"Mind you," Bandini added with a tone of caution. "Lorenzo is armed with a saber."

"But neither Lorenzo nor Giuliano is wearing a breastplate beneath his tunic," Francesco assured them. "This I made sure of myself just a few moments ago."

Inside the cathedral, the crowd was large. The four conspirators had to shove their way through the throng to get into position. Stefano the priest, and Volterre, a notary by trade, pushed their way toward the front of the church where Lorenzo was standing not far from the altar. Inch by inch, they moved to within an arm's length of Lorenzo's shoulders, Stafano just behind and to the left, Volterre to the right. Meanwhile, Giuliano had decided to remain in the back of the church so as to afford a quick exit should his stomach ailment overcome him. Francesco and Bandini positioned themselves so that the younger Medici brother was between them.

As the service was about to begin, a sweating Archbishop Salviati of Pisa rose from his pew in the first row.

"Excuse me, excuse me," he said as he pushed his way through the throng to the back of the church. He was having second thoughts about participating in what was about to take place. Coming across Giuliano standing near the exit, he blanched and stammered out an explanation.

"Giuliano. I . . . my mother is ill," he lied. "I have just this minute received word of it. I must go to her."

"I am sorry to hear it," Giuliano relied. "Go, by all means. I shall pray for her."

"May God be with you, Giuliano. You are a kind man, truly a kind man," the Archbishop said, meaning every word of it. He then turned and scurried out of the church.

The Archbishop held no grudge against Giuliano Medici. In fact, he felt a genuine affection for him. It was the tyrant, Lorenzo, who had to be replaced. But if the scheme were to be pulled off successfully, both brothers would have to be killed. Of that there was no doubt, for either brother alone could sway the sentiments of the public against the Pazzi.

The Archbishop's job, once the vile deed had been done, was simple. He was to direct his mercenaries to the Palazzo de Signoria, the seat of Florentine government, and to secure the reins of official power there. Stopping in the street, he looked back at the Duomo once more. Then, darting around a corner, he made directly for his troops at the Santa Croce.

And so the mass began. A hush fell over the congregation as the cathedral priest, his back to the gallery, led the assemblage in Latin. Bowed heads dutifully recited prayers as the priest, glancing into a small mirror embedded in the altar, observed his flock behind him. Then came the moment for the Elevation of the Host.

"Hoc est corpus Christi, corpus novi et aeterni testamenti," the priest spoke in Latin, lifting the small communion wafer with both hands to his chin. Then, as prescribed by the ceremony, the priest stretched up his arms toward heaven while an altar boy lifted a bell and rang it vigorously. This was the signal, a signal that could both be seen and heard in the cavernous cathedral. With that, the assassins struck.

Chapter 3

At 11:10 AM, Prester set the carved mahogany box on his desk as his Comprehensive World History class settled in. It was December 21st, the final day and final period of instruction before the winter break. This fact did not make holding the attention of an adolescent audience any easier. But Prester was a history teacher, and a good one by his own estimation. True, he was not the accomplished professor his father had been. His father had thrived at the post-graduate level teaching history to students at Harvard University. Prester, however, had made the conscious decision to remain at home, on Block Island, teaching at the same high school he had attended.

Prester stood before the class waiting for them to quiet down. He had faced students like this many times before – jaded, disinterested, anxious to be somewhere else, anywhere else. He knew he had to challenge them.

"HISTORY!" he shouted at the top of his lungs, shocking them into silence. "What is it?" he continued. There was no response, as anticipated. Prester edged through the rows of desks, stopping in front of Annie Sage. In the back of the room, Kirk Renzo looked on with foreboding.

"Hello, Ms. Sage," Prester said.

"Um, hello Mr. John," Annie responded.

"May I ask you a question?"

"I guess."

"When I walked into class today, I noticed that you were telling a story to your friend, Melissa. And from her reaction, it looked like a pretty good story too."

Annie gave an embarrassed glance in Kirk's direction.

"I was just telling her about some stuff that happened," Annie said, "that's all."

"Okay, so here's my question for the class," Prester said. "Why do we like stories? Can anybody tell me?"

"Because they're usually about boys?" a soft-spoken reply came from a girl in the third row.

"In this case, just one boy," another girl ventured as she glanced toward Kirk. A peel of general hilarity resounded through the class as Kirk sank into his chair.

"So we like stories about other people, whether it's her story," Prester said, gesturing toward Annie, "or his story," he added, pointing toward Kirk. "Is that about it?"

"Sure, I guess," Annie said. In the back corner of the room, Kirk recoiled further and gripped the desk hard.

Prester moved to the front of the classroom and picked up a piece of chalk. He then wrote two words on the blackboard in large block print, speaking each word aloud as he did so.

"HIS," he wrote in capital letters. "STORY," he added. He underlined the two words together. "History. A story told by people, for people, about people. Isn't that what we're really talking about? It's not the battlefields or the sailing ships or the ancient buildings that interest us. It's the people, the people who fought in those battles, who sailed in those ships, who lived, worked and worshiped in those buildings. They were just like you. They had teachers and parents and little brothers and big sisters. They had boyfriends and girlfriends and secret passions. They whispered gossip in each other's ear."

He turned again to Annie.

"That story you were telling Melissa," he said. "Was it true?"

"Yes," Annie said.

Prester looked at Melissa.

"Do you think it was true?" he asked her.

"Maybe."

"So you're not sure," Prester said, causing the class to tumble into laughter again. Melissa began to turn red.

"She probably made it up," Luke, a boy in the front row, interjected.

"Why would Annie make it up?" Prester asked the class.

"To cause trouble," another boy offered.

"Cause she's a gossip," a girl from the far left suggested.

"Hey!" Annie protested.

"Or to make someone jealous," Melissa blurted out, stealing a glance toward Kirk. "I mean, could be. I'm just saying."

"But it was true, mostly," Annie said, stirring up another cycle of laughter. "I mean, I didn't make it up. I just sort of told the good parts. That's not lying, is it?"

"No, that's not lying," Prester said. "That's just how stories are. Annie told what she thought would be interesting and important for Melissa to hear, and skipped over the rest. That's what makes it her story. And you know something? That's the way history is too. History depends on the choices made by the storyteller." Prester turned again to Kirk. "Do you think I'm right about that?"

Kirk looked up at his teacher with contempt.

"This is stupid," he snarled and looked away. Unfazed, Prester ignored the look and pushed on.

"Stories are passed down generationally from person to person with each person telling it the way he or she wants it to be heard. Maybe one person leaves out a detail. Maybe another embellishes something. Each teller of the story changes it slightly, which raises a very interesting question, doesn't it? Are the stories true?"

Prester crossed the room once more, letting his question float in the air.

"As we move forward in this class, I want you to peel back the layers of history. Look at the motivations of the people involved in the making and the telling of the stories. Question what you read, and consider whether it really happened that way. Once you do that, you will begin to understand history."

The class was with him now, each student hanging on his every word, except for Kirk Renzo. Sitting in the back near a large window through which snow could be seen hurtling by in horizontal streams, Kirk was a coiled venomous snake. His eyes narrowed as he looked with disdain upon the scene. History, he thought. What a colossal waste of time.

Chapter 4

Florence, Italy - Sunday, April 26, 1478.

Bernardo Bandini grasped Giuliano by both arms, pinning them back, as Francesco de' Pazzi plunged his dagger deep into Giuliano's chest. The young prince staggered backward, then turned and began to stumble away, the bejeweled dagger still protruding from his torso. With his strength failing him, he pulled the knife from his body and dropped it to the marble floor. Faltering, he fell face first to the ground gasping for breath in the shadow of the cathedral door. A moment later, having retrieved the dagger, Francesco was on top of him, hacking at the back of the defenseless body. Over and over he thrust the knife into Giuliano's back, shoulders and neck, stabbing him on both sides of his rib cage, blood spurting in all directions. Again and again, thrusting downward, the knife found its mark. One last time, Francesco brought the dagger down, but this time his foot slipped in the burgeoning pool of blood and the knife plunged into his own thigh.

"Augh!" he screamed, pulling loose the knife and flinging it away.

Meanwhile, in the front of the church, the priest Stefano drew his dagger and raised it high above the head of Lorenzo while Volterre reached forward to pin Lorenzo's shoulders. The knife came down just as Lorenzo flinched to his left. Lorenzo's neck was sliced just below his right ear.

"Lorenzo!" shouted the voice of Poliziano, Lorenzo's boyhood friend. He had by chance turned just in time to see the assassin's knife come down. Leaping to his right, Poliziano fell upon the priest Stefano, knocking the dagger from his grasp and sending it skidding away.

With a muscular twist of his limbs, Lorenzo shook loose from Volterre and drew his sword with one hand while wrapping his cloak around the other for a makeshift shield. Volterre, having backed away, now swung at Lorenzo with a long single edge cutlass that he had pulled from within his flowing cloak. Lorenzo dodged to his left, and then thrust his own hard steel blade toward the man, drawing blood from Volterre's upper right shoulder.

"Behind you," Poliziano shouted again. Turning, Lorenzo saw three monks in full-length brown frocks running toward him, knives at the ready. Lorenzo raised his sword and swung it horizontally in front of him, bringing the charging assassins to a stand still.

"Il Magnifico," spat one of the monks as he lunged forward with his blade. Lorenzo, reacting rather than thinking, came down hard with his sword and sliced two of the man's fingers from his hand.

"My Lord, they are all around us," came the voice of another Lorenzo ally, the stonemason Sigismondo Stufa. "Della Robbia, della Robbia," Stufa shouted. Lorenzo understood and leapt across the low railing that separated the altar from the main apse. He then darted toward the protection of the New Sacristy with its large bronze doors that had been so finely carved by Luca della Robbia some 34 years before. Poliziano, running now directly behind Lorenzo, pushed him inside as he pulled the heavy ten-panel doors shut behind them and threw closed its bolt lock.

From inside the sacristy, Lorenzo and Poliziano could hear clashing swords and shouting voices just beyond the door. Suddenly, Lorenzo dropped his sword and fell to his knees. His neck was bleeding, and he had already lost sufficient blood to soak his blouse. Poliziano rushed to his aid, laying his friend down and cradling his head across his lap.

"Lorenzo," Poliziano whispered. "Lie still."

"Giuliano," Lorenzo muttered as he raised his hands to his neck. "Where is Giuliano?"

"Lie back, my friend," Poliziano said. "We are safe for the moment, but I fear that the priest's dagger may have been poisoned."

"Giuliano," Lorenzo mumbled again.

"I know not of your brother's fate. All in good time, Lorenzo. Now lie back while I suck this poison blood from your neck."

"No," Lorenzo said. "If indeed it be poison, you shall die."

"But you may live," came Poliziano's brief reply, and with that Poliziano pressed his lips against the bleeding neck of his friend.

Spitting blood from his mouth, Poliziano drew again and again from Lorenzo's wound. After a few moments, he stopped and wrapped the wound with a bandage torn from his tunic. He then eased Lorenzo's head to the floor, and lay down next to him as the sounds of clashing swords continued beyond the door.

Looking up, the two exhausted men could see the organ loft above.

"Lorenzo," Poliziano whispered. There was no answer. "Can you hear me?"

"I am not dead just yet," Lorenzo mocked.

"Are you all right?" Poliziano asked.

"I feel my strength returning. And you?"

"Fine. It seems that God has seen fit to spare us both."

"I pray He has not taken Giuliano in our place," Lorenzo said.

In every part of the cathedral, panicked parishioners were fleeing towards the exits. Those leaving by the main entrance had to step over the dead body of Giuliano still laying in a pool of his own blood. In the middle of the cathedral amid the chaos, Francesco de' Pazzi stood bleeding from his self-inflicted wound, and cursing his ill fortune. Giuliano was dead, he knew, but Lorenzo de' Medici was safely ensconced behind the thick bronze doors of the New Sacristy.

"We shall kill him when he comes out," Bernardo Bandini said. He had just run up to where Francesco stood next to a wounded and bleeding Antonio da Volterre. Francesco looked at Bandini with disdain.

"Do you not comprehend anything?" Francesco said. "Lorenzo lives. All is lost."

"But he cannot hide in there forever," Bandini replied.

"You are a boil-brained lout," Francesco spat in disgust. "Did you not see the people depart in haste from this treacherous place? Before the sun sets, every merchant, smith and barmaid in Florence will know of our failure. The people might well have conceded their fate to the Pazzi if both Medici brothers had died. But once they hear that Lorenzo is alive, they will not follow us."

Bandini and Volterre looked upon Francesco with vacant stares.

"Then what do we do?" Bandini asked.

"Do? You ask me what you should do?" Francesco said half laughing. "There is nothing to do. Leave the city post-haste. That is my advice. None of us is safe here now."

"But my family, my business," Volterre said. "I must go home."

"Go home then. But know this. Lorenzo and his followers will not let this rest," Francesco replied. As he spoke, a shriek came from across the cathedral near the chapel of Saint Zenobius. Adjacent to Ghiberti's fine bronze urn, a group of Medici loyalists had surrounded the three conspiratorial monks and were poking at them with all manner of swords, pitchforks and sticks.

"I am innocent," one of the monks was screaming as he raced back and forth within the closed circle, being pushed into the center first by one angry parishioner and then another. "I knew nothing of this," the monk shouted. Just then, a large wooden club struck him squarely atop the head. He fell to the floor in a heap.

"Get me to the street," Francesco de' Pazzi ordered. Bandini and Volterre complied, grasping Francesco under his arms on either side to brace him. The three men hobbled out of the Duomo and made for the Via del Proconsolo that led to the relative safety of the nearby Pazzi Palace.

Within ten minutes, the cathedral was nearly empty. The mob that had surrounded the monks had departed, dragging along the beaten and tattered remains of their victims. Just six men remained from the original congregation, Medici supporters all. With swords drawn, the brave six had taken on the conspirators and driven them away. The men now moved as a group toward the New Sacristy. One of the group, Santino, banged hard on the bronze doors.

"Lorenzo," he shouted. "It is a friend. All is safe."

Inside the sacristy, Poliziano had by this time managed to climb up to the organ loft above the door and peek over the edge.

"I recognize this man," Poliziano shouted down to Lorenzo. "We have worked together, and he is loyal."

"Then come down so that we may stand side by side," Lorenzo said. Poliziano climbed back down.

Lorenzo and his friend together pulled open the heavy bronze doors. Lying just beyond the doors were the mortal remains of Sigismondo Stufa. Lorenzo looked at the body and clenched his fists.

"For whom did this man die?" he said, a deep-seated anger building in his voice. "For Florence, or for me?"

"You are Florence," one of his loyal followers from the group responded.

"Quickly now," said another. "We must get Il Magnifico home before they strike again."

The six men, along with Poliziano, enveloped Lorenzo in a protective circle of swords and knives. They escorted him through the south side door of the Duomo, intentionally directing him away from Giuliano's body that now lay covered with a cloak. Hustling along the Via Cavour, they arrived at Lorenzo's home within minutes and entered into the foyer where several servants barred the doors behind them. Fearing further attack, the men began to arm themselves with additional weapons as best they could.

"Giuliano!" Lorenzo called throughout the house. Hearing no response, he turned to his followers.

"Where is my brother?"

The men looked at each other, and then back to Lorenzo.

"Where is he?" Lorenzo asked again.

"Giuliano has been stabbed, my Lord," Santino, one of the group, finally said.

"Is he badly hurt?" Lorenzo asked. "Where is he?"

"He is in the cathedral," Santino answered.

"Why was he left behind?" Lorenzo shouted. "Go and fetch him home immediately," he said, pointing toward the door.

"He cannot come home, my Lord," Santino replied, tears beginning to streak down his face. "He is with God."

Lorenzo stopped upon hearing the words. With his arm still outstretched, he turned to stare at the group.

"No," Lorenzo said. "It is not true. You are lying. You are all lying. They have no reason to kill Giuliano. Tell me where he is?" Lorenzo suddenly drew a long blade from his cloak and brandished it, but Poliziano stepped forward and grasped his arm.

"He is dead, Lorenzo," Poliziano said. "God in His wisdom, it is true."

Lorenzo's gaze drifted toward Poliziano, as if in a dream. He then bowed his head and closed his eyes as he let the knife fall from his hand. No one spoke.

"He must be brought here," Lorenzo spoke in a near whisper. "My good and loyal friends, please, go to the cathedral and bear my brother's body home."

And so they did.

Reprisals came swiftly. Word spread from house to house that Lorenzo had survived the assassination attempt, but that Giuliano was dead. From the Signoria, bells rang out as a signal to one and all that their city was in danger. Angry mobs, loyal to the Medici, flowed into the streets. The gates to the city were closed and locked before the approaching conspiratorial soldiers from Urbino could arrive. Worse for the Pazzi clan, all exits from the city were blocked.

Archbishop Salviati, more a diplomat than a warrior, arrived at the Palazzo della Signoria with fifty armed soldiers, only to botch the take-over attempt. His men were disarmed, placed under arrest and locked in the bell tower overlooking the piazza below. The mob, however, would not be put off. Enraged citizens burst through the locked doors where the soldiers had been situated and cut the hapless men down where they stood. Survivors of the initial carnage were thrown from the windows of the 308-foot tower to the gathering crowds below who then stripped them of their clothes and hacked them to pieces. Their body parts were carried through the city streets in mock parade.

Francesco de' Pazzi, still bleeding from his wound, was brought from his home by twenty men to the Signoria where he was questioned and beaten. Within the hour, a rope was put around his neck and he was hanged from the tower, followed immediately by the Archbishop of Pisa. Their bodies were left hanging for all to see, and were soon joined by many of their fellow conspirators. To the boisterous throng below, each hanging was a public statement of revenge and civic pride. These were, after all, Florentines. They would not be ruled by anyone at the point of a sword.

Cries of "Palle! Palle!," a reference to the six spheres depicted on the Medici coat of arms, echoed in the streets. Banker stood beside baker, wool merchant with silk merchant, farmer next to physician, each person shouting for the hangings to continue. Even an artist stood among them, dipping his stylus in ink. Then, looking up, the twenty six year old Leonardo da Vinci sketched the hanging lifeless figure of Bernardo Bandini.

By some accounts, over two hundred conspirators were dispatched at the hands of the mob over the next five days. Most were hanged in or near the Palazzo della Signoria. Many others were thrown to their deaths from the tower. A few were unceremoniously and quite clumsily beheaded. The bodies of the conspirators were stripped naked. As rigor mortis set in, they were propped up around the perimeter of the Piazza della Signoria as if on guard over the city they had betrayed. But even in death the conspirators were not safe from the outrage of the citizens. Noses, ears and tongues were cut away from the rotting corpses and nailed to the doors of the Pazzi palace.

The Pazzi, of course, the perpetrators of the conspiracy, paid the heaviest price of all. Jacopo de' Pazzi, patriarch of that old and noble family, managed to get out of the city, but was soon captured by peasants and borne back to Florence. He too was hanged from the Signoria bell tower. In respect for his high status, the ruling Gonfaloniere, a government official named Cesare Petrucci, ordered that he be cut down and buried. Four days later, however, his body was unearthed, tied to a horse, and dragged through the city streets before being tossed into the Arno River.

In the succeeding weeks, the Pazzi name was erased from the Florentine landscape. Ships bearing Pazzi cargo were seized by the governing Council of Eight, as were all Pazzi homes, lands, crops, live-stock, jewelry, clothing, and business records. All those owing money to the Pazzi now had their debt obligations transferred to the Republic. A new law was enacted requiring that all remaining Pazzi family members change their name and give up their twin dolphin coat of arms. They had little choice but to comply. Every public emblem of the Pazzi was ordered removed, and all members of the clan barred from ever again holding public office. Indeed, nothing of the Pazzi legacy remained, or nearly nothing.

On the first day of October 1478, a special box was presented to Lorenzo de' Medici by the men at arms who had protected him on the day of the attempted assassination the previous spring. The box itself was made of fine polished mahogany. On the lid, in high relief, was carved a fanciful image depicting Lorenzo in the Duomo with sword drawn, holding off his attackers, while Giuliano lay dead in the fore-ground. Displayed inside the box, atop a red velvet lining, were the twin jewel-encrusted daggers that had been used against them. Exhibited upon the stock of each knife were the twin dolphins of the now defunct Pazzi coat of arms.

Chapter 5

Prester opened the hinged lid of the wooden box on his desk, turned it around, and tilted it up for the class to see. Inside, displayed against red velvet, were two identical bejeweled daggers. The twin knives lay side-by-side, each having a black handgrip, and each inlaid with a ruby set off by an S-shaped hand guard. Incrusted on the stock of each knife was a coat of arms depicting twin dolphins.

Prester handed the engraved box to Annie and motioned for her to take a look at it and then pass it along to her neighbor.

"I want you to look at these," he said, "but don't touch them. These knives are over 500 years old, but they're still very sharp."

As the students began passing the display box from person to person, Prester went on with his story.

"The knives once belonged to a young prince from Florence, Italy named Lorenzo de' Medici. They called him Lorenzo the Magnificent, or in Italian, Il Magnifico. Has anyone ever heard of him?"

From the blank stares, he could see that no one had a clue of whom he was talking about.

"Lorenzo lived in Florence around the time another fellow by the name of Columbus was trying to raise money for a little sailing trip he had in mind. I take it you've heard of Christopher Columbus."

The class laughed.

"So while Columbus was getting ready to set sail, Lorenzo was busy holding court in Florence as one of the most powerful and influential bankers in the western world. In 15th Century Europe, having money, or even access to money, meant that you had political power. That hasn't changed much in 500 years, has it?"

The class laughed again.

"Now here's the thing. The Medici were powerful bankers and a political powerhouse for generations. They were the leading family of Florence. Lorenzo in particular was greatly admired and respected by the people. He was also a very generous man. He donated large sums of his family fortune to charitable causes, and he sponsored many great artists such as Michelangelo."

"Michael who?" came the sarcastic voice of a round-faced boy sitting in a middle row.

"You've all seen pictures of Michelangelo's works, whether you realize it or not – his giant statue of David, his superlative Pieta, the ceiling of the Sistine Chapel."

"Oh, that Michelangelo," the boy grinned.

Kirk Renzo, observing the scene from his back row seat, watched as the twin daggers were passed from desk to desk.

"Of course," Prester continued, "not everyone in Florence was happy with Lorenzo. The Pazzi clan hated the Medici. They were the second most powerful family in Florence at the time."

A smirk curled up on Kirk's lip as he saw the daggers coming closer.

"Eventually, the Pazzi clan decided that Lorenzo had to go. So they put in motion a plot to kill him, and these were the knives they used to do it."

As Prester spoke, the engraved box finally reached Kirk Renzo. Kirk lifted the lid, and stared down at the knives. Then, with one swift motion of his right arm, Kirk removed one of the twin daggers and slid it into his book bag.

"When we come back after your vacation, we'll talk about that attack, and what happened to the Medici and the Pazzi clans."

As the class listened, the engraved box was passed back to the front of the class and to the last student, Luke Wilson.

"Florence in the late 15th Century was a place of great violence and intrigue. It was also a city of great genius – Leonardo da Vinci, Raphael, Machiavelli, Donatello, Brunelleschi, Michelangelo all lived there. The question is, how did this explosion of talent and intellect occur at this one place and time in the world?"

Luke peeked into the box, and then shut it quickly. He took a deep breath, and peeked again. A look of fear washed over his face. He raised his hand.

"Why did the people of Florence excel in the arts, science, political theory, architecture, medicine, philosophy, far beyond what random chance would suggest is possible?"

"Um, uh, Mr. John?" Luke whispered.

"In almost every field of human endeavor, the people of that time and place transcended all that humankind had accomplished in the previous thousand years."

As he spoke, Prester moved toward Luke and took the box from his outstretched arms. Catching the look in the boy's eyes, he opened the lid. One of the daggers was gone.

"All right," Prester said. "Very funny. Where is it?"

"It wasn't me," Luke said, choking back tears.

Prester looked across the classroom.

"That's enough now," he said. "I'm sure that whoever took the knife meant it as a joke. But the joke's over."

Prester watched for any sign from the class as to which of them had the dagger.

"We can't begin our winter break until we get this settled," Prester said. "Whoever took the knife, please pass it forward now."

Wide eyes looked from face to face as the students squirmed in their seats.

"We are not leaving this room until the dagger is returned," Prester warned again. "Now before this thing gets out of hand . . ."

In the second row, Melissa finally spoke up.

"He's got it in his book bag," she said, pointing at Kirk. "I saw him."

As all eyes turned towards him, Kirk reached into his book bag and pulled out the dagger. He held it out in front of him.

"Kirk?" Prester said as he stepped forward. "That's not a toy. Please hand it to me."

Kirk glared across the room, tears beginning to form in his eyes as he stared at Annie.

"Don't be such a showoff, Kirk Renzo," Annie said.

Prester stepped closer. "Just set the knife down, Kirk, so we can all get back to what we were doing."

Kirk's anger boiled over and spilled forth from the corners of his black eyes. "You people are pathetic," he blurted out. "You're all just so stupid, and I've had enough of it." Then, with the dexterity of a gymnast, he leapt up onto his desk. Pushing open the large window behind him, he jumped out into the deep and blowing snow.

Prester looked on in disbelief. He should have never brought his father's rare and priceless heirlooms to school, he thought. But this was no time for self-recriminations. In the next instant, reacting more than thinking, Prester was up on the desk and springing through the open window after the boy.

Prester's feet landed with an icy crunch. Some twenty yards in front of him, Kirk raced along the side of the building, his boots leaving deep footprints in the snow. Prester gave chase, his unprotected shoes filling with ice as he high-stepped his way through the pack. A moment later, he saw Kirk round the corner of the school building and move beyond his view. Prester, twenty years Kirk's senior, realized that he could never keep up. Thank God for the footprints, he thought.

Prester raced forward, rounding the corner and pumping his legs for all they were worth. The boy's tracks now veered away from the building and out across the open field toward the Block Island Oak. Prester hurried on toward the tree, following the trail before him. The boy was nowhere in sight. He must have continued beyond the tree, Prester thought as he plunged through the snow. The leafless branches and trunk of the old oak loomed before him.

Upon reaching the tree, Prester stopped to catch his breath. Looking up into the branches, he saw only bare limbs devoid of life. He stepped around the large trunk to pick up the trail.

But there was no trail. There were no footprints. There were no tracks in the snow. There was nothing, nothing but white, pure unbroken snow spreading out before him like a sheet upon a freshly made bed.

Prester stood still, looking, listening for any hint of movement. He heard not the screech of a crow, not the dull rumble of distant street traffic, not the rustling limbs of the old tree. There was only the wind. Then, in the distance, the bell from the Chapel Street Church came crisp and clear, the sound carrying over the distance, twelve strikes of the bell in all.

From around the corner of the school building, a crowd began to approach, teachers, students and administration personnel. They trudged through the deep snow toward where Prester was standing. Prester watched them as they came. They were shouting questions, but he had no answers for them. He would have no answers for the police or for the private investigators who would question him over and over again in the coming months. Where was the boy? Where had the boy gone? What had he done with the boy? Why had he given the boy a knife? Prester had no explanation. He knew just one thing. The boy and the dagger had vanished.

Chapter 6

Providence, Rhode Island (Reuters) – Present Day

L ocal police and F.B.I. jointly announced today that the investigation into the disappearance of Kirk Renzo is being closed for lack of evidence. Renzo, who vanished without a trace one year ago, was the 16-year-old son of prominent New York investment banker Chas Renzo. Kirk Renzo was a sophomore attending the Block Island Academy at the time of his unexplained disappearance from the grounds of his school. The investigation into the incident, which authorities have categorized as a missing person case, has centered on a former teacher, Prester Charles John, whom authorities have referred to as a "person of interest." John served as Assistant Principal of the school.

"Our investigation has turned up nothing but dead ends," Providence Police Chief Patrick Morris said. "But people don't just vanish."

No arrest has been made in the case that created nationwide headlines at the time and has remained a topic of public interest. Unnamed sources report that Mr. John, who was suspended without pay from his teaching position, continues to be viewed unofficially as a suspect.

"Prester John was the last person to be seen with the boy," said Chief Morris. "He was right there when the boy disappeared. He must know something. But at this point, we can't prove it."

Chapter 7

Manhattan Island, New York

"It is now 5:15. The museum will be closing in fifteen minutes. Please exit through the main lobby," Annie Sage announced as she had been trained to do. Across the gallery, her supervisor smiled and nodded. "Thank you all for coming," she continued as she motioned for the remaining stragglers to move along.

It had been a long day, the first of her winter-session internship. She was tired, having been on her feet for most of her on-duty time, but she was happy. Working at the Metropolitan Museum of Art was going to be good, she thought.

"Okay, that's it," her supervisor, Milo Clarkson, said after the last of the hangers-on had gone. "Let's go home."

"Mr. Clarkson?" Annie ventured. "May I speak with you a moment?"

"Good job, Annie," Clarkson said. "You handled the mob well for your first day."

"Thank you, sir," she said. "I enjoyed answering people's questions and helping them find their way around."

"Glad to hear it."

"Sir, do you have time for a question?"

"Tell you what, Annie, can we do it tomorrow? I'm trying to get out of here. Knicks tickets."

"Oh, sure, of course," Annie said. "See you tomorrow then."

"You did good today, Annie," Clarkson said over his shoulder as he headed for the exit. "Tomorrow, bright and early."

"Good night, Mr. Clarkson," Annie said.

Annie watched as Clarkson walked away, his black heels clicking against the hardwood floor of Gallery 604, the European Paintings Collection – Fifteenth Century Florence Section.

Left all alone, Annie listened to the quiet of the empty gallery and thought about the curious thing she had noticed earlier in the day. She gathered up her things, including the large coffee table book she had purchased in the museum store, and headed for the elevator. Perhaps she should keep it to herself. She was brand new on the job, after all, and there were probably all kinds of odd things she would notice over time. Still, it was very odd.

Could it be an elaborate test, she thought? Maybe the whole idea was to see whether she would notice. Maybe they tested all the interns this way. That must be it, she thought, or at least that could be it. How else could you explain it?

Annie tucked the large book up under her arm, stepped aboard an employee-only elevator, and pressed the button for the third floor administrative offices. Upon exiting, she turned left around a corner and walked down a long hallway to the glass double-doors of the Office of A. Joseph Brennan, the Museum Director. She tapped on the glass, and then entered.

Standing before a large mahogany counter, she waited for the secretary to finish typing on her computer. Sixty seconds passed. Then ninety seconds. The secretary continued to type. The woman was dressed in a severe black suit and delicate white blouse. A single string of pearls surrounded her neck, and her hair was pulled up in a bun completing an ensemble that to Annie could only be described as persnickety. Annie thought the woman must be somewhere north of eighty years old. Perhaps she couldn't hear well. Perhaps she didn't realize someone was standing there. Annie noticed a nameplate depicting the name Elaine Trumbull.

"Hello?" Annie called out, "Ms. Trumbull is it?"

"One moment, young lady," Trumbull said as she found a stopping point and looked up with irritation. "Mrs. Trumbull, not 'Ms'. I am not inclined to favor the contemporary penchant for epitomizing the female marital status. Now, how may I help you?"

Annie stared at her for a long moment, and then grinned. "Is the Director in?"

"You're new here, aren't you?"

"It's my first day, actually."

"Who would have guessed? Tell me, young lady, do you have an appointment?"

"An appointment? No, no, I don't have an appointment. I just . . ."

"You'll need an appointment. That's the procedure, and procedures must be followed. Mr. Brennan is a busy man," Mrs. Trumbull said, "a very, very busy man. No one sees the Director without an appointment."

"I'm sure he's busy. It's just that I wanted to report a problem."

"What kind of problem?"

"Well," Annie hesitated, "it's kind of hard to explain. If I could speak with the Director for just a moment."

"You'll need an appointment," the secretary said. "That's the procedure."

"Yes, and a very fine procedure it is too, I'm sure, but this may not be able to wait."

"Would you like to make an appointment?"

"Sure, I guess so," Annie said.

"Please call the main desk between the hours of nine and five, Monday through Friday. I'm sure you'll be able to locate the number. They can set up an appointment for you," Mrs. Trumbull said as she returned her focus to her typing.

"The main desk?" Annie said.

"That's the great big one down in the lobby, dear."

"But wouldn't you know when the Director is available?" Annie asked.

"There is a procedure, and procedures must be followed. The procedure is that you call the main desk between the hours of nine and five, Monday through Friday," Mrs. Trumbull repeated.

"So the main desk will know when the Director is free?" Annie asked.

"They will check with me," Trumbull said as she looked back at her computer screen. Annie stared at her.

"Can't you just tell me when the Director will be free, sort of cut out the middle man I mean?"

Mrs. Trumbull looked up at her again.

"Listen dear," she said, "you're new here. I remember when I was new here. It was during the Kennedy Administration, something called the Cuban Missile Crisis – U.S. versus Soviet Union, world on the brink of nuclear holocaust? Perhaps you read about it in your history books at school. In any case, President Kennedy called here and said he needed to speak with the Director right away. You know what I told him? I told him that there are procedures that must be followed. Didn't they tell you during orientation that there are procedures that must be followed?"

"Well, sure, I know there are procedures," Annie said.

"That must be followed," Mrs. Trumbull repeated herself.

"But it's just that I think there might be a problem with one of the pictures," Annie said.

The secretary stopped dead.

"What did you say?" Mrs. Trumbull asked, holding one hand to her forehead and closing her eyes.

"I said, I think there may be something wrong with one of the pictures."

"Your name? What is your name?" Mrs. Trumbull demanded.

"Annie Sage."

"Firstly, Miss Annie Sage, they are not 'pictures.' They are paintings, very valuable paintings. This is the Metropolitan Museum of Art, not the Department of Motor Vehicles. If the Director heard you refer to them as 'pictures' he would fire you on the spot. Don't thank me. I just want to avoid the extra paperwork. Secondly, any problems you may think you perceive with the paintings may be referred to your supervisor, whomever he or she may be. Thirdly, to see the Director – and at this point, in all candor, I wouldn't advise it – you will need to call the main desk for an appointment. That's the procedure."

"And then they will call you to see when the Director is available?" Annie confirmed.

"Now you've got it," Mrs. Trumbull said, her words dripping with disdain.

Just then, the large door behind the secretary opened, and the Museum Director emerged, hat and coat in hand.

"I'm going home early, Mrs. Trumbull."

"Are you feeling all right, Mr. Brennan?" she asked.

"I'm fine," he said.

"Very good, sir. See you in the morning."

"Good night, Mrs. Trumbull," he said as he pushed through the glass double doors and headed down the hallway. Annie took her cue.

"Thank you so much, Mrs. Trumbull, for explaining the procedures," Annie said as she headed for the exit. "I'll be sure to speak with the main desk right away."

"You do that," Mrs. Trumbull said as Annie dashed out into the corridor. "Remember, there are procedures," she shouted after her, but Annie had already gone. Mrs. Trumbull looked back down at her computer screen. "And procedures must be followed," she mumbled as she resumed her typing.

Rushing down the corridor, Annie made the quick right just in time to catch the door of the closing elevator. She stepped aboard, out of breath, and stood next to the Director. The elevator doors shut, and they began their descent.

Annie smiled and nodded. The Director responded by allowing a flicker of a smile to cross his face, and then stared up at the floor indicator light.

"This is my first day," Annie said to get the conversation rolling. There was no response. "I really think I'm going to like it here," she added. The elevator passed the second floor.

"So you're the director of the museum, huh?" Annie looked at the Director and extended a hand. He did not react, and she put her hand down. "Love the pictures . . the paintings that is," she tittered. "They are paintings, of course. I said 'pictures' because I was thinking of the pictures of the paintings in this book I bought at the museum store," she said, holding up her coffee table book. The elevator reached the ground floor, and the door opened.

"Good night," the Director said as he stepped out of the elevator.

"I think one of the paintings in Gallery 604 is a forgery," she blurted out, thrusting her left foot forward to keep the door open.

The Director stopped and rotated toward her.

"Did you say you work here, young lady?"

"I'm an intern. It's my first day, yes sir," she said.

"Where do you work?"

"Gallery 604, Fifteenth Century Florence Section, European Paintings Collection."

"And what is it that you think you saw?"

"Well, sir, I can't be sure of course, it's only my first day."

"Tell me. What did you see?" he asked again.

"One of the paintings isn't right, sir."

"What do you mean it isn't right?" he inquired. "What is not right about it?"

"Well, have you seen this book, from the museum store?" She held up the book again. "I bought it yesterday, even though it was really expensive. But I've been looking at my paintings, you know, the pictures of the paintings from my gallery, I mean Gallery 604. One of the paintings is called 'Portrait of a Young Man,' artist unknown."

"Yes."

"It's one of the paintings in my gallery," she reiterated.

"I'm familiar with it," the Director said.

"Oh, well, of course you are. The thing is, I noticed this particular painting, you see, because, well, it looks just like a boy, Kirk, I used to know in school. I mean, how crazy is that, right? And so I made a point of looking it up in the book."

"Young lady, what are you trying to tell me?"

"The painting on the floor, in Gallery 604?"

"Yes?"

"The thing is, it's not the same face."

Chapter 8

Philadelphia, Pennsylvania

The front door buzzer woke him from a dead sleep. Prester pushed the pillows away and looked at the far wall of his disheveled studio apartment. Blinking both eyes nearly in unison, he tried to focus on the microwave oven clock. A quarter past seven? Was that morning or evening?

The buzzer rang again. A small television sitting atop a plastic milk crate near the foot of his bed crackled with some form of game show.

"Leave it by the door," Prester shouted as he pulled a blanket up over his head.

The buzzer sounded once more.

"Oh, for God sake."

Prester rolled across the bed, threw his feet to the floor, and shuffled toward the sound of the buzzer while pulling on a terry cloth bathrobe. Tying the cloth belt, he peeked through the peephole.

Standing in the hallway beneath the yellow light of a naked bulb was a short, ruddy-faced older man wearing a chauffeur's cap, white button-down shirt, and black bow tie. Prester peered at the man for a moment before backing away.

"You've got the wrong place," he shouted through the door.

"Sorry ta bother ya, sir," the chauffeur shouted back in a thick Irish accent, "but might ya be Prester Charles John?"

Prester peeked at him again. He then turned the triple security locks, unlatched the chain, and pulled open the door.

"Who are you?" Prester asked the chauffeur.

"Brophy's the name. Victor Brophy, at your service," the man said. "Are ya Prester Charles John then?" the man asked again.

"I used to be. What do you want?"

"I've an invitation, sir, from my employer," the man said, holding out a small white envelope.

"Invitation?" Prester asked as the envelope was slipped into his hand.

"He'd like it very much if ya'd join him for lunch tomorrow in New York City. It's a bit of a drive from here, so I'm to pick ya up at 10:00 AM I trust that'll be satisfactory, sir," the chauffeur said. He then tipped his cap and, without another word, beat a hasty retreat. Prester watched as the man scurried down the dim corridor and turned out of sight. He then turned the envelope over in his hand.

"Who's your employer?" Prester shouted, but the man was already gone.

It was a formal invitation, engraved on high quality bond stationery and gilded in gold leaf. Embossed on the flap was some sort of stylized symbol. Scrutinizing the envelope again, Prester realized that the symbol consisted of the overlapping initials "CR". He grimaced.

"Oh no," he said aloud to himself. "No, no, no."

Prester ran to the window and threw it open. A cold December wind blew in as he peered down upon the lamp-lit street from his third-story perch. Perhaps he would catch sight of the old man exiting the building. But the street was empty.

"Hey," he shouted into the darkness. "Tell your boss I'm not interested."

Stepping back inside, Prester crossed the room and closed the front door of his apartment, re-securing the triple dead bolt locks. He then propped up the unopened invitation against the toaster that sat on the bent metal table that served as his bookshelf, pantry, dining room and entertainment center. Switching off the television, he sat on the cold ledge of the open window and listened to the muffled sounds of the city below.

"How many times do I have to say no to this guy?" he said aloud to himself. He had been an educator at a prestigious private academy. He had risen to a position of importance. He had lived in the same house in which he had grown up, and had been both respected and trusted by everyone who knew him. His had been a quiet, comfortable life, ordinary in most respects perhaps, but satisfying. Then Chas Renzo had put the kibosh on all that. Chas Renzo, with his money and his influence, with his statements to the press and his insinuations of evidence that did not exist, had turned his friends and coworkers against him. Chas Renzo had run him off Block Island. Now the only job he could get was tutoring the dense and ungrateful children of desperate Philadelphia parents.

It was all so unfair. He had done nothing wrong, and there was no evidence to even suggest that he had done anything wrong. The authorities had searched the entire school a year ago, inside and out, and found nothing. They had searched all the homes on the island, every single house and apartment, and every shop and business besides. Nothing was found. The storm that morning had shut down the Point Judith ferry and had halted all travel to and from the island for two solid days. No boats, no planes, no helicopters had come or gone during that time. No one could have gotten on or off the island unless they swam, and people do not swim in the Atlantic Ocean off Block Island in December.

The possibility that Kirk Renzo had somehow made his way down the hill from the Block Island Academy, had crossed Water Street, and had for some reason jumped or fallen into the icy Atlantic waters was certainly considered, but there were no footprints in the snow to suggest it. No one had reported seeing the boy later that day, nor that week, nor in the months that followed the disappearance, or even the following spring after the ice had thawed.

When the weather cleared, the Rhode Island State Police began dragging the bottom of the coves and inlets around Block Island. Divers were sent down to visually inspect the sea floor. Underwater cameras, and even water-trained search dogs, were employed to no effect. Chas Renzo brought in a team of specialists from Hawaii at great expense to employ a side scan sonar system wherein a transducer housed in a tow-fish was towed through the water just above the bottom. They searched for weeks, but through it all found nothing.

One problem, of course, was the lack of any reliable "point last seen" information. The authorities had Prester's explanation, of course, but that was not credible. People don't just disappear. As a result, the search area had to be extended from tens to hundreds of acres. Having nothing solid to go on, the Rhode Island State Police called off their search after 21 days. Chas Renzo had his people continue with the side scan sonar for another three weeks, but still they found nothing. There was no sign of the boy on or off the island.

Prester looked out at the illuminated street. No one was about, except for a man walking his golden retriever. As the man and dog passed a parked sedan, the dog barked and strained at the leash. The man pulled the dog back, appeared to wave to someone in the parked car, and moved on.

Prester kept his eye on the parked car after the man and dog left. In the darkness, he thought he saw the red glow of a lit cigarette pass across the inside of the windshield. He watched for a long time, but no one emerged from the car.

Prester closed the window, and pulled tight the curtains. Crossing the room to where the invitation lay waiting like an unexploded land-mine, he picked it up with both hands and stared at it. After a moment, he slipped the tip of his right forefinger beneath the lip of the seal and tore open the flap. Inside, on a simple white card in black hand-lettered calligraphy, were the words, "The honor of your presence is requested for lunch tomorrow, December 18th, at the home of Mr. Chas Renzo." A Manhattan address on upper 5th Avenue was included.

Prester read the message out loud with a laugh. He knew he spoke aloud to himself often these days, but had long since ceased to consider it a failing. "Right."

He was being summoned. Well, to hell with that, he thought. He was not about to expose himself to more questioning at the hands of Chas Renzo. He'd been through enough of that. He had been inter-rogated nearly a dozen times by the state police, by local authorities, and by the privately paid thugs hired by Kirk's father. He was sick of it. Chas Renzo could go to hell.

Chapter 9

Prester spent the rest of the evening as he usually did. He graded the abysmal papers of his students, ate a turkey pot pie and watched an old movie on TV until he drifted off to sleep. He slept, it seemed, 12 hours a day now, and he could not think of a reason why he should do otherwise.

The next morning, he awoke earlier than usual. He made himself a breakfast of burnt toast, hard boiled eggs and coffee. He dressed in khaki pants and a sweatshirt. On his feet, he wore simple gumshoe boots, appropriate for winter weather. He didn't bother any longer with leather wingtips. A heavy overcoat and wool scarf lay over the back of a kitchen chair ready to go, just in case he should need them. By eight thirty he was sitting on the edge of his bed waiting for the buzzer. It rang at ten o'clock.

Victor from the previous evening smiled when Prester opened the door.

"Good mornin', sir. Are ya ready to go then?" he asked.

"I have a question," Prester said. "How did Chas Renzo find me?"

"I couldn't say, sir," the chauffeur said.

"Well, what does he want? What else could he possibly have to ask me?" Prester asked.

"Again, sir, I couldn't tell ya even if I knew myself," the chauffeur repeated.

Prester had been thinking about the invitation all night, turning the thing over in his mind. What did Chas Renzo want with him this time? Was it just to ask him the same questions all over again about what he had seen and what he had heard? Or were his intentions more sinister this time? Did Chas Renzo intend to do him harm, perhaps to kill him out of some twisted sense of justice? And if so, why warn him with an invitation at all? Why not just burst into the apartment and do him in? Of course, that would be rather messy, Prester thought. That would not be the smartest way to do it. Better to lure him out of his apartment, down onto the street and into a waiting car. That way, Renzo could control the situation, and Chas Renzo was a man who liked to be in control. He could make it look like an accident, a mugging, a hit and run, anything. Chas Renzo was many things, but careless was not one of them.

"Look," Prester said to the chauffeur. "About this, this invitation thing." There was a long drawn out pause.

"Sir?"

"Tell Mr. Renzo I'd rather not. I have things to do today. Just tell him I'm busy, okay?"

"Sir," the chauffeur said, "ya really must come with me."

"Yeah, here's the thing," Prester said. "I've thought a lot about this, and I'm not going. Thanks anyway."

Prester began to close the door, but the chauffeur stuck in his foot.

"I'm afraid, sir, Mr. Renzo will insist upon it," the chauffeur said.

"He always was kind of pushy that way," Prester said. "Look, what's your name? Victor is it? Look, Victor, I understand that you've got a job to do, but I've got my own issues. So just tell Mr. Renzo . . . tell him I said no."

Prodding Victor's toe away, Prester closed and locked the door.

The buzzer sounded.

"I'm not going, Victor."

The buzzer sounded again.

"Go away, Victor."

The buzzer sounded twice more.

"Is this going to go on all day?" he shouted again through the door.

"Mr. Renzo asked that I secure your attendance," Victor shouted back. "If I go back without ya, it'll be my job."

Prester opened the door again and stared at the elderly little man.

"You're not going to give up, are you?"

"I'm afraid not, sir," Victor said.

"Okay," Prester said. "You win." With that, Prester threw on his overcoat, wrapped the scarf around his neck, and stepped outside of his apartment door. He pulled it shut tight, and triple locked it.

"Lead the way," Prester said.

"Very good, sir."

Victor turned on his heels and started down the hallway. Prester followed close behind. At the end of the dingy hall, the men descended a narrow staircase before entering the small lobby, replete with a plastic palm tree and broken floor tiles. They then stepped outside onto Cuthbert Street.

"So," Prester said as he tucked the ends of his scarf into his overcoat, "where's the car?"

"Just there, sir," Victor said, pointing to the left. Prester nodded his understanding.

The chauffeur cantered down Cuthbert Street toward where he had parked the black limousine near a fire hydrant.

"Just follow me, sir," he said over his shoulder as he strode across the icy street. "It's just here a bit further."

Half a block down, Victor stopped to let a car pass. It was then that he noticed it. There were no footsteps behind him. He turned around. Prester was already a full block away, scampering in the opposite direction.

"Ah, bleedin' hell," Victor muttered under his breath.

Sprinting toward the limousine, Victor began snapping his fingers and pointing back in Prester's direction. As he reached the car, two large men in gray hats and top coats emerged from the back seat.

"He's there, right there," Victor shouted at the two thugs. "I t'aught he'd come along a'right, but he's makin' a run for it." The two men nodded and bounded off at a quick pace up the street.

A block away, Prester was not quite running. He had no reason to run, or so he thought. As he reached the corner, however, he glanced back at the limousine to see what had become of the little chauffeur. What he saw were two gorillas barreling towards him at full tilt. He didn't stop to think, but rather darted left and broke into a sprint.

The Philadelphia streets were difficult to navigate. Two snow-storms had blown through within the previous six days covering the City of Brotherly Love with 28 inches of snow, most of which was now piled along the curbs. Prester plunged into the deep crusty slush as he scurried across and down the road.

Running south on North 2nd Street, Prester did not look back until he reached the gated brick entrance to the Colonial era Christ Church, its tall white steeple towering high above. Turning around, he saw the two dark figures still running toward him. Unbelievable, he thought. He scanned up and down the street for a cop, but saw none. What would he tell the police if he did find one, that he was being invited to lunch against his will? It was all too bizarre.

Glancing again at the church tower, he made his decision. They wouldn't dare try anything in a public place, he thought. He ran through the iron gates of the church courtyard, and darted into the small gift shop foyer of the church.

"Good afternoon," a frail woman shopkeeper looked up from behind the counter where she had been setting miniature pocket-sized bibles onto a display. "Welcome to Christ Church."

"Hi," Prester replied. He thought about asking the shopkeeper to call the police, but wasn't sure what he could tell them that would make any sense. "I'm just . . . mind if I look around a bit?"

"By all means, come in," the woman said.

"Thank you." Prester stomped up and down to knock the ice from his pants and boots.

"Where you from, friend?" the woman asked.

"Up the street. I live here," Prester responded.

"Oh, a native."

"Not exactly," Prester said.

"I see," the woman said, although she did not see at all.

Prester stepped through the foyer and into the church proper. White and brown pew boxes lined both sides of the hardwood center aisle. On either side, tall white columns held up a second-story balcony, leading the way to a white altar topped by a triple pane window. The effect was inspiring without being grandiose, a perfect complement to the humble heroes and heroines of the Revolutionary period who had worshipped there.

Only a handful of people were in the church, it not being the tourist season. He had been hoping for a crowd within which he could seek safety. Prester walked up the center aisle, his eyes scanning the perimeter for another exit. He did not see one. Behind him, he heard the shopkeeper greeting additional visitors. Turning, he saw the two gray clad thugs step into the church.

Prester looked into the black eyes of the goons as they made their way up the aisle. How he wished there was a crowd. Glancing from pew to pew, he saw what he was looking for. He stepped into a large pew box designated with a gold informational plate.

"Ladies and gentlemen, gather up, please," Prester spoke in an authoritative voice. "Yes, that's it, this way everyone. Gather around."

The people scattered throughout the church turned to look, then began to migrate toward where Prester was standing.

"My name is Prester John, and I would like to give you a brief yet fascinating history lesson on Christ Church."

Soon a small crowd had formed around the pew box where he stood, perhaps a dozen people in all. Among the crowd were the two thugs.

"This, ladies and gentlemen, is the very pew where George Washington regularly sat while attending Sunday services."

The crowd exuded a collective sigh of satisfaction at this revelation, and moved in a bit closer.

"Indeed, there were lots of very famous people from the Revolutionary War period who used to attend this church. Let's see, there was, there was, George Washington, of course, and Robert Morris, a signer of the Declaration of Independence. And there was Benjamin Franklin. He attended here. And Betsy Ross."

The two thugs waded through the crowd, squeezing past people in an effort to get to where Prester stood.

"The church itself was founded in, in, 1730," Prester said.

"I read that it was founded in 1695," a young girl in the front spoke up.

"Yes, 1695, exactly. That's when it was originally founded," Prester said, trying his best to recall any facts he had read about the place. "They then lost it for a while before it was founded again in 1730."

Several people in the crowd nodded their understanding.

"Gather around, yes, that's it. Come on," Prester encouraged a few stragglers. The crowd grew larger, entangling the two hoodlums a bit more.

"Now, the baptismal font over here," he continued, pointing first to his right, and then to his left, "was designed by the famous American architect, Robert Smith."

"It was the steeple," the young girl chimed in again.

"I'm sorry?" Prester asked, looking past the girl toward the two men behind her trying to push their way in closer.

"It wasn't the baptismal font that he designed, it was the steeple. Robert Smith designed the steeple," the girl said.

"Yes, that's right. Of course that's right," Prester said. "I just wanted to be sure you were listening. Say, where are you from, little girl?"

"Me?" the girl began. "Well, I'm from a little town way out in . . ."

"How about you two," Prester asked, pointing now toward the two brutes. "Yes, the two of you, with the gray hats. Where are you from?"

The men stopped and looked around at the faces now staring at them.

"We're not from here," one of them said.

"Say," the little girl chimed in again, "I was just about to say where I'm from. I'm from a little town way out in . . ."

"I know where you're from," Prester said to the two men, cutting off the little girl again. "You're from New York City, aren't you? See, I know where you're from. And you work for Mr. Chas Renzo. Chas Renzo, ladies and gentlemen. Now we all know where you're from, and for whom you work. And you're here to kidnap me, isn't that right?"

The faces in the crowd fogged over as they oscillated between the two large men and Prester and back again.

"What I want to know is," the little girl interjected again, "where in this church did Benjamin Franklin sit?"

"What was that, dear?" Prester asked, never taking his eyes off the two stooges.

"Benjamin Franklin," she said again. "Where did he sit?"

"Where?" Prester repeated. He had no idea. "I'll tell you where he sat. Benjamin Franklin sat right there," he said, pointing to the pew directly behind the two thugs. As he had hoped, the crowd turned en masse and stepped toward the opposite pew, pinning the two men against the far side of the aisle.

"Right there?" the little girl asked, craning her head to see through the crowd. "I don't think that's right. I think you're making that up," she said, and then turned back to chastise Prester for his comment.

But Prester by this time was gone, his gumshoe boots squeaking down the aisle and out of the church. The two big men, hemmed in by the throng, pushed tourists out of the way to get free, and then lumbered after him, knocking down a Japanese couple in the process.

The two men burst like cannon balls from the church doors and ran out into the open space of the brick courtyard. They looked around for any sign of their prey, hesitated, and then split off in two separate directions. One ran south toward Market Street and Penns Landing. The other ran north toward Filbert. Prester, meanwhile, had already sprinted the three blocks necessary to reach City Tavern, and was holed up in the back corner of the cellar bar.

Chapter 10

It's called the luck of the Irish, and Victor Brophy had it in abundance. Many times he had gotten the unexpected break, had heard tell of the good deal, or had been in the right place at just the right time. Once he found a raffle ticket in the street, picked it up by chance, and won first prize – a portable record player complete with a collection of long-playing albums, or as he called them, "Turty tree and a turds."

And so it was that a police officer had forced Victor Brophy to move his limousine from in front of the fire hydrant on Cuthbert Street. Victor obliged the officer with a tip of his cap, then looped the car west on Arch Street before turning south onto North 2nd. He wanted to find a nearby place to wait so that he would be accessible if Prester were spotted. By chance, Victor found an open parking space near the City Tavern.

It was from here, having settled back into his seat to await a report from his goons, that he happened to see Prester making his headlong dash across the snow-covered sidewalks and into the famous eatery. A quick cell phone call later, and Prester was being manhandled into the back seat of the limo. The two goons sat next to him on either side, and by eleven o'clock the limousine was speeding north along the Delaware Expressway toward Manhattan.

By 1:00 o'clock that afternoon, the car was rolling down Park Avenue. It turned left onto 81st Street, and came to a stop half a block from the Metropolitan Museum of Art. Prester was yanked out of the car, hustled through a side door, pushed through a parking garage, and dragged into a freight elevator. The elevator rose to the top floor of what now appeared to be an apartment complex. Prester was then led down a long corridor, pushed around a turn, and hauled before the door of a corner suite. Victor Brophy rapped on the door before opening it with a magnetic card-key.

"This way, Mr. John, if ya please," Victor said, sweeping his arm toward the door to invite Prester's entrance.

Prester stepped into the apartment and looked around at the marble and glass foyer. Victor entered behind him, followed by the two goons.

"Mr. Renzo is waiting for ya in the den, sir, if ya'd be so kind." Prester followed Victor across the foyer.

Wealth emanated from the residence like luster from gold. On the foyer walls, Prester observed three small paintings of ballet dancers that he recognized as Degas originals. Near them was a large canvas that looked to him to be an English garden done in the distinctive pixel style of George Seurat. Across from that was a Cezanne still life.

"This way, sir," Victor directed. Prester stepped from the airy foyer through a doorway and into a wood-paneled study complete with tall-backed leather armchairs, oak bar and green shaded table lamps.

"Mr. John has arrived, sir," Victor announced to the empty space as Prester entered the room. Then, with a slight bow of the head, Victor departed, closing the door behind him.

Prester looked around. No one was in the room. Hesitating a moment, he turned toward the door and reached for the knob.

"Welcome, Mr. John," a voice emerged from within. Prester turned in the direction of the voice. There was no one there.

"So nice of you to join me," the voice came again. Prester's eyes were drawn to the back of a tall leather chair.

Rising above the high back chair, the thin frame of Chas Renzo stood and turned around. He was dressed in a tailored gray three-piece suit, white shirt with gray pinstripes, and a purple tie crisscrossed with white diagonal lines. He reached out his hand toward Prester, but Prester let the hand hang in the air.

"Why am I here?" Prester insisted.

"Please sit down," Chas Renzo directed. Prester recalled that there was nothing warm or inviting in this man's manner. Ignoring the command, Prester remained standing.

Chas walked across the room to where a dozen bottles and an assortment of glassware sat displayed on the bar. He poured two tumblers of Johnnie Walker Blue Label and started to sip from one glass when he noticed Prester still standing.

"I assure you, Mr. John, I mean you no harm."

"It's early yet," Prester replied.

"Give me a chance to explain. I believe you will find that your trip here today has been a worthwhile venture."

Chas Renzo spoke with an accent, not English exactly, but definitely aristocratic. To Prester, the man spoke as if he were rolling wine across his tongue to savor its full flavor before swallowing.

"I'm going to ask you one more time," Prester said. "Why am I here?"

"All in good time, I assure you. A drink?"

Prester shook his head.

"No? Straight to business then. Let me first apologize for the manner in which my associates obtained your attendance," Chas said. "Although they mean well, they can on occasion be rather roguish."

"Roguish? They kidnapped me."

"I suppose they did, in a manner of speaking. It's my fault, really. You see, I instructed them to bring you here. They don't like to disappoint me."

"Well, I'm afraid I'm going to have to disappoint you," Prester said, "but I had nothing to do with Kirk's disappearance."

Chas Renzo held up the second glass again and rocked it from side to side.

"It's really very good stuff. No?"

"I told the police, I told your private investigators, I told everybody. Your son just disappeared. I don't know what happened to him."

Chas set down the second tumbler and again sipped contemplatively from his own. He then stepped closer to Prester, perhaps too close, and peered into his eyes.

"My son is a tortured soul, Mr. John," Chas said with a tone of genuineness Prester had never before noted in the man. Breaking off, Chas sat on the leather sofa. Prester sat opposite him.

"Kirk is not comfortable around other people," Chas continued. "He was never comfortable around me anyway. His mother, God rest her soul, tried her best with him. She died when Kirk was only seven. One cannot, I find, be both father and mother to a troubled boy. That, at least, has always been my excuse."

Prester watched as Chas took another sip from his glass and stared into space. Prester had no idea what if anything he should say to this man, what he could do for him, or why he was here.

"We cannot seem to see eye to eye on things, that's the trouble in a nutshell," Chas continued. "Perhaps we're too much alike. Sometimes I think we put on a show for each other. Do you know what I mean?"

"Yes, I think so," Prester replied.

"He is very independent in his way, you know. Nothing scares him. As his teacher, perhaps you've noticed that."

"Mr. Renzo," Prester interrupted, "you speak as if Kirk is alive, and maybe he is. I'd give anything if that were true. But he's gone, and he's been gone for nearly a year. There's nothing I can do about that."

"Yes, well," Chas said as he placed his drink on a side table. Rising to his feet, the thin man crossed the room to where a large wood-panel painting in the style of the Renaissance masters hung on the wall. The painting depicted a formal banquet with servants bringing food to people seated at two long cloth-covered tables receding back under a series of arches. Grasping the painting, he gently lifted it from the wall.

"I'd like to show you something, Mr. John," he said. "I think you will find this rather interesting."

Prester said nothing, but continued to look on.

"This is entitled *The Story of Nastagio degli Onesti*. Botticelli painted it in Italy over half a millennia ago at the height of the Italian Renaissance. I acquired it some twenty years back as an investment. Once per year, I have all my collected works of art taken down and cleaned in order to preserve them."

"Did you bring me here to tell me about your art collection?" Prester asked with irritation.

"Recently," Chas continued, ignoring the comment, "while this painting was being cleaned, I noticed something unusual on the back. Something was written there that I had never seen before."

"Mr. Renzo, this is all very interesting, but . . ."

"I'd like you to read what is written on the back. I cannot help but think that in some way it has something to do with Kirk's disappearance."

Prester, now intrigued, stepped forward and took hold of the masterwork. Turning it over, he looked at the back and read the words written there. His eyes grew wider.

"That's from BIA exactly."

"Yes."

"Did Kirk write it?"

"I had the ink tested," Chas said. "There is no doubt it was written 500 years ago."

"An astonishing coincidence," Prester said, handing the painting back to Chas.

"I do not believe in coincidence, Mr. John," Chas said, setting the painting down.

"How could it be connected to Kirk's disappearance?" Prester asked.

"Yes, regarding that, I want you to know that I don't blame you. Oh, I did. Most assuredly, I did, and for a long while too, but no longer. I apologize for all the inconveniences I've caused you. You see, I was in a great deal of pain, and as such I relished in hearing of your troubles - your time in jail, your termination from BIA, your friends and associates turning on you. I've kept a close watch over your declining career during this past year."

"Let's be honest, Mr. Renzo. You did much more than watch my decline," Prester said.

"Um, yes, yes, I will admit to that. But I have recently given the matter a great deal of second thought," Chas continued. "Would you like to know what I have concluded?"

"Not really," Prester said, his anger welling up again.

"I've concluded that you are not cunning enough to have orchestrated my son's disappearance. Don't misunderstand me. I'm not suggesting a lack of intelligence on your part. Your students, I know, once considered you quite brilliant."

Prester jumped to his feet.

"I think it's time for me to leave," Prester said as he turned and started walking toward the door.

"Please, Mr. John, I am clumsy at this business of apologizing. It's just that over the past year I've found nothing in your life to suggest that you've ever been in the slightest deceitful."

"No one asked you to look into my life. Good day, Mr. Renzo," Prester said as he opened the study door to leave.

"Which is why I wish to make you an offer," Chas said. "I need your help, Mr. John, and I'm willing to pay you handsomely for it."

"You want me to work for you? I don't think that would be a good idea," Prester said as he started through the open door.

"I'm prepared to pay you one million dollars to help me find my son," Chas said. "I'm sure you could use the money."

"I don't want your money," Prester shot back as he crossed over the marble floor.

"Won't you at least hear my proposition?" Chas shouted.

"Not interested," Prester shouted back as he approached the entryway and began to open the large main door to make his exit.

"I'm offering you a chance at redemption, Mr. John," Chas shouted after him. "I'm offering you your life back."

Prester stopped.

Chapter 11

Florence, Italy - Sunday, April 8, 1492

Lorenzo de' Medici lay in his sick bed. In his head, a cacophony of cannonballs fired against the inside of his skull. His eyes were shut against the stinging candlelight, yet he was awake and could hear his personal physician, Lazzaro de Pavia, discussing his treatment with a medical intern.

"It is a special potion of my own design," came Lazzaro's voice, "consisting of a small amount of olive oil mixed with the dust of distilled precious gemstones."

"Ideal, I'm sure, doctor," the intern responded, "and yet the patient grows worse by the day. Perhaps he is in need of another bloodletting, possibly from a vein in his other arm."

"No, not from his arm," Lazzaro explained. "If the patient's head is in pain, then the proper procedure is to bleed him from the feet so as to draw the illness away from the head. Do you understand?"

"Ah, yes doctor, most logical. Should I secure more leeches?" the intern asked.

"I fear there is not sufficient time for that method," Lazzaro said. "A slow release of blood over an extended time will not do in this case. The patient would prosper best from a gush of blood such as to induce fainting."

"I have read about this procedure in the Galen text," the intern confirmed. "Do you think it is the best way, doctor?"

"I do. Hand me the scalpel," Lazzaro the physician ordered, "and brace him should he awake."

"Enough!" Lorenzo de' Medici barked, raising a feeble hand in the air. "Leave me."

"But my Lord," said the physician, startled to find that his patient was not asleep. "You are very ill and in need of our care."

Lorenzo opened his eyes and looked up at the red and gold drapes that hung around the dark carved wood posts of his bed. He saw his physician staring down at him.

"No more bloodletting," Lorenzo said. "I do not wish for you to take another drop. Leave me with what little I have left, for I find that I still have need of it."

"You are delirious, my Lord," the intern interjected. "Let us do our jobs."

"You have done what you can," Lorenzo said. "Now we must leave things to God."

"But my Lord," the physician protested. "There is yet more we can do for you."

"Go now, good doctor," Lorenzo said. "Come back tomorrow and we shall discuss the matter once more." Lorenzo's tone was quiet and resigned. He smiled through half closed eyes as the physician Lazzaro and his intern bowed and departed.

"Angelo," Lorenzo's cracking voice called out after the medical men had left.

Angelo Poliziano drew back the curtains and leaned in close. "I am here, old friend," he said.

Lorenzo's eyes fixed on the face of his childhood companion and lifelong ally, the man who had saved his life in the Duomo those many years ago during the Pazzi conspiracy.

"What time is it?" Lorenzo asked.

Poliziano looked up beyond the bed curtain to the fading light beyond the window.

"Dusk," he said.

"How long have I been asleep?"

"Not long enough," Poliziano answered. "You need to sleep more."

"Yes, yes, I know I should," Lorenzo said. "And soon enough I will, but there is much to attend to."

"Of course," Poliziano said, always willing to defer to his master despite their long familiarity.

Poliziano raised a cup of warm red wine to the lips of the sick man. The pungent liquid soothed Lorenzo's inflamed throat, a welcome relief as he considered the weight of his present position and the political dilemma it presented.

"Tell me of our financial accounts," Lorenzo said.

Poliziano picked up a large double-entry ledger that was kept near Lorenzo's bed. He opened it to the middle and ran his finger down the page.

"Our merchants in the Netherlands are late again on their interest payments," Poliziano said, "but an envoy has already been dispatched to meet with the Duke of Burgundy to discuss the matter."

"Very good," Lorenzo said. "Anything else?"

"Oh, a point of some interest," Poliziano added, "you may recall the young sea captain from Genoa who was seeking funds for a westward exploration into the open sea?"

"Yes, yes, I recall the matter," Lorenzo said. "We turned down his loan request, did we not?"

"We did. It seems, however, that he has at last acquired financial support from the Spanish crown. Reports are that he will set sail from Spain this very August."

"I am surprised that Ferdinand and Isabella have the funds for such adventures, given their military campaigns in Granada."

"I am given to understand that the investment is a rather modest one. Only three ships," Poliziano said.

"Not an expedition likely to change the world," Lorenzo added. "Well, perhaps for the King and Queen the voyage will at least serve as a temporary diversion from their incessant persecution of the Jews," Lorenzo observed. "Where is Nicolo?"

"I shall send for him," Poliziano said, and immediately gave the order to summon Lorenzo's chief political counselor, Nicolo Machiavelli.

The short, stern faced man arrived moments later, having been called from his writing desk.

"Pray I have not pulled you away from something too serious," Lorenzo said when Machiavelli came near to his bedside. "But we must speak, Nicolo."

"Certainly, my Lord," Machiavelli said. "I was just making notes for a theme I have been considering on the nature of princely political power."

"And what of your history of Florence?" Lorenzo asked. "How is it progressing?"

"Steady progress, my Lord. But I trust you did not call upon me to inquire as to my literary pursuits."

"Your literary pursuits are worthy of the greatest attention," Lorenzo said, "but no, I have called you for another purpose. We must speak together now."

As Poliziano laid a cold cloth across Lorenzo's forehead, Machiavelli pulled a chair close to the bed.

"What news is there of Savonarola?" Lorenzo asked.

"He continues to preach daily in the Duomo, my Lord," Machiavelli said.

"And does Florence listen?" Lorenzo asked.

"The throng grows larger by the hour," came Machiavelli's reply.

Lorenzo shook his head. "Why do they not see him for what he is?"

"I think, Lorenzo," Poliziano interjected, "that the people see in Savonarola not just a pious monk, but a Paladin of the faith."

"But Savonarola advocates for the death and destruction of Florence, and says it is God's will," Lorenzo said. "He calls for repentance, but offers no mercy. He tells the people that they are sinners, and that Florence is evil. He tells them that God shall forsake them merely because they wish to live in His greater glory rather than in His shadow. It is madness, and yet the people listen and follow. He speaks against me too, I know. I have become the antagonist in his apocryphal predictions."

"That is true, my Lord," Machiavelli agreed. "Yesterday, while you slept, three armed men came to the palace demanding vanities."

"Vanities?" Lorenzo asked.

"They were not particular," Machiavelli responded. "They demanded that we turn over to them anything of humanistic art: statutes, paintings, books."

"Did you send them away?"

"Of course, but they went away with curses, curses against you, my Lord, I am sorry to say."

"They are simple people," Poliziano said. "They do not understand what is happening to them."

"Simple, yes, but dangerous," Machiavelli clarified. "Although we gave them nothing, others could not as easily resist. They and other roving bands like them went house to house throughout the city, demanding anything of classic beauty."

"My God," Lorenzo said. "Does Savonarola think we need to sacrifice all our earthly graces to that of the heavenly Father?"

"Savonarola's thugs seized paintings, statuary, vases, pottery and books, many, many books," Machiavelli continued. "All this was thrown into a bonfire. Oh, it was a lamentable thing to behold."

Lorenzo shook his head. "It is time," he said. "Send for Savonarola. Tell him that I wish to speak with him."

"What if he refuses to come?" Poliziano asked. The thought had not occurred to Lorenzo.

"He will come," Machiavelli said. Indeed, they had always come, the kings and queens, the princes and lords, the popes and priests and monks, the artists, the poets and the thinkers. They had all come to meet with, to speak with, and to pay homage to Lorenzo the Magnificent. They had come, most of them, not from fear, but from love, or at least from respect. Even Lorenzo's enemies respected him for his calm leadership in the face of mounting dangers, and for his unrivaled abilities at diplomacy. It was the consensus that Florence would not exist as a free city-state but for the talents of Lorenzo, and thus Lorenzo's wishes were granted tremendous deference by all.

"Nicolo," Lorenzo said in little more than a whisper, for his strength was already beginning to wane. "Come closer."

Machiavelli leaned in so that his cheek brushed Lorenzo's lips.

"Yes, my Lord," he said.

"Tell me, old friend," Lorenzo murmured. "Have I not always done well for them? Have I not earned their trust and loyalty?"

Machiavelli thought a moment before answering.

"You are the chief merchant and banker of Florence and of the surrounding territories," he began his explanation. "As such, you provide to the citizens of Florence a sense of security, for they know that among all things your first love is for Florence. It is for this same reason, however, that news of your illness has filled the people with doubt and fear, a fear that is quickly turning to hostility, for it is in the nature of people to feel contempt for that which they fear may desert them."

"I am not dead yet," Lorenzo said.

"No, master, and pray that God keeps you with us for many years to come. But the people, my Lord, the people fear for themselves and for their well-being should you pass on prematurely."

"Have you talked with the physician?" Lorenzo asked.

"Yes, my Lord."

"He is not hopeful, I think. He and his young assistant do not tell me this with their words, but with their sighs and silences. Nicolo, you must tell me. What do they believe?"

"Master, I am your political adviser. It is not my place to speak for your physician," Machiavelli said.

"Then you, Angelo. You have always spoken the truth to me, even when it was not pleasant to hear. Now I need you to speak the truth again. Tell me, old friend, what is the physician saying? Will I live or die?"

Angelo Poliziano looked up at Machiavelli, and then lowered his gaze again toward Lorenzo.

"I have heard," Poliziano said, "that he cannot be sure. He is confounded as to the reason for your malady, and he is equally puzzled as to its cure. But . . ." his voice trailed off.

"Tell me," Lorenzo pleaded.

"He is not optimistic," Poliziano added.

"Please, Angelo," Lorenzo said, "be plain in your meaning. It is important that I know."

"Yes, my friend, you will die," Poliziano said, a tear forming in his eye as he spoke. "Your physician cannot be absolute in his prognosis, of course, but he is confident in his ignorance. He does not know how to help you, and your condition grows worse by the hour. And so yes, Lorenzo, he believes that you will die, barring a miracle from God."

"I have always believed in miracles," Lorenzo said.

"As have I, old friend," Poliziano agreed, "and God has always been there for us."

"I suppose God will take me in His own good time. If it is soon, then perhaps there is need of me in heaven," Lorenzo said smiling.

"There is need of you in Florence," Poliziano said, squeezing Lorenzo's hand. Lorenzo smiled, and turned again toward his political adviser.

"Nicolo, our time together may be short," Lorenzo said. "As to this damnable priest, what is your counsel?"

"Savonarola has presented himself to the people of Florence at the very moment of your physical and hence your political weakness," Machiavelli said. "As I see it, Savonarola would be well positioned to wrench power away from the Medici in Florence but for the presence of the new papal prince."

"That boy?" Lorenzo protested. "He is a mere youth of no discernible lineage, is he not?"

"I have not met him, master, but I am told that he is a young lad of considerable knowledge and insight," Machiavelli said. "He is called Prince Kirkrenzo, and none other than Leonardo da Vinci has befriended him. The new Borgia Pope, Alexander VI, has taken both Leonardo and this new prince into his court."

"I have been too much inside these walls," Lorenzo said. "What have you heard about this boy, this Kirkrenzo? Where is he from?"

"His origins are unknown, but since his sudden appearance three months ago, he has become the talk of all Italy," Machiavelli said. "He has brought much public favor upon the Church in Rome. They say that his knowledge of advanced science and mathematics, and his felicity with technical invention, seems far advanced for one of such tender years. But there is more."

"More?" Lorenzo asked. "What more?"

"It is said that he can foretell the future."

"No, this cannot be."

"One would think not, and yet he has already predicted some remarkable events. Poliziano mentioned, for example, that you were discussing the Genovese sailor who had sought a loan from us, Captain Cristopher Columbus."

"Yes, I believe that was his name."

"It seems that Prince Kirkrenzo informed Pope Alexander months ago that the Spanish crown would finance the venture even before Ferdinand and Isabella had decided the matter for themselves, indeed even before Columbus had been informed of the grant. The boy also correctly predicted the names of the three ships that would be commissioned for the voyage. Pope Alexander has deemed the boy to be a miracle from God, and the people have come to view him as divinely blessed."

"Such a remarkable prince adds greatly to the power of the Pontiff," Lorenzo pointed out.

"Indeed," Machiavelli agreed. "With this boy prince by his side, and the public adulation he brings, Pope Alexander has become the third leg of a politically balanced stool. Savonarola will not move against the Medici while Prince Kirkrenzo remains in the public favor, for to do so would only cause the public to turn their support to Rome. Similarly, the Pope will not attempt to silence Savonarola's heretical pronouncements while you yet live, for by doing so the Church would lose the favor of the public and serve only to strengthen the Medici, whom the Pontiff also fears."

"But should I die?"

"Yes, my Lord, should you die, the stool will be upset. The people will, in your absence, turn to the strongest leader, and this young prince may in time give Pope Alexander the superior mantle in that regard."

"Then Savonarola, for all his ranting against me, should more properly fear Rome," Lorenzo concluded.

"That is undoubtedly the case," Machiavelli said.

"I must speak with Savonarola myself, and soon," Lorenzo said. "I must reason with him. I must make him see that his success can come only from working with, not against, the Medici."

"Master," Machiavelli said, "Savonarola does not strike me as a man who can be reasoned with."

"Did you not tell me once, Nicolo, that all men are capable of humility, given the proper incentive?"

"Yes, my Lord," Machiavelli said. "But Savonarola has already humbled himself before God. Would that he were to also humble himself before any man is less certain."

"I must try, Nicolo," Lorenzo said as he slipped into a fit of coughing. Machiavelli placed a cup of water to his lips and held his head until the coughing subsided. "I must reason with him, for the good of Florence," Lorenzo continued. "I must make him see that his war against me can only destroy us both."

"I will send for him," Machiavelli said.

"Do so without delay, Nicolo," Lorenzo said, and then closed his eyes and sank into the pillow.

Chapter 12

Machiavelli eased the door closed as he and Poliziano left Lorenzo's bedchamber. Waiting just beyond the door, with tears welling up in his eyes, was Lorenzo's 17-year-old ward, Michelangelo Buonarroti.

"May I see him?" the boy asked.

"He is very ill, son," Machiavelli replied. "I think he had better rest."

Michelangelo looked pale and tired. Moisture dripped from one nostril of his crooked nose, and he wiped it with his dust-covered sleeve. The nose had been fractured by a sucker punch from a jealous, former student some two years before.

"Will he die?" Michelangelo asked.

"Shouldn't you be in the Garden with the other students?" Machiavelli chided.

"Master Bertoldo granted me permission to come here," Michelangelo said. Under his right arm, he carried a marble tablet.

"Ah, special favors for a special student, eh?" Machiavelli said, but the boy did not smile.

"I want to show him my sculpture," the boy said.

Machiavelli looked at him for a long moment.

"All right," he said, "but just for a few minutes, no more."

Michelangelo wiped the tears from his cheeks and entered Lorenzo's room. The door creaked as Michelangelo pulled it closed behind him. He then eased his way across the wooden floor to Lorenzo's bedside and hovered over the reclined body of his benefactor before venturing to speak.

"It is I," he whispered. Lorenzo's eyes opened, and the older man looked up at the boy.

"Ah, Michelangelo," Lorenzo smiled. "You have come to see me. I knew you would."

"I could not stay away, sir," he said.

"How are you, my boy?"

"I am well, sir. Just today I have finished my second piece. I brought it for you to see," Michelangelo said.

"Splendid," Lorenzo said. "Show me."

Michelangelo held up the marble base-relief sculpture for Lorenzo to inspect.

"It is a companion to my first relief," Michelangelo explained. "Master Bertoldo read to me the myth of the battle of the Lapiths against the Centaurs, and I was taken by his descriptions. He spoke of the wild forces of life being locked in heroic combat. This I tried to depict through the male form at war."

"It is very different from your first piece. What did you call that one?"

"The Madonna of the Stairs," Michelangelo replied.

"Yes, I remember it: Mary upon a rock, the child Jesus curling into her body, and she already envisioning his death and eventual return to God on the stairway to heaven."

"Yes, my Lord. The two works have opposite and complimentary themes. The first was spiritual in form, while this one is of the earth and mortal men," Michelangelo commented.

"Yes, I can see that. Michelangelo, you have come a long way since joining our little school," Lorenzo said. "How old were you then? Fourteen?"

"I was but thirteen, my Lord."

"Only thirteen. Do you remember when I first saw you sculpt? You were making a copy of a piece from antiquity, the head of an old faun. It was perfect in every way. I was truly amazed. Indeed, it was too perfect, for I noticed that you had given it all its teeth. Do you remember what I said to you?"

"I do," Michelangelo said. "You told me that old people never have all their teeth; there are always some missing?"

"Yes, yes, that is what I said. And no sooner had I said it than you took your chisel and broke off one of the faun's teeth to make it look as if it had fallen out from decay," Lorenzo laughed. "The skill with which you wielded your chisel even at that tender age was something to behold. I knew then, Michelangelo, that you would be a great artist if given the proper training and discipline. That is why I asked your dear father, Lodovico, to let me keep you here in my household, so that I might raise you as my own son."

"Yes, my Lord. I am forever grateful that you did," Michelangelo said.

"You should be grateful to your father, Michelangelo, for it was he who made the greatest sacrifice."

Michelangelo nodded, a tear forming in his eye.

"I love my father, of course, but you are like a father to me as well."

"That is kind of you to say. And now look at the fine young man you are becoming," Lorenzo continued. "You will have great success, I have no doubt of that, my boy. Ah, the things you will do as you grow. The works you will create."

"And you will see them all," Michelangelo said.

Lorenzo smiled and grasped the boy's hand.

"Your birthday," Lorenzo remembered. "It was your birthday last month."

"March the 6th, my Lord," Michelangelo said.

"Yes, yes. I have not been myself, or I should have remembered. Michelangelo, I want you to have something for your birthday. There, upon the mantle across the room, bring me that box," Lorenzo said, pointing to a spot above the fireplace.

Michelangelo crossed the room and retrieved the wooden box from atop the mantle over the fire. He brought it back to Lorenzo.

"Open it," Lorenzo instructed him.

Michelangelo opened the top. Inside were twin jewel-encrusted daggers displayed against a background of red velvet.

"These knives represent my good fortune, and my great sorrow," Lorenzo said. "I want you to have them, and I want you to always remember that as we go through life, happiness and sorrow go with us hand in hand."

Michelangelo looked at the knives. He had heard Lorenzo tell of their treacherous history, and he knew what they represented to him.

"My Lord, these are very special to you."

"They are yours, Michelangelo," Lorenzo said. "Now listen to me, my dear boy. Come closer and listen carefully to what I have to say."

Michelangelo drew in closer to Lorenzo.

"Florence is your home," Lorenzo continued. "It has been a wonderful place for you. It is where you have grown up. It has offered you sculpture, painting, architecture, all the finest examples of art for your studies. It has provided you sustenance for your soul. Your own mother died when you were very young. In her place, Florence has been your mother," Lorenzo said. "But Florence is changing, Michelangelo. She is becoming rigid and unforgiving. She is growing stern in her old age. Her old eyes are failing her, and she can no longer see the beauty in things as you can. And so as with all young men, it is time for you to leave your mother. Go to Rome, Michelangelo. There are great fountains in Rome, and piazzas, and grand buildings such as you have never imagined. Your talent is great, my boy. It is time for you to leave your mother in her old age, and go find your future."

"I have always valued your counsel, my Lord," Michelangelo said, "and I respect your opinions more than any man alive. But I cannot leave Florence. You have much still to teach me."

"Think about what I have said," Lorenzo stated. "Go now, back to school, for I am expecting another visitor."

Michelangelo rose up, clutching the boxed daggers to his chest, and looked at Lorenzo for a long moment. Lorenzo smiled a half smile and nodded. Michelangelo understood that it was time for him to go, and slipped from the room.

Lorenzo lay still for some time. He could not be sure how long. In due course, he heard the door to his bedchamber open again, and Poliziano was at his side, smiling down at him.

"My dear friend," Lorenzo said, grasping Poliziano's hand. "Has Savonarola come?"

"He awaits you just outside."

"Then bring him in. I feel the sands of the hour glass slipping too quickly by."

Poliziano burst into a flood of tears.

"Oh, Lorenzo," Poliziano said. "To you I owe everything. Why has God done this?"

"Now, now, Angelo," Lorenzo said. "You will be fine. Let us not question God's wisdom. He has given me many years of happiness on this earth, and it is now time for me to go home."

"It is I who should be comforting you, Lorenzo. But instead you comfort me."

"You are here," Lorenzo said. "In that there is great comfort for me."

Poliziano leaned down and kissed the hand of Lorenzo the Magnificent.

"Bring Savonarola to me," Lorenzo wheezed.

Poliziano walked across the room, opened the door, and ushering in the priest.

Savonarola, tall and gaunt, was dressed in a black robe and hood, with simple leather sandals on his feet. Upon entering the room, he stood in the doorway and glared at Lorenzo before proceeding across the floor. Poliziano pulled a chair near to the bed, and Savonarola sat down.

"Thank you for coming," Lorenzo said, his voice weaker now than it had been moments before. Despite his physical frailty, Lorenzo pushed himself up in the bed. Poliziano took hold of his shoulder, helping him forward to meet the priest.

"They tell me you are dying, Lorenzo," Savonarola said in a matter-of-fact tone.

"You come right to the point," Lorenzo responded.

"Others may temper their remarks with you," the priest replied, "but I have never forsaken truth in favor of false comfort."

"Of course. I know of no honest friar but you, and that is why I have asked you here." Lorenzo coughed. "Father, my mind is haunted by specters of the past."

"And so you call upon me for absolution?" Savonarola asked.

"Yes, for absolution, and so that we may speak one last time of our city."

"What have you to tell me of Florence?" Savonarola asked.

"I tell you, I implore you, I humbly beseech you to understand her for all that she is. You, Father, can be of great service to her. Florence needs your steady, guiding hand. But be gentle with her, for she is temperamental in her affections. Guide her, but do not push her away from all that is beautiful in nature and in man. Remember that Florence needs her beauty as much as it needs her piety."

"Your thoughts are of self-interest," Savonarola said.

"No, father. They are of your interest," Lorenzo responded. "I will soon be gone, but Florence will remain. The question is, will she live in peace and tranquility, or in turmoil? You, Father, hold the key to her future. Should you push her too far, you will lose her. You know yourself that the Holy See has shown displeasure with your talk of visions, your proclaimed revelations, your threats of coming ills, and your harangues against the church. Rome will not hesitate to act, perhaps even to the point of your excommunication, should they determine that you have gone too far. Father, I fear for the destruction that may rain down upon our fine city should you falter."

Savonarola said nothing in response to Lorenzo's warning. He listened, but showed no emotion. After a moment's contemplation, he spoke.

"Regarding your absolution, Lorenzo," he said, "what sins do you wish to relate to me?"

Lorenzo sank back into his pillow, and exhaled a lengthy sigh. He had done his best. The future of Florence was now out of his hands.

"I have tried to live a decent life, Father, but as with all men I have committed many sins," he said to Savonarola. "Still, of them all there is one I am especially anxious to confess."

"God is good. God is merciful," Savonarola said. "Tell me of your sin."

"You are aware of the Pazzi conspiracy?" Lorenzo asked.

"I was but a student in the Dominican Order at Bologna at that time," Savonarola replied, "but certainly I have heard the stories."

"Then you must know that the Pazzi killed my younger brother, Giuliano, and they very nearly killed me. The treachery of the Pazzi in attacking us in the Duomo was unparalleled, as were the bloody reprisals that followed."

"I am given to understand that it was a terrible episode," Savonarola commented.

"I was young then, and my sadness turned quickly to anger. I could have stopped the killing, father. I could have stopped the retribution. But I did not. The Florentine people are a forgiving people, but I did not ask them to forgive. I allowed them to seek their revenge without limit. Many died in those days and weeks following the attack. In looking back, I have always regretted that I did not intervene. When Florence needed my wisdom, they got only my silence. When they needed my compassion, they got only my fury, and I allowed it to happen."

"And it is for this sin that you now seek forgiveness?"

"Yes, father."

Savonarola sat back and considered the situation for a long moment. He then leaned forward again.

"Three things are needed before I can offer you absolution," Savonarola said.

"What things, Father?"

Savonarola extended his right hand and began to count them off one bony finger at a time.

"Firstly, you need to possess a great and living faith in God's mercy," Savonarola said.

"I have the fullest faith in God and His mercy," Lorenzo replied.

"Secondly, you must restore all your ill-gotten wealth, or charge your heirs to restore it in your name after you are gone."

At this, Lorenzo seemed to be struck with surprise, followed by grief. Nevertheless, making an effort, he gave a nod of assent.

"I will make provision for it in my last will and testament."

Savonarola then stood up, his black robe flowing down as he seemed to soar above the dying prince.

"Lastly," Savonarola said, "you must restore liberty to the people of Florence by having the Medici relinquish all control of their financial interests and political authority." Savonarola's face was solemn, his voice severe, his eyes fixed on those of Lorenzo as if seeking to divine Lorenzo's response.

Gathering up his remaining strength, Lorenzo took a deep breath. "You ask too much," he said.

"I ask only what God requires," Savonarola proclaimed.

Lorenzo stared up at the defiant priest. Then, without uttering another word, he rolled over, showing his back to Savonarola.

"You have made your choice," Savonarola said, and then turned and left the room without granting him absolution.

Lorenzo, racked with regret, spent a restless night. As dawn approached, he breathed his last.

Chapter 13

Manhattan Island, New York

A. Joseph Brennan, Director of the Metropolitan Museum of Art, stood before the 'Portrait of a Young Man,' and stared at the canvas in disbelief. It was now forty-three minutes past closing.

"Let me see the book," he commanded. Annie handed him the large coffee-table book she had purchased the day before in the Museum shop. He opened it and turned to the photographs of the paintings from Fifteenth Century Florence. There on the printed page was a four by six photograph of the 'Portrait of a Young Man,' artist unknown, in full color. The photograph in the book showed a young man in his mid to late twenties, brown eyes, straight Roman nose, and jet-black hair with no part, the hair coming down such that it covered all but the lobe of the left ear. The boy was dressed in a black collar with a red fur-trimmed tunic. He was depicted from the waist up, sitting serenely with hands folded in front of him, looking to the left of the canvas.

Looking up from the book, the Director glared at the painting that hung on the museum wall. There within its 15 by 11 inch wooden frame was what purported to be the 'Portrait of a Young Man'. The figure in the painting was dressed in the same black collar and red fur-trimmed tunic as the figure in the book, but it was not the same young man. In the painting, the young man held his chin higher. Also, the cut of his hair was noticeably different, with a part to one side. And in the painting the boy's nose deviated as if it had been broken.

"That is not 'Portrait of a Young Man,'" the Director whispered almost to himself. "Annie?" he asked.

"Yes, sir?"

"Listen to me very carefully now. Are you listening?"

"Yes, sir."

"I want you to do exactly as I say. Exactly. Can you do that, Annie?"

"Yes, sir."

"Take that painting off the wall. Do it right away. Then take it to my office and give it to my secretary, Mrs. Trumbull. Do you understand me, Annie?"

"Yes, sir. You want me to take the painting off the wall, and then . . ."

"You don't need to repeat what I said, Annie. Just do what I said, exactly."

"Yes, sir."

"Very well. Now, after you've removed the painting and delivered it to my office, I want you to go home or wherever it is you go after you leave here. But do not breathe a word of this to anyone, do you hear me?"

"Not a word, sir. I mean, yes sir, I hear you."

"Report back to my office at 9:00 sharp tomorrow morning. Will you do that, Annie?"

"Yes, sir, of course."

"Very good."

Annie smiled and nodded.

"Annie?" the Director added.

"Yes, sir?"

"Is there something wrong?"

"No, sir."

"Then go, go, do."

"Ah, right," she said, and then reached out and removed the painting from the wall. With a half curtsey, she turned and carried the painting through the gallery toward the elevator.

"Oh, and Annie?" the Director called after her.

"Yes, sir?"

"Thank you for showing me this."

"Oh, don't mention it, sir."

"Mum's the word, eh?"

"Oh, yes sir. Not to worry," she said.

After she had gone, the Director dialed his cell phone and held it to his ear. It rang only once before being answered.

"It's me," the Director said into the phone. "We have another one."

Chapter 14

Prester turned in the middle of the foyer and glared back at Chas Renzo.

"What sort of game are you playing?" he asked.

"No game, Mr. John."

"I don't want your money," Prester assured him.

"I believe you."

"What do you mean, you can give me my life back?"

"I mean just what I say."

Prester hesitated. He did not like Chas Renzo. He did not trust him. Every instinct within him was telling him to just walk away. But what more did he have to lose? Returning to the study, he sat down.

"All right, I'm listening," Prester said.

Chas smiled. "What I'm about to tell you may not initially seem to you to be rational. Quite frankly, I didn't believe it myself at first. I ask only that you bear with me until you have received the full explanation."

"I said I was listening," Prester repeated himself.

"There is a scientific facility on Long Island known as the Brookhaven National Laboratory. Have you heard of it?"

Prester shook his head.

"I hadn't either. But they have there a machine, an atomic accelerator called the Relativistic Heavy Ion Collider. With this machine they are able to study all manner of things having to do with how the world works on a subatomic level."

"Quantum mechanics," Prester said.

"Exactly. Recently I was visited by one of their scientists, a brilliant young physicist from Pakistan named Dr. Akram Ponnuru. He told me that he had read about Kirk's disappearance, and had a theory about what may have happened to him. Moreover, he said he thought he could help find him. Well, of course, I agreed to listen to what he had to say."

"A physicist?" Prester asked. "I don't understand."

"I would like you to meet with Dr. Ponnuru."

"Meet him? Why?"

"Because he asked to meet with you."

Prester was dumbstruck by this.

"How does he even know me?"

"Again, he read about the disappearance. Your name was, of course, prominently mentioned."

"And when is this meeting supposed to take place?" Prester asked.

"Now," Chas said. "He will be joining us for lunch. In fact, he's waiting for us as we speak. I hope you don't mind."

Prester could only admire the fact that Chas Renzo was a man who did not waste time.

Chas Renzo rose, gesturing for Prester to follow. They stepped from the study and crossed the foyer into a formal dining room replete with ornate crown moldings. As they entered the dining room, a small dark skinned man rose to greet them.

"Dr. Ponnuru, so good to see you again," Chas said, extending his hand.

"Thank you please for your very kind invitation," Ponnuru said, nodding his head.

"This is Prester Charles John, formerly of the Block Island Academy."

"Ah yes, Mr. John," Ponnuru said, extending his hand. "I am so glad to be making your acquaintance."

"I'm told you wanted to speak with me?" Prester asked.

"Indeed, this is a true thing. You see, I have read of the terrible tragedy of last year. I refer of course to the boy who disappeared. Terrible, terrible."

"Mr. Renzo tells me you have a theory as to what happened to him."

"This will require some explanation," Ponnuru said with something of a twinkle in his eye.

"All right," Prester said, taking a seat at the table. "Have at it, doctor."

Ponnuru smiled, took a deep breath and paced across the room to gather his thoughts.

"We must be beginning," he said, "by looking closely at the nature of time itself."

Prester peered at him. "Okay," he said.

"Einstein tells us that time is like a river, and that we, you, I, all of us, are like people in a boat floating upon this river that winds out of sight ahead of us, and curves back beyond our view behind us. We are seeing nothing of this river except that portion upon which we float, and yet we should not by this be concluding that the river ahead and behind does not exist."

"Hum," Prester grunted. "I presume this is going somewhere?"

"We are speaking of the past, the present and the future because these words are convenient to our daily experience," Ponnuru pressed on. "In truth, however, time, like Einstein's river, is existing all around us, all at once. The events of the past, present and future are, in reality, all happening at the same time."

Prester crossed his arms and sat back.

"You know, this is all very intriguing in its own way," Prester said, "but how does any of it relate to the disappearance of Kirk Renzo?"

"I am speaking to this point momentarily," Ponnuru answered, "but first I must be asking you a few questions about the day of the boy's disappearance."

Prester grimaced. Here we go, he thought. He had answered and answered and answered such questions. He was sick of such questions. He was sick of being accused of something he had not done, and his contempt showed on his face.

"I assure you, Mr. John," Chas spoke up. "I have no idea what Dr. Ponnuru wants to ask you."

Prester stared at Chas Renzo. He considered getting up and walking out. He squirmed in his chair, and looked at the door.

"What questions?" he finally asked, looking back at Ponnuru.

"The boy, when he disappeared, was standing near a very old tree, is this not true?" Ponnuru asked.

"He was running," Prester replied. "I was chasing him. He was maybe twenty yards ahead of me when he turned the corner. I followed his footprints directly to the old Block Island Oak."

"And what time was this being, Mr. John? Please be as precise as possible, if you would."

Prester thought a moment. "It had to be 11:45 in the morning," Prester said. "No, no, wait, it was right at twelve noon. I remember hearing the church bells chime."

"It was December 21st, correct?" Ponnuru asked.

"Yes."

Ponnuru pulled a notebook from the breast pocket of his jacket and leafed through it.

"And young Mr. Renzo, he was carrying something unusual, isn't that right?"

Prester squinted at the physicist.

"He was carrying a dagger," Prester said, "one of a matched set from the Italian Renaissance period."

"And the dagger, the matching twin, was never recovered?"

"That's right," Prester confirmed.

"Tell me please about the twin daggers," Ponnuru said. "Where did they come from?"

At this point, Prester stood up.

"Look, what's this really all about? What difference does it make where the daggers came from?"

"Please, Mr. John," Chas said. "Bear with us just a bit longer. I assure you, everything will be explained in good time."

"I am believing there is an expression – in for a rupee, in for a pound," Ponnuru said smiling.

Prester shook his head, but sat down again. "What do you want to know?"

"What is the history of the daggers?" Ponnuru asked.

"Their history? Well, they once belonged to Lorenzo de' Medici. That much is clear," Prester said. "My father left them to me, just as my grandfather left them to him."

"Yes, but how please is it that your grandfather is coming to acquire them?" Ponnuru inquired.

"It was during the First World War. My grandfather fought along side a British soldier by the name of Henry Whitney, and they became good friends. Unfortunately, Whitney was killed at a place called Ypres, Belgium. After the war, my grandfather went to visit Whitney's parents in England. He wanted to deliver Whitney's personal effects, you know, and to tell them that their son had died bravely. I guess he felt he owed that to his friend. Well, apparently Whitney's father was so grateful for the visit that he gave my grandfather a gift – an engraved box containing twin daggers depicting the Pazzi coat of arms."

"Ah, yes. And from where is the Englishman getting them?" Ponnuru persisted.

"My grandfather told me that during their brief discussion Whitney's father had mentioned that he was a great fan of Charles Dickens."

"The writer?" Chas Renzo chimed in for clarification.

"Yes," Prester confirmed. "In fact, the man apparently was such a Dickens fan that in 1883 he purchased The Old Curiosity Shop in London from one Mr. Charles Tesseyman, who had owned the shop for over 50 years."

"I've read most of Dickens' novels," Chas said, "including *The Old Curiosity Shop*. But I didn't know there really was such a place."

"There is," Prester said. "It's still there at number 13 Portsmouth Street in London. The shop, or at least the building, dates back to the 16th Century."

"Amazing," Chas said.

"The way I heard it, shortly after Whitney's father bought the shop he found the engraved box with the daggers buried in an old crate in the cellar. The crate, according to the shop account books, had been stored there since 1840. Unfortunately, that was as far back as my grandfather was ever able to trace the history of the daggers," Prester said. "But then a few years ago, while I was in London doing unrelated research for an article on the history of the Bank of England, I quite unexpectedly came across something rather fantastic."

"This is most interesting, Mr. John," Ponnuru said. "Go on, thank you please."

"In the archives of the main branch of the Bank of England," Prester continued, "I happened upon a receipt issued in 1840 by the London and Westminster Gaslight and Coke Company for the laying of a gas lamp line. On the back of the receipt was a list with a caption entitled 'Unprofitable assets for Removal.' Apparently, a gas line was to be laid in the basement of the Bank of England, and to make room for it the bank had to get rid of some old crates and boxes that had been stored there for years. I was curious to see exactly what items had been removed, and so I matched up the date on the receipt with the account books of the bank. There in the accounts was a list of the actual items removed and sold at auction. Included in the list was an item described as an antique boxed set of two knives with Pazzi seal. Also listed was the name of the man who purchased the knives at the auction. It was none other than Mr. Charles Tesseyman, the owner of The Old Curiosity Shop."

"So the daggers had been owned by the Bank of England," Chas observed. "But where did the bank get them?"

"Well, when I realized that my grandfather's knives had once been the property of the Bank of England, it was a relatively simple matter to trace their origin back through bank records."

"And what is it that you are finding?" Ponnuru asked.

"Turns out, the Bank of England received the knives as part of its initial capital investment when it was founded in 1694."

"Capital investment?" Ponnuru asked.

"Money and other assets put together as the initial stake when a bank is created," Chas explained. "But who put up the initial capital investment for the Bank of England?"

"Another bank, of course," Prester said, "the Banca Villani, which was founded in Florence in the late 15th Century. Unfortunately for the Villani family, their bank was not very well run. Internal family squabbles had become unmanageable. So some of the senior family members liquidated their shares, pooled their resources, and placed their investment under new management. Basically, the old Italian bank became the newly formed Bank of England."

"A Florentine bank," Chas noted. "The Medici were bankers, isn't that right?"

"They were. In fact, lots of banks were centered in Florence. You see, unlike Venice or Genoa, Florence was not a port city and so it could not rely on sea trade as its primary source of wealth. Instead, it specialized in banking. By the beginning of the 15th Century, many Florentine banks had branches in cities as far away as Brussels, Stockholm and London. In fact, the gold florin, named for the city of Florence, was the most widely accepted currency of Europe for over two hundred years."

"So you are saying that the knives were at one time being owned by a Florentine bank?" Ponnuru asked.

"Well, not 'owned' exactly. More like they were on loan. In going through the Banca Villani records, I found something askew in its *God's Account*."

"Did you say 'God's Account?'" Chas inquired.

"Yes. Banks of that time used to carry on their books things called 'God's Accounts,' which were basically money set aside for the Church and charities. You see, the Catholic Church viewed money as a dead thing, and believed that any attempt to make a dead thing reproduce was unnatural."

"Reproduce? Are you talking about interest?," Chas said.

"Exactly. In the opinion of the Church, using money to generate interest was an offense against God. Despite this, the Church needed to borrow money for its various projects and military adventures. In fact, the Pope was generally the biggest customer of most banks."

"So it would seem that the Church and the banks were needing each other, no?" Ponnuru noted.

"Precisely. But to justify the interest they made, bankers typically would share their profits with the Church. Many bankers of that day genuinely believed that interest and profits were inherently evil. That's why so much of their money was spent on commissioning great works of art to glorify God."

"You said you found something awry in the Banca Villani accounts," Chas said.

"Yes, I found a bookkeeping error. Many Italian banks of that time were just beginning to use the double-entry system of accounting first introduced by the Medici in the 14th century. By entering every transaction in two different places, the double-entry system was designed to ensure the integrity of the accounts, or at least it was supposed to. The trouble was, some of those early banking clerks didn't really understand how it worked. What I found was a mistake, an entry within an entry. The records from the old Banca Villani made reference to a *scatola di lengno* or wooden box being deposited with the bank in the year 1517, apparently as collateral for a loan. The same box was then deposited into the bank's God's Account. But they screwed up the double entry."

"They lost track of it?" Chas asked.

"Yes. Not physically, of course. They had the box all along. But they improperly listed it in their accounts," Prester said. "As a result of the error, the box lay there for all those years, being moved from place to place, never coming off the books, but never being properly accounted for. Years later, when the Banca Villani merged into the new Bank of England, it was still there, just another box to be transported with the furniture."

"An amazing thing indeed," Ponnuru said.

"So, who was it?" Chas asked.

"Excuse me?" Prester asked.

"The loan. You said someone deposited the knives as collateral on a loan. Who was it?"

"Oh, right," Prester said. "The bank records showed that the loan was made to a woman by the name of Nanna Masina. Near as I can tell, she ran some sort of a boarding house in Rome. The fact that a woman was given a loan is in and of itself pretty amazing considering women typically couldn't get loans of any kind. But the bank records actually describe Nanna Masina as being a 'gray haired matron of stable disposition.' They probably also thought the knives had value. In any case, she got the loan."

"So you were able to trace the knives all the way back to this woman, Nanna Masina?" Chas asked.

"Yes, all the way back to the year 1517," Prester said. "But the records end there. The bank probably didn't care, and certainly didn't write down, where Nanna Masina got the knives. So that is as far as I could trace them."

"It would interesting to be finding the connection all the way back to Lorenzo Medici," Ponnuru commented.

"As I said, we know from history that Lorenzo was the original owner of the knives," Prester said. "We'll never know how they got from Lorenzo to the innkeeper."

"Maybe Lorenzo once stayed at that inn," Chas conjectured. "Perhaps he left them behind by mistake?"

"Not likely," Prester said. "Lorenzo Medici would have had no reason to stay at a common inn."

"One final question, Mr. John, if you please thank you," Ponnuru said. "This is most important of all. Did anyone, anyone at all, observe young Mr. Renzo while he was standing at the old tree, holding the antique dagger, at the precise moment of his disappearance?"

Prester looked at Ponnuru, and then over at Chas, for any clue as to the intent of the inquiry.

"You mean, did anyone actually see him disappear? No," Prester said. "After he ran around the corner of the building, no one saw him. He just seemed to vanish."

Ponnuru smiled as he looked again at his notebook.

"Yes, it all is fitting, everything perfectly into place," Ponnuru said. "I am believing I know what has happened to him."

Prester stared at Ponnuru in disbelief. "So?," he asked. "What happened?"

"Trans-temporal equilibrium shift," Ponnuru said.

"What does that mean?" Prester asked.

"I am thinking that our young Kirk Renzo is alive and well and living in 15th Century Italy."

Chapter 15

Rome, Italy - 1498

Pompeo Gispare ran at full tilt from the chapel of Santa Petronilla out into St. Peter's Square. He had news for his master, Cristoforo Solari, and such news it was. Through the narrow cobblestone streets he sprinted, his short green cloak and gray hose a blur as he dashed past the shops of wool merchants, tanners, silk weavers, druggists, furriers, notaries and shoemakers. These people of Rome, he thought, these clothiers and butchers, these bakers and vintners, these simple blacksmiths, carpenters and rope makers, none of them had shown the proper respect for his master. But now that would all change. They had called Solari "Our Hunchback of Milan," but they had never understood, never appreciated the long, weary hours and great physical pain he had endured for his art of sculpting stone.

Solari was a great artist, Pompeo thought as he ran, or at least he believed him to be so. He had watched his master at work, and he had seen the care with which he approached each sculpture. Pompeo himself did not comprehend art or sculpture. He did not understand why some of his master's works were said to be beautiful while others were criticized as simplistic and forced.

Solari made a decent living for them both with his commissions of portrait busts and memorial tombs. He had received great praise from the good citizens of Milan for his recumbent effigies of Prince Lodovico il Moro and his beloved but too soon departed wife, Beatrice d'Este. Solari had even sculpted a Madonna and child for one of Rome's wealthiest families. Yet with all of this, with all his popularity, Solari had never been accepted in the higher ranks of Roman society. These bawdy Romans, Pompeo thought, were too crude, too base to appreciate true talent. Perhaps he and his master should have stayed in Milan.

But this turn of events would change everything for Solari, indeed for them both, Pompeo thought as he coursed towards the Ponte Sant'Angelo, the bridge crossing the Tiber River near Hadrian's ancient Castel Sant'Angelo mausoleum. His quickening steps followed the path of the ancient Roman Via Borgo Sant'Angelo, and as he ran he thought of what he had seen.

This new pietà, this unblemished configuration of the Virgin Mary cradling the dead body of Jesus that had just been placed in the chapel, was unlike anything Solari had ever achieved. It was magnificent, even to Pompeo's untrained eye. That it was upon its debut being praised so highly by the multitudes confirmed its allure. But that it was being attributed to his master Solari . . . well, that was nothing short of divine intervention.

Pompeo dashed across the old stone bridge and turned up the street where Solari kept his studio. Breathless, he ran inside and interrupted the master at his work.

"Master," he puffed as he bent over to catch his breath. "They are praising you in the streets," he said.

"What is this?," Solari said with an annoyed tone, putting down his hammer and chisel. "Why do you fly in here like a pigeon?"

"You must come and see," Pompeo continued. "They are saying that you are the greatest artist of them all," he gasped, taking in air between syllables.

"Who is saying this?" Solari asked. "What do you mean?"

Pompeo looked about the small studio covered in granite and marble dust and spied a stool nearby. He sat and heaved another deep breath before continuing.

"A new pietà has been placed in the Santa Petronilla chapel," he said. "It is the most beautiful thing I have ever seen, that anyone has ever seen," he said, "next to your own works, of course," he added quickly.

"And what does this pietà have to do with me?" Solari inquired.

"It is a sign from God," Pompeo said. "The whole city is praising you for this sculpture. They say that you are the artist who carved it. I tried to explain to three gentlemen from Lombardy that it was not your work, but they would not believe me. 'Certainly it is the work of Solari,' one of them said to me. They all agreed that it must be your work, and that I was a fool for doubting it."

"You spoke to these men about me?" Solari asked, now growing interested in Pompeo's frantic report.

"As I say, I tried to tell them that the artist who carved the work was not the great Solari, but they just laughed at me. 'Who else could have accomplished this?' one in particular kept saying."

"Who else, indeed," Solari said. "Whose work is it?"

"I don't know, master. I made some inquiries, but could not determine its true origin. Probably an unknown amateur."

"Take me to this new pietà," Solari said, placing his tools on his workbench.

Master and servant made their way back through the busy afternoon streets, back across the Tiber on the stately bridge toward the Borgo region of the city, and eventually toward a throng of people who had gathered on the steps of the small Santa Petronilla chapel. As they approached the throng, not yet in sight of the statue itself, a young woman turned and looked at them.

"Solari," she shouted for the benefit of the gathering. "He is here, the artist himself."

With that, several heads turned to look at him. In another instant, the crowd turned en masse to stare with excited expectation in his direction. Someone shouted from within the swarm.

"It is a masterpiece, Solari."

"Your best work yet," bellowed another.

The horde converged around him, eager to see the celebrity and to shake his hand. Solari, taken by surprise, could do nothing but smile and respond with cordiality. He nodded, and shook the hands of the assembled audience one by one. All present heaped praise upon him, and there was no talking to them. They were not there to listen, but to flatter. Solari tried on three occasions to explain the truth, as he would later recount in defense of himself. But in fact he did not know the truth of who had carved the statue, a statue he had not yet even seen. In any case, the assemblage did not want to hear the truth, but rather wanted to exhibit their adulation for the artist.

Breaking free of the mob, he strode toward the exhibit itself. Laying eyes for the first time upon the marble composition, the polished figure of the dead adult Christ reclining in the lap of the young Virgin Mary, he stopped and stared at it for a long moment.

The facility of this unknown artist was extraordinary. This was his first thought. The pose of the Christ figure exhibited the very perfection of anatomical exactness – every muscle, vein, and nerve being displayed. And there was a most exquisite expression on the countenance of Mary. So too the limbs of the figures were affixed to their trunks in a manner that was flawless.

Solari stepped closer and peered into the face of the Madonna. She was represented as being very young, too young to have an adult child. That was a flaw in the artist's design, no doubt, and yet there was an incorruptible purity in her face that seemed to him as fitting as it was incongruous. What had this unknown artist in mind? What was he trying to say with this too youthful visage?

Solari excused himself to the crowd and hurried away. Pompeo ran to accompany him. They walked swiftly, more swiftly now than before, back along the road toward the Ponte Sant'Angelo. As Solari crossed the bridge, he stopped midway and stared out across the river.

"*Vergine madre, figlia del tuo figlio,*" Solari said aloud to no one in particular.

Pompeo, at the heels of his master, looked up at Solari, hearing but not understanding.

"It is from the Divine Comedy," Solari continued. "Dante's *Paradiso*, the third Cantica of the poem," he clarified, although Pompeo had no knowledge of his reference. "In the poem, Saint Bernardo, in a prayer to the Virgin Mary, speaks those words."

"What words?" Pompeo asks, realizing that the conversation had already moved beyond his grasp.

"'Virgin mother, daughter of your son,'" Solari repeated the phrase as if holding it up for examination. "Of course. I understand now. Don't you see what this artist has done with his pietà? Don't you see what he is trying to say? Christ is one of the Trinity, three figures of a single whole: the Father, the Son, and the Holy Ghost. Although Jesus was the son of Mary, the artist is telling us that Mary was also his daughter, just as we are all his sons and daughters," Solari said.

"I know that what you are saying is very profound," Pompeo groaned. "But I do not understand."

Just then, Solari's eyes widened and he gasped audibly.

"Nor do I understand," he said. "For suddenly I see that there is yet another explanation. Yes, yes, of course, now I see it ever more clearly."

"Master, I have not eaten today," Pompeo whined. "Perhaps if we had some little bite to eat first, then I might be able to . . ."

"My God, of course. Brilliance, sheer brilliance. I see now what this artist has done. It is an issue of perspective, an issue of time, don't you see?"

"Time, yes. It is past dinner time I think," Pompeo implored.

"The Madonna is too youthful, to be sure. But that is not a mistake. This artist, whoever he is, is too gifted to have drawn her thusly without intention. No, no, it is not a mistake by any means. Don't you see, Pompeo? He has made her young, because through her eyes, from her perspective, the perspective of the Virgin Mother, she is young. We see that she looks down, placidly, calmly, serenely, upon Jesus. There is no horror on her face, no pain, no grief of loss. Her arms are natural and serenely splayed. This is because, in her eyes, she is holding her infant son. From her perspective, she cradles the baby Jesus. But to us, the viewer, looking at this pietà from beyond the stone, removed from the marble by space and time, we see instead the future image of Jesus, the fallen Christ, dead by crucifixion. The artist is playing God with us. Don't you see Pompeo? He is showing us the past and future together, time as God created it."

Pompeo had ceased to listen. Whenever Solari paused, Pompeo nodded. Whenever he looked at him, he smiled. Whatever his master's point was, he would agree so that they could go to dinner.

"All right, Pompeo," Solari at long last said, realizing the futility of his one-sided conversation. "Let us go and eat."

"A splendid idea, master," Pompeo said, pleased to understand something truly concrete.

Chapter 16

The mind of man has always been adept at rationalizing ill behavior, and so it was with Solari as he considered the pietà over his evening meal.

"It is a most beautiful work, to be sure," he said to Pompeo, "and the true artist, whomever he is, deserved credit."

"These olives are exceptional," Pompeo said between chews, dipping his fingers into a ceramic bowl to fish out another.

"But equally true is that many an artist has starved on such works, and acclaim alone does not put food on one's table. That I can tell you," Solari said. "Still, this could be a wonderful opportunity. For me, certainly, but also for him."

"That was my thinking exactly," Pompeo added.

Solari bit down on his roast mutton and considered his options. Pompeo, meanwhile, compressed a loaf of saltless bread between his teeth and ripped away a hunk.

"A work like this pietà will mean larger commissions in the future," Solari continued, "but only to the artist who is well established as being able to produce the desires of his patrons in a timely and consistent manner."

"I quite agree," Pompeo mumbled with his mouth full as he took a sip of cheap Chianti wine.

"What will this artist have to say when his patrons demand to know whether he can produce three, four or perhaps even five pieces within a year's time?" Solari asked rhetorically.

Pompeo shrugged his shoulders in response, but did not stop eating.

"And despite whatever answer may be forthcoming," Solari added, "how is a patron to know that the predictions and promises of this new artist are not mere puffery?"

Pompeo nodded again, scanning the assortment of savory meats, yeasty breads, and tasty black and green olives before him.

"An unproven artist, you see, could never sustain more than a modest level of commissions," Solari concluded, half believing his own logic. "On the other hand, if I were to accept the acclaim for this pieta that the public seems so desirous of thrusting upon me – mind you, I did not ask for the acclaim – but if I were to accept it, then, then we would have something of true value here," he said. "This pietà, coupled with my notoriety, would mean greatly increased future commissions. I would profit, certainly, but more importantly so too would he."

"I see large purses in our future, master," Pompeo said smiling.

"I want to be fair to this artist, of course," Solari said.

"Oh yes, we must be fair," Pompeo agreed. "He deserves something."

"He deserves more than something," Solari corrected him. "He deserves to be well paid for his work, both for this pietà and for his future, our future, endeavors."

The two men chewed as they mulled it over.

"How much should he get?" Pompeo asked.

"That is hard to say. I would want to know what commission he may have agreed to for this pietà, and from whom it is to be received," Solari said. "But however much it is, we will pay him . . . double . . . yes, double his earnings. That is more than generous on my part, don't you think?"

Pompeo bowed his head. "You are a generous man," he said.

"We must find this sculptor," Solari concluded. "We must speak with him in reasonable and prudent tones. If he is a true artist, he will understand that the art is what matters, not the fleeting fame that comes with it."

"An excellent idea, master," Pompeo said, and then resumed eating.

The next morning, upon Solari's instructions, Pompeo set out at first light to conduct his investigation. His first stop was the Santa Petronilla chapel where the parish Priest told him that he did not know who had commissioned this new pietà, but that Solari as the artist could certainly tell him. Pompeo did discover, however, the address of the workmen who had moved the large marble composition to its current location, and so he set off to inquire of them.

The address he had been given was a small shop with a courtyard just beyond the outer wall of the city through the Porta del Popolo, the centuries old main entrance to Rome. Pompeo arrived there at exactly 10:00 o'clock in the morning, according to the bell tower of the distant San Paolo fuori le Mura church. The shop itself consisted of four white-washed stone walls, with a red door, red window sashes, and a red tile roof.

"Excuse me, sir," Pompeo shouted up to the fat sweaty man in the white apron who appeared to be in charge, for the man was standing on the roof at the time.

"Both of them, both of them," the man hollered down to his subordinates in the courtyard. "The oxen work as a pair, you imbeciles," he shouted. In the courtyard, two young men dressed in white smocks with leather vests were attempting without success to attach a heavy wooden yoke to the thick necks of two large grayish white beasts of burden.

"Sir," Pompeo shouted up again. "If you please."

"Who are you?" the sweaty man said, finally taking notice of him below.

"My name is Pompeo Gispare," he shouted back. "If you please, I have a question of you."

"Are you in need of carting services? We specialize in heavy loads," the man said.

"No, thank you, sir. I have a question about a delivery you made recently."

"You are not in need of my services?" the man said, sounding now even more annoyed than he had been. "I am a busy man," he added with a dismissive wave of his meaty hand.

"I work for the artist Cristoforo Solari," Pompeo shouted back. "He is a sculptor of great works. I'm sure you have heard of him, no?"

"No," the towering man shouted back at him.

"All the same, I simply need to know from where you moved the pietà that now graces the Santa Petronilla chapel."

"No, no, the other way around, you dimwits. Do you want the animals to push the load or pull it?" the man shouted to his befuddled helpers.

"Where did you pick up the pietà?" Pompeo shouted up to the fat man again, afraid now that he was losing the fight for the man's attention.

"The what?" said the man looking down at him.

"The large marble statue of the Madonna and Christ that you delivered recently to Santa Petronilla."

"What business is it of yours?" the man shouted back.

Pompeo withdrew a gold florin from the purse tied to his waist and held it aloft.

"This makes it my business," he said.

The large man looked down and rubbed his unkempt whiskered chin.

"One florin begets three," the man said, a slight smile breaking over his face. "If I could only recall," he added with feigned concern.

Pompeo reached into his purse again and withdrew two more gold florins for the man's review.

"Do these help your memory?" Pompeo said, holding up the three coins to glimmer in the morning sunlight.

"Throw them up to me," the large man instructed Pompeo.

"Have your full faculties returned?" Pompeo shouted.

"Throw them up. You'll have your information."

One by one, Pompeo tossed the gold coins up to the roof where the fat man caught them, inspected each, and dropped them into the pocket of his white apron. When all three had been safely deposited, he looked back down at Pompeo.

"The statue you speak of was taken from the studio of a young sculptor who lives near the house of Lorenzo Manilio. The studio is just before the gate to the Ghetto degli Ebrei," the large man said. "Go there and look for a house decorated with ancient fragments of a Roman relief. There you will find a large inscription in bold letters above the door that looks like it came from an old temple. It is only Signore Manilio's name inscribed in Latin and Greek letters, but he is a vain man and likes how it looks. Directly across from Signore Manilio's door is the entrance to the studio where we picked up the statue."

"Thank you," Pompeo shouted up at him and then turned and began to sprint back toward the Porta del Popolo. Suddenly he stopped and turned his head once more toward the elevated figure.

"One more thing," Pompeo called up to him. "Did you happen to get his name," he said.

"Whose name?" the burly man responded.

"The name of the young artist whose work you transported," Pompeo shouted.

"Oh, him." The man rubbed his whiskers again, this time in genuine reflection. "Buonarroti, I think it was," he shouted down. "Michelangelo Buonarroti."

Pompeo waved once more to the lofty man.

"Many thanks, kind sir," he said, and then rushed back toward the city.

Chapter 17

That afternoon, in his studio near the Ghetto degli Ebrei gate, Michelangelo put quill to parchment.

"Dearest Father," he wrote, "I have had a letter from you today which gave and still gives me great anxiety as it tells me of your recent illness. I beg of you, as soon as you have read this, to let me know how you are, because if you are really very ill, I will come by the post to Florence during this ensuing week; although this would be the greatest hindrance to me, for two reasons. Firstly, I have earned and am to be paid four hundred and fifty ducats upon the return to Rome of my most recent patron, the Cardinal of St. Denis, a Frenchman named Rovano. This is the agreement I have made with him, and I am hopeful that as many more he will give me should he find pleasure in my work. But he has lately gone from here, leaving me no orders whatever; so that I find myself without money, nor do I know what to do if I go away. I should not like him to despise me, and lose me my earnings, in which case I should be badly off. I have written him a letter, and am awaiting the answer. Secondly, all Rome has heard of the Friar Savonarola's excommunication, and that Florence is now being led by a young and untested prince. Whether any artist may prosper in Florence at present is uncertain, and I must trust that you are staying well away from the mobs. Yet if you are in danger, dear father, let me know about it, because I shall leave everything." He signed the letter, "Your Michelagniolo, sculptor in Rome."

Michelangelo sprinkled pounce powder upon the paper, blew on it to dry the ink, and then folded the paper twice. Just then, beyond his open door, he spotted the old woman who was his landlady.

"Nanna," he called to her, but she did not hear him and continued hanging her laundry on a line just outside his door. "Nanna Masina," he shouted. She stopped, wiped her hands on her apron, and stepped inside.

"This is to go in the post this afternoon," he commanded.

"You owe me my rent," she said in return.

"Yes, yes, you will get your rent," Michelangelo said. "There are tumults in the world far more serious than your rent, but rest assured, you will get your rent."

"When?" she persisted.

"When I am able," he said. "You know my dilemma. It is already more than a year since I have received a penny for my work, although it is clearly owed to me."

"Then why do you not demand it?" she insisted.

"You know nothing of art. Don't ask me about my work," he said.

"Your work, your work, always your work," she said. "Why don't you get a real job?"

"Why don't you mind to your own affairs and leave me to mine?"

"I want my rent," the old woman said, then snatched the letter from his hand and strode away, tired of arguing with her disagreeable tenant.

Michelangelo watched her go, her dusty gray frock dragging on the ground behind her. Turning back to his workbench, he slammed the door behind him and looked around at the decrepit state of his studio. Blocks of poor marble, cracked and inadequate for any good use, stood in stacks in one corner. In another, a marble Head of a Faun sat upon a bench, staring back at him with a mocking grin. He had created it while just a boy studying in Lorenzo de' Medici's sculpture school at the Garden of San Marco in Florence.

Lorenzo had started him on his career. He had given him his education. He had given him a place to live in the palace amongst his family. Most importantly, he had given him the confidence he needed as a young artist. But Lorenzo had been dead these six years, and what could be said of his career now? What of his hoped for success? It had all seemed so possible from the perspective of Lorenzo's Garden. But now, here in Rome, he wondered whether his work was all mere folly.

"I am spending my time fruitlessly," he thought to himself. "All around me I see many men with steady incomes, earning perhaps two or three hundred scudi per year, and living in clover, while I, with the greatest toil, succeed only in impoverishing myself." He flung his hammer across the small room.

Just then a knock came at the door. He looked up and stared in the direction of the disturbance. A second, louder knock came. Michelangelo did not move. He had no desire to see anyone. He had no friends of any sort, and wished for none. He did not have time to waste on trivial friendships, nor on unannounced visitors.

"Buonarroti?" a voice called to him from beyond the door. He did not answer. "Michelangelo Buonarroti?" came the voice again. "Are you there? I have good news."

Michelangelo stepped toward the door and opened it a crack. There, just beyond the threshold, was the artist Solari whose work and reputation he had come to know while in Rome. Behind him was Pompeo. Michelangelo peered out at the two of them.

"Good day, sir. I am Cristoforo Solari."

"I know who you are," Michelangelo said.

"Your landlady told us that you were at home," Solari added.

"I am working."

"Ah, of course you are. We artists must continue to work, always work," Solari said.

Michelangelo stared at him without smiling.

"You are Michelangelo Buonarroti, are you not?" Solari asked.

"Suppose I am. What do you want of me?"

"Are you the artist who carved the pietà that stands in the Santa Petronilla chapel?" Solari persisted.

"You have seen it?" Michelangelo asked.

"I have, sir. May we come in to discuss it?"

"Discuss what?"

"The pietà, of course," Solari said.

Michelangelo looked them over top to bottom. He did not like intruders.

"The pietà has been sold," Michelangelo said.

"I'm sure it has, sir. Please, if we might have but a moment of your time. It could be worth a great deal of money to you," Solari said, growing tired of this temperamental sculptor, but striving to maintain his façade of politeness.

Michelangelo stepped aside and Solari entered without waiting for a further invitation. Pompeo followed close behind.

Inside the small studio, Solari saw at once that here lived an artist who, try as he might, had not yet tapped into the soul nor the purses of Roman society. The floors were filthy, marble dust covered every surface, and there was a distinct odor of urine in the air. Against one wall was a pile of hay covered with blankets that appeared to serve as a bed.

"Ah, so this is your studio. Very nice, very cozy," he said and then looked at Pompeo with a grin. "Pompeo, what do you think?"

Pompeo lowered the kerchief he had been pressing against his nose to filter the smell. 'What did his master want him to say?' he thought. He wished he were of quicker wit.

"It is a little dark perhaps," he said.

"Dark, yes, perhaps a little too dark," Solari repeated, turning again toward Michelangelo. "From one artist to another, you might want to consider bringing the morning light in through that wall," he said, pointing to the south wall beyond the straw pile. "A window there would do nicely."

Solari could already see in Michelangelo's young face the struggle for survival and the pained determination of a much older man. The mouth of the young artist curled with torment, and the bridge of his nose was flat and misshaped as if having suffered a break. More obvious was the anguish in the young artist's eyes, as if time – that heartless thief of dreams – had already begun to steal his opportunities for success.

"You mentioned money," Michelangelo said.

"May I sit down?" Solari asked.

Michelangelo nodded his approval, but took no steps to offer his guests a stool or chair. Solari looked at Pompeo, who reached for the nearest stool, dusted it off with his sleeve, and set it next to his master. Solari flipped up the back of his cape and sat.

"Michelangelo," Solari began his pitch. "Do you mind if I call you Michelangelo?"

"Call me what you like."

"Do you consider yourself to be a practical man, Michelangelo?" Solari asked.

"I consider myself to be a private man," Michelangelo responded.

"And our presence here is disturbing you, I can see that. Quite clearly, you are a pure artist and we are intruding upon your valuable time."

"You are, that is true. It is, I know, a failing of mine that I am not a more pleasant host, but I think of nothing but my work day and night," Michelangelo said.

"As well you should, Michelangelo. The work is the most important thing. Which is precisely why I have come to see you today."

"Listen carefully to him," Pompeo interjected. "He has a proposal for you." Pompeo underscored his remark by making a gesture with his right hand, an upturned palm with the thumb and fingers rubbing together.

"Forgive my saying so, Michelangelo," Solari continued, "but it would appear that perhaps you have been somewhat lacking in financial remuneration of late."

"He means you look poor," Pompeo said.

"I know what he means," Michelangelo responded. "In truth, my work has brought me little more than the greatest inconvenience. But then, I live very simply. I do not require much. I am fortunate in that regard, if no other."

"What about your family? Are there not others who count on you?"

"I have several brothers and an elderly father in Florence, all of whom seek my assistance constantly," Michelangelo said.

"Then you have not had it easy, Michelangelo. If I may say, you appear to live in great anxiety and in extreme bodily fatigue."

"I do not deny it," Michelangelo said.

"Perhaps there is a way that I can help you," Solari said.

"With charity?"

"No. I do not offer you charity," Solari said. "I come instead with a business proposition."

Solari rose from his stool and, looking about him, picked up from Michelangelo's worktable an unfinished sculpture of a sleeping cherub.

"This piece, this little angel that you are sculpting," Solari said, holding the child-size work with one hand, "what do you think this is worth?"

"Worth?" Michelangelo repeated the word.

"For what amount might it sell?" Solari clarified.

Michelangelo looked at Solari, and then at the sleeping marble cupid.

"Perhaps thirty crowns," he said. "It is difficult to say."

"Would it surprise you to know that I could sell this for, oh, perhaps two hundred crowns?" Solari asked him.

"Are you an art dealer as well as an artist?" Michelangelo asked.

"Not an art dealer," Solari said. "But I know these Romans. I know their likes and dislikes. I know their prideful tendencies, and I know their petty pretensions. I know that this little cherub would sell for two hundred crowns if . . .," Solari let the statement dangle in the air.

"If what?" Michelangelo asked.

"If I had carved it," Solari said, "or, more precisely, if the public believed that I had carved it."

Michelangelo stared at him, still unsure of what he was trying to convey.

"Let me be more direct," Solari said, setting the small sculpture down. "Have you heard the rumors on the street about your pieta? Are you aware that the public has come to believe it to be my work?"

"Your work!" Michelangelo said, his voice rising. "Why would they think it is your work?"

"Well, to be fair, it is a very nice piece," Solari explained. "The craftsmanship is superb, a fact of which you ought to be proud. That is not to say that the trained eye cannot discern a few flaws, particularly in regard to the choice of composition, but your flaws are mostly of a minor character. Still, the work is of such advanced quality that the public simply presumed it to be mine. After all, they know me, and they know my work."

"Then they ought to know that your work is nothing as compared to mine," Michelangelo retorted.

"I'll let that pass," Solari said. "In truth, the public cares less for the quality of a work than for the fame of its creator. Can you understand that, Michelangelo?"

"I understand my art, or at least I strive to," he said. "I do not claim to understand the vagaries of the public's taste."

"But we are also, you and I, in the business of art, don't you agree?" Solari pressed. "Creating fine works is all well and good, but to survive, to last so that you can create in the future, you must sell, and you must sell at a good profit. Otherwise, it is all simply dust and sweat."

Michelangelo looked at this man with narrowing eyes. "What are you proposing?" he asked.

"What I propose is a merger of sorts, for our mutual benefit," Solari said. "The public thinks that I created the pietà. So let them think it. Indeed, let them think that all your works from this day forward are from my hand. Let my fame be a companion to your labor. They shall pay far more for the works if they think I created them, for they know me well, and they do not know you. As an unknown here in Rome, your labor has not the value of my own. But by joining my reputation with the sweat of your brow, we shall together earn a far greater reward than you could ever earn alone."

Turning to Pompeo, Solari waived his hand. Pompeo stepped forward and tossed thirty gold florins onto the workbench.

"Let this be a down payment on our mutual and secret union," Solari said. "Let this bind us together as brothers of the arts so that we may both find profit in our work."

Michelangelo looked at the coins splayed out in front of him, but made no motion to retrieve them.

"Tomorrow morning," Solari continued, "I have arranged a small gathering at the chapel Santa Petronilla where we will officially unveil the pietà as my own work. As I say, the public already presumes that it is mine, but by making it official, my fame will increase all the more rapidly, and our commissions on future works will increase proportionately. Meanwhile, you continue your work here, working as rapidly as you are able. As you complete your pieces, we will sell them under my name for a handsome profit, and you will get your fair share."

With that, Solari readied himself to leave, dusting the marble dust from his cape.

"You may attend the unveiling, of course, Michelangelo, but bear in mind that secrecy is essential to our success. Whisper to no one of your connection to the pietà, for only in complete confidentiality can our scheme flourish."

Nodding his head toward Michelangelo and flipping his cape over his shoulder, Solari stepped back out into the open air of the lengthening afternoon. Without looking back, Solari and Pompeo strode across the street and vanished between the narrow buildings of the Ghetto degli Ebrei.

Chapter 18

Anger comes in many guises. It may boil slowly and simmer like a gruel, or explode suddenly like a geyser. It may linger like the foulness of a latrine, or dissipate unnoticed in the still, night air. For Michelangelo, anger came like a cancer, a spreading nausea turning into sharp pangs of pain as the realization of Solari's proposal engulfed him.

After Solari and Pompeo departed, Michelangelo sat alone in his studio and stared at the gold pieces that lay before him until their color vanished with the fading light of the setting sun. The things he could do with that money, he thought. He could help his father, Lodovico, who was ill, and his brother, Buonarroto, who was in constant financial distress. He could also help himself, of course, to live in better circumstances, with better food, better clothing, free of the stresses of the daily struggle for life. He would not have to freeze in his cold studio in the winter with too few blankets to warm him. In the hot summer months he could journey to the coast where the tepid winds made a pleasure of every day. He could work at his art without interruption. All he had to do was sell his soul.

Rising from his hard chair, Michelangelo lit an oil lamp, and then crossed the studio to where several boxes were covered with the canvas of an old Genoa sail. Lifting back the canvas, he moved a few boxes until he found the one he was seeking. With great care, he withdrew from beneath the canvas a small wooden box festooned with relief carvings depicting the long-ago Pazzi conspiracy. Setting the box on his workbench, he opened it to reveal two matching bejeweled daggers, each engraved with the Pazzi twin dolphin coat of arms.

Closing the box again, he pushed it into the middle of the dusty workbench near the gold coins of which he took no further notice. He then set about collecting his few belongings – his meager clothes, his chisels and hammers, the few odd trinkets for which he held some sentimental value – and stuffed them into a large leather satchel. Taking quill and parchment in hand, he sat down near the lamplight and began to write a note to his landlady.

"Signora Masina," he wrote, "Please forgive my sudden departure and accept this notice as the termination of my tenancy. Circumstances very soon will make it impossible for me to remain in Rome, and thus I am returning to the home of my father. The coins here do not belong to me, but are rather the property of the artist Solari. I beg that you see to their safe return to him. As for the payment of my indebtedness to you, I have but insufficient currency of my own. I beg you to accept instead these twin knives given directly to my hand by Lorenzo the Magnificent on his deathbed. These knives are worth all and more than what I owe in rent. Sell them if you choose, but take no less than fifty gold florins for them or be ill served in the bargain." He signed the note, "Michelangelo in Rome."

Michelangelo slid the note partway under the wooden box just as the anger within him welled up so that he felt he might vomit. He had no doubt as to what he must do next to relieve the pain. Grabbing his gear, and pulling open the door, he set off into the Roman night and did not look back.

Rome at night was a hazardous venue. Oil lamps flickered in the windows of the few merchants kept up late by the necessity of accounting for their goods. Distant taverns echoed their raucous cacophony from unseen narrow lanes. Harlots sauntered brazenly along the moonlit streets, and the downtrodden and treacherous lingered in the shadowy alleys.

Michelangelo weaved his way through the streets, a hooded cape draping his slender frame, his leather satchel slung over his muscular shoulder. A full moon gave a silvery glow to the damp cobblestones that paved the roads leading from the Ghetto degli Ebrei and toward the Santa Petronilla chapel.

He arrived shortly before 9:00 PM The chapel was empty. The pietà, his pietà, sat unattended in the small alcove where it had been placed only a few days before. Setting down his satchel, he removed a hammer and two chisels, one small and one large. He approached the statue and ran his fingers across the silken smooth surface of the Madonna's gown. It was a flawless piece, and he had labored long on its perfection. Grasping the hammer in his right hand, he positioned the larger of the two chisels just below the flowing head cover of the Virgin Mary.

Michelangelo struck the first blow upon his most divine work at 9 o'clock. Upon that hour, the bell tower of the Basilica Santa Maria Maggiore began to echo its traditional tone calling the faithful to prayer. Masked by the cover of the bell, the artist's chisel drove deep into the polished Carrara marble. A second blow followed, and then a third, and a fourth, his hammer marking his raw graffiti upon the glistening pietà. Who were these men to think that he could be bought, that his soul was for sale? Who were these tyrants who deigned to usurp his work and steal the essence of his being? His task did not take long. When he was done, he stepped back and gazed upon his statue.

Across the breast of his once perfect pietà, he had chiseled a ribbon from the Madonna's left shoulder to her waist. Within the ribbon he carved a lapidary inscription in Latin letters, *"MICHEL ANGELUS BONAROTUS FLORENT FACIBAT,"* Michelangelo Buonarroti, Florentine, made this.

Chapter 19

Manhattan Island, New York

Trace Gilmore leaned his massive bulk across the table and held his illuminated magnifying glass an inch above the canvas. Annie, who had arrived at the Director's office at nine o'clock sharp as instructed, stood off to one side next to Mrs. Trumbull.

"Hum," Gilmore grunted.

"Well?" Director Brennan said.

Gilmore ignored him as he moved the magnifying glass slowly across the surface of the painting.

"Um hum," the large man grunted again.

"What do you think?" the Director asked.

"What do I think," Gilmore repeated the question to himself. "Hum," he snorted again as he bent in for a closer inspection.

"Well?" the Director said.

"Mr. Brennan," Gilmore said, straightening up. "I'll tell you this. I think it's unbelievable, that's what I think. Most unbelievable."

"It's another fake, surely," Brennan offered. "It's not the same face."

"No, it's a different face all right. But it's good. Damn good."

"It's outrageous," Brennan added.

"Yes, it is that, but still. Don't get me wrong. It's clearly not the 'Portrait of a Young Man', but my God what a work. All I'm saying is, if it's a fake, it's very, very good. Truly, there's not one thing about this painting that would lead me to conclude it was not painted during the Italian Renaissance."

"That's impossible."

"Impossible maybe, but look at the brush work, look at the pigments, look at the pigments, look at the age of the canvas. Even the frame is perfect. I'll take some X-rays, and run a white lead test, of course, but everything about this painting appears to be authentically Italian Renaissance."

"How could this be happening again?" Brennan asked. "The security cameras show absolutely nothing unusual occurring in the gallery."

"This has happened before?" Annie interjected.

"Young lady," Mrs. Trumbull jumped in. "This does not concern you."

"No, no, it's all right, Mrs. Trumbull," Brennan said. "Annie discovered the most recent problem last night. She has a right to know what's going on."

"Yes, of course, Mr. Brennan," Mrs. Trumbull said in monotone, taking a step back.

"So?" Annie asked. "Are there others? Other paintings I mean?"

"Unfortunately, yes," Brennan answered.

"What's going on?" Annie asked.

"You're asking the wrong question," Gilmore said, holding the framed canvas up to the light. "What is going on is fairly obvious."

"It is?" Annie asked, feeling a bit embarrassed at her ignorance. "Could you maybe go over it again? I think I missed it."

"What's going on," Gilmore said with a note of irritation, "is that genuine Renaissance artwork is being stolen from the walls of this museum, and being replaced by other genuine Renaissance artwork, or if not genuine then extremely good fakes."

"Replaced?" Annie asked. "But why? Why would any thief do such a thing?"

"That I cannot tell you," Gilmore said. "Perhaps to gain time before the thefts are discovered, who knows? But quite frankly, the fakes, if they are fake, are as good as the originals. They're perfect. In all my years, I've never seen anything like this."

"They must be fakes," the Director said. "A thief would not steal a masterpiece only to replace it with another masterpiece."

"It must be the work of some sort of criminal genius," Mrs. Trumbull chimed in.

"And this has happened before?" Annie asked.

"Twice before," Director Brennan said.

"The first was five months ago," Gilmore explained. "A little librarian lady from Omaha, Nebraska noticed that a sketch by Leonardo da Vinci called 'The Hanging Body of Bernardo Bandini' had an inconsistency from the original that she remembered having seen in a book. In the original sketch, the body of the hanging man has his hands tied behind his back. But in the drawing that the librarian found on display here in the museum that day, the hanging man had his hands tied in the front."

"We told the lady that Da Vinci had actually drawn two versions of that same scene," Brennan said. "She seemed skeptical, but it appeared to satisfy her for the moment."

"But there is only one such drawing," Mrs. Trumbull sighed. "There's only ever been one, and the hands are behind the back, not in front."

"So the sketch left behind was changed from the original?" Annie asked for clarification.

"Except for the hands, it was exactly the same in every detail down to the smallest flick of Da Vinci's pen," Gilmore said. "It's as if Da Vinci himself snuck in and changed the drawing."

"If a forger had the talent to fake a sketch so perfectly, why would he intentionally include so obvious a change?" Annie asked.

"He wants us to know they're fakes," the Director conjectured. "That's the only explanation. They must be fakes."

"Tell her about the second time," Gilmore chuckled, his rotund belly jiggling as he laughed.

"The second one we found was even more strange," Director Brennan said. "Two months ago, a small girl with her mother noticed something peculiar about the 'Madonna and Child with Saints' by Girolamo dai Libri, 1520."

"Tell her what the child saw?" Gilmore chuckled. "You'll never guess."

"Well, in the painting, the real painting that is, the painting that was supposed to be hanging on the wall, three angels appear in the foreground. One angel is holding a vihuela, an instrument that looks like a small guitar. A second is holding up a page of sheet music. And a third angel, the one in the middle, isn't holding anything. That's what's in the real painting. But in the painting that the little girl found, the fake painting that was hanging where the original should have been, the middle angel was holding something."

"God bless us and save us," Mrs. Trumbull muttered out loud.

"Holding what?" Annie asked.

The Director gulped. "A paper airplane," he said.

Annie just stared at him, and then began to smile.

"Okay," she said, "okay, I get it. Very funny. This is some sort of hazing thing for the new kid, right? I got it. You really had me going there for a while."

"I don't blame you for not believing it," Gilmore said.

Annie looked at the Director, and then at Trace Gilmore, and then at Mrs. Trumbull. None of them were smiling.

"A paper airplane? Are you serious?" she asked of the collective group.

"I'm afraid so," Brennan said.

"Oh my God," Annie whispered under her breath.

"I must ask you," the Director said to Annie, "not to speak of this to anyone, do you understand?"

"I don't think she understands," Mrs. Trumbull said.

"I understand," Annie insisted.

"The museum cannot afford to have this come out," Brennan added. "We cannot have the public thinking that some of our paintings are fakes. It would ruin us. I mean that quite literally. Do you understand me, Annie? It could mean bankruptcy for the museum. Until we can figure out who is doing this and why, we need to keep this under wraps."

"Of course, sir," Annie agreed. "Mum's the word."

"God bless us and save us," Mrs. Trumbull said again.

Chapter 20

Block Island

Prester stood and stared at the Block Island Oak. In the morning sun, it looked very much as it had exactly one year before on the day of Kirk Renzo's disappearance. Unlike that day, however, there was no wind now. But as before, the ancient tree stood alone in a snowy field, its limbs folded under itself like a great sleeping lion. It was December 21st and the Academy had been vacant since the previous day owing to the start of the winter break.

At precisely two minutes and twelve seconds past noon, the earth's axis would be at its maximum 23° 26' tilt, and the North Pole would be at its furthest distance from the sun. It would be the precise moment of the winter solstice, and, as Ponnuru had explained it, the optimum point for a trans-temporal equilibrium shift.

A mere 72 hours before, Prester had been introduced to the concept in Chas Renzo's 5th Avenue apartment.

"Trans-temporal equilibrium shift," Ponnuru had explained, "is occurring when the past and present come into perfect synchronization. Strongest at the precise moment of the summer or winter solstice, such a shift is nonetheless extremely common and is taking place all around us all the time. For example, Mr. John, has it ever been that you are experiencing a feeling of déjà vu?"

"Sure," Prester had said, thinking back to an occasion when he was a child. "Well, once anyway."

"Please, tell me about it," Ponnuru inquired.

"I was at my uncle's house. I was just a kid, and my cousins and I were playing in my uncle's basement. It was a finished basement, very nice. We used to play there all the time, so there was nothing unusual about it at all. But I remember at one point all my cousins had gone upstairs, and I was still downstairs by myself getting dressed to go out to dinner. I was walking across the hardwood floor of the basement to where my mother had set a small cosmetic case that she often took with us when we would travel. I opened the case and began to fish around in it for a belt she had packed for me. As I lifted the belt from the cosmetic case, I remember suddenly feeling that I had done it all before. I felt sure that I had walked across that same basement floor, had opened that same cosmetic case, and had reached for that same belt, all at some point in the past. I'll never forget the feeling."

Ponnuru smiled. "Was it being summertime by any chance?"

Prester thought a moment. "You know, now that I think about it, I remember that my cousins and I were excited because it was the longest day of the year."

"The day of the summer solstice."

"Yeah, I guess so."

"In all probability, you were undergoing a momentary trans-temporal equilibrium shift. That is to say, for a very brief instant, you were crossing into a parallel dimension of time such that you were experiencing, or more precisely re-experienced, an event that from your perspective had already been taking place in the past."

Prester rolled his head. "I don't know. That sounds pretty crazy."

"To understand this, you must be realizing that we do not actually live in a 'uni-verse,'" Ponnuru explained. "Rather, nature provides for us what is better described as a multi-verse, with numerous, perhaps an infinite number, of parallel universes all existing at once. It is as though there were individual pieces of paper being stacked on top of one another, with each individual page representing its own universe just as real and complete as the one you and I are experiencing now. On occasion, we can momentarily shift from our universe into a parallel one, sometimes coming out ahead or behind where we were. That is what is happening when we experience déjà vu, or for some people precognition."

Prester grinned and nodded. "Okay," he said, "let me ask you this. If this phenomenon of yours . . . what did you call it?"

"Trans-temporal equilibrium shift," Ponnuru repeated.

"If this shift of yours really happens, and if it is as commonplace as you say, wouldn't people see it? That is, wouldn't there be reported sighting of people momentarily disappearing and then reappearing all over the world? In fact wouldn't someone by now have taken a video of such a thing and thrown it up on YouTube?"

"That is an excellent question, Mr. John, but easily explained. The fact is, the phenomenon cannot be taking place if anyone is actually observing the event. You see, the observation of an event entails the transfer of photons or light from the object of the event to the observer. Since light carries with it information, it actually is defining and locking into place the time element of the event for the observer."

Prester stared at him with raised eyebrows.

"Perhaps some further explanation, yes? Yes, okay," Ponnuru said before taking a deep breath.

"Let us be taking the hydrogen atom, for example," Ponnuru continued. "In a hydrogen atom, a single electron spins rapidly around its nucleus. Curiously, however, when we are attempting to measure the precise location of this single electron at any given moment, we are always finding it in exactly the same place – right in front of us. It is never being off to one side or behind the nucleus. Rather, it is always being directly in front of us, no matter how many times or in how many ways we are attempting to measure it. In a sense, it is as though the single electron is being in all places at once, and yet we know this cannot be because only a single electron is existing there. What is happening is that, by the mere fact of our measuring the electron, we are affecting it, thus freezing in place the three-dimensional reality of its location relative to our observation."

Prester lowered his eyebrows as well as his expectations of comprehending Ponnuru's explanation.

"All right," Prester had said. "For the sake of argument, let's assume you're right and that there really are these momentary shifts going on. So what happened to Kirk Renzo? If he experienced a trans-temporal equilibrium shift, why didn't he reappear immediately? Why was his shift permanent?"

"With young Mr. Renzo, there were occurring two critical differences from the normal experience. These two differences were so unique as to rarely, if ever, occur by chance."

"What differences?" Prester had asked.

"Firstly, at the exact moment of trans-temporal equilibrium, young Kirk must have been in physical contact with a timetree."

"A timetree?"

"Yes. The Block Island Oak, you see, is a timetree. It is not the only one, of course. There are many timetrees now existing around the world. The living tissue of such aged trees can, under the right circumstances, act as a bridge between our present reality and a parallel universe."

"Timetrees, huh? You said there was a second difference?"

"Secondly, we know that Kirk was holding in his hand an artifact that has been existing for centuries – one of the twin daggers. This artifact was serving to not only pull Kirk across to a parallel universe, but also down the chain of events of that parallel universe to some previous time, such as when the knife was relatively new."

"How can you be sure of exactly where in that parallel universe Kirk may have landed?" Prester asked.

"I cannot be sure," Ponnuru admitted. "But we have a great advantage at our disposal. We have the twin dagger, or to be more precise, you have it. In theory, we can recreate the same trans-temporal equilibrium shift that happened to young Kirk. If you are holding the twin dagger, then I believe you should be shifting to the exact place where young Kirk is now."

"In theory?" Prester gulped.

"I'm afraid so, Mr. John. While I am being extremely confident of my calculations, it is still just a hypothesis."

Prester felt both amused and uneasy as Ponnuru concluded his explanation. In his heart, he didn't believe a word of what he was hearing. But if Chas Renzo wanted to pay him a lot of money to stand by a tree and hold a knife in his hand, who was he to argue? And yet, in his gut, he could not help but feel a strange queasiness at the prospect that it might all be true.

As Chas Renzo had promised, the trio boarded a private helicopter the day after their meeting in New York and flew to Block Island. Upon landing, Prester made his way to the local bank where he kept the remaining twin dagger in a safety deposit box. Two days later, they assembled in front of the Block Island Academy. Now, standing before the ancient oak as the noon hour approached, Prester knew only two things to be true. One, Kirk Renzo had disappeared exactly one year ago to the day without a trace and without explanation. And two, Prester was now being asked to engage in a fantastic enterprise designed to find him.

"Are you possessing the dagger?" Ponnuru asked for the fourth time that morning.

"I have it, I have it," Prester said.

"And we should stand facing away from the tree?" Chas Renzo asked. "Is that right, Dr. Ponnuru?"

"Yes, always looking away," Ponnuru answered.

Prior to their arrival on the island, Ponnuru had arranged for about a dozen students of quantum physics from Boston University, his alma mater, to be present. Having briefly explained the intent of his experiment, and having sworn them all to secrecy, Ponnuru assigned each student to their own thirteen-foot pole upon which was stapled a twelve-foot wide continuous roll of opaque purple silk. The cloth-covered poles were then laid around the ancient oak so that, when lifted up and pressed into the snow, they created a complete curtain around the tree.

Now with the students all at their posts, Ponnuru spoke to them with his final instructions.

"Today," Ponnuru announced, "we are conducting a very interesting and important experiment. If we are to be succeeding, you must follow my instructions absolutely and without question. Is there any-one among you who is not feeling that they can do this?"

The students as a whole remained silent in the face of this rhetori-cal question. Hearing nothing, Ponnuru continued.

"I am thinking today of the biblical story of Sodom and Gomorrah. God decided that for their sins, He would be destroying these two cit-ies and all of their inhabitants. But God was making a special favor to one man, Lot. God was allowing Lot and his family to leave before the destruction, and God made to them only one warning. God said to them, do not be looking back. But as we know, Lot's wife did not obey God. She did look back, and things did not turn out so well for her."

The students laughed at his understatement.

"Now," he continued, "I cannot say what God may be thinking of quantum physics or of our little experiment here today. I can say, how-ever, that as with God's instructions to Lot, you must not be looking back. This experiment requires that no one observe the trans-temporal equilibrium shift phenomenon. You all are knowing that observation equals measurement, and measurement destroys the quantum effect. And so, as much as you may be wanting to, you cannot watch. You cannot be looking back. You must allow the experiment to play itself out unobserved. Only then can we be seeing the results. Do you all understand?"

The students murmured their assent.

"Very well," Ponnuru shouted, holding a small device high over his head. "I am holding here a portable air horn. When the horn sounds, you will lift your poles and spread out around the tree until the cloth is taut. You must be holding the cloth tightly so as to prevent any move-ment should a gust of wind be suddenly upon us. And most importantly, you must be looking away, always away, from the tree."

Like a director on a Hollywood set, Ponnuru shouted his instruc-tions in staccato bursts, all the while pointing and waving his hands.

"Once the screen has been erected, be ever watchful," he continued. "Be scanning the horizon. Watch for anyone who might be moving or looking in your direction, and shout out if you need assistance. Keep in mind, the screen will draw attention, so we must be moving quickly.

From the moment you hear the horn, we will need only thirty seconds. I will sound the horn a second time for the all clear."

Prester watched as the students each squatted down, ready to grasp their poles and lift them into place at Ponnuru's order.

"Are you ready, Mr. John?" Ponnuru asked.

"Sure thing," Prester said, smiling at the theatricality of it all.

"Very well, then. Please move to the center of the ring, directly next to the tree. Be sure you have the dagger, and be touching the tree with one hand. When you hear the horn and see the curtain rise around you, I want you to close your eyes tightly. Do you understand?"

"Aye aye, Captain," Prester said with a mock salute as he touched the dagger in his waistband and walked toward the tree.

Ponnuru, ignoring the sarcasm, surveyed the scene one last time. He then checked his watch again. It was one minute after twelve and counting.

"Okay, everyone, we are going now. Good luck," Ponnuru shouted. He then lifted the air horn high above his head. One moment passed. Then two. Then three. Suddenly, shattering the stillness of the air, Ponnuru pulled the trigger on his portable horn, one long, loud blast. With that, the students lifted up their silk-covered poles and stretched them taut as they turned their heads and eyes away from the fabric circle they had created.

Inside the circle, Prester pinched closed his eyes and, with the dagger firmly tucked into his waist, reached out for the tree with his right hand, laying his bare palm upon the cold bark. He waited. In his mind, he counted off the seconds: fifteen, twenty, twenty-five. Now thirty seconds had passed, and then thirty-five and forty, and now forty-five seconds. Where was the horn? Perhaps he had miscounted. Perhaps the seconds seemed to be going by faster for him, but certainly by now it must be at least one minute, possibly two minutes or even three.

"Dr. Ponnuru?" he shouted. He waited, still with his eyes tightly closed, but heard nothing. Where was the second horn?

"Can I open my eyes now?"

He listened carefully. There had been another sound, the sound of snow under shuffling boots, but that too was now gone. Again he listened, and he began to count anew. Finally, confident that a sufficient time must have passed, he opened his eyes.

Blinking several times, Prester stared straight ahead. The purple curtain was gone. Blue sunlit sky touched upon yellow daisies and tall green grass. Warm air caressed his cheeks and lips. The aroma of wild honeysuckle filled his nostrils as a hummingbird hovered in midair. Turning, he saw that his right hand was touching an olive tree near a stone archway leading to a small garden where roses were in full bloom. The snow was gone, it was spring, and he was no longer on Block Island.

Chapter 21

Prester heard the sound of laughter in the distance. Looking off, he saw three young boys playing with sticks, wielding them as if fighting with swords. He began walking toward them, and immediately noticed the crunching sound of the dry dirt path beneath what he now saw were unfamiliar black leather boots.

Looking at his sleeves, Prester realized he was dressed in strange clothes. In place of his polyester blend microfiber winter coat, he was wearing a tan felt sleeveless vest with silver ringlets tied with black lace. A collarless white cotton shirt that tied in a bunch around each wrist had replaced his forest-green nylon sweater. He also realized that he no longer possessed the dagger. Instead, tied to his waist was a small leather pouch.

It was mid-morning. The sun was just a quarter of the way into its arc across the sky. He looked up to gauge the sun's position. As he lowered his head again, the three threadbare boys stood squarely in front of him.

"*Chi sei tu?*" one of the boys asked him.

He shook his head to show that he did not understand.

"*Egli e' perduto,*" another said, and the boys all laughed. Prester could only smile.

"What is this place?" he asked, but the boys just looked at him. One of the boys, bolder than the others, stepped forward and touched the leather of his vest. Prester saw that his vest was much nicer than any of the tattered rags the boys were wearing.

"*Tu sei ricco,*" the bold boy said as he ran his small hand across the soft felt.

A second boy, emulating his friend, stepped forward and glanced toward Prester's pouch.

"*Che cosa e' nella borsa?*" he asked.

Prester, seeing where the boy was looking, opened the pouch and, quite to his surprise, withdrew two gold florins. After examining them for a moment, he dropped them back into the pouch. "Well, look at that," he said to himself.

"*Questo e il mio,*" the second boy grinned, and they all laughed again.

Suddenly, the first boy reared back and kicked Prester hard in the shin.

"Hey!" Prester protested, pulling back from the boys. But the second boy had grabbed hold of his pouch and was yanking it in the opposite direction. As he did so, the first boy began hitting Prester with his stick.

The boy pulling on the pouch abruptly shifted direction and threw his small body against Prester's left side, knocking him off his feet. As they both fell to the ground, the pouch came loose from Prester's waist. In the next instant, the two boys were racing away with their loot.

Prester pushed himself to his feet and dusted himself off. Nearby, standing just out of reach, the third little boy, smaller than the others, eyeballed him.

"Nice friends you have there," Prester said, but the boy did not understand.

In the distance, down the road where the boys had run, Prester now noticed what appeared to be a high stone wall at the end of the path.

"What is that?" Prester said to the remaining boy. "What's over there?" Prester pointed in the direction of the wall.

"*Ci?*" the boy said. "*E 'Firenze.*"

Firenze. Prester recognized the word.

"Is that the city of Florence?" he asked the boy. "Is that Firenze?"

"*Firenze, si,*" the boy confirmed.

Ponnuru had done it, he thought.

Prester began walking toward the stone wall, unsure of what he would find beyond what he now understood to be the city perimeter, but eager to explore this new reality. Stopping, he looked around. The boy's fascination with him had apparently worn off, for he was gone.

Prester walked down the path toward the wall. As he drew nearer, he could see that the wall rose perhaps twenty feet above the path. To one side, the wall extended out along flat ground for about two hundred yards before curving inward to surround the city. In the other direction, the wall climbed up and over a hill, bending out of sight at the crest.

As he reached the city wall, he saw a massive stone arch that supported heavy double wooden doors held by enormous iron hinges. The doors were wide open, and no one seemed to take any notice of him as he passed under the arch and stepped into the city proper.

No sooner had he entered the city than he began to see peddlers and shopkeepers, bakers, weavers, and blacksmiths, all employed in their work. Slowing his pace, he stared at the people passing by. He saw men dressed in flowing capes, some black, some red and some blue. One man with a beard had a black cloth draped over the crown of his head, almost in the fashion of a nun. Another much younger man had reddish brown hair cut in a bowl style.

A woman passing nearby carried in her arms a basket of freshly baked bread, the aroma trailing behind her as she walked. Crossing in front of her, a woman was wearing a brown and white head covering that looked to Prester like a potato sack. He noticed a third young woman standing alone, the long curve of her white neck set against long black hair that was bundled together at the shoulder before being allowed to flow halfway down the fabric of her bright red dress trimmed in black velvet.

"Attento!" shouted a man from a donkey cart as it rolled by, almost knocking Prester over. He realized he had been standing in the middle of the road. Stepping aside, he noticed several young men standing near the corner of a building, chewing on grass reeds, and staring in his direction. One of them, the apparent leader of the pack, was dressed in a red cape and blue tunic, his yellow floppy hat tilted forward atop his shoulder length black hair.

"Hey, amico. Vieni qui," the leader shouted at him, waving his hands in a mocking gesture inviting him to approach. They were like young thugs anywhere, Prester thought, and they did not look friendly. He decided to move on.

As he continued walking, he came upon a cobblestone street more heavily traveled than any he had seen to that point. Suddenly the people all around him seemed to be rushing ahead, all hurrying in the same direction as he, but eager to get to their destination. He was swept along with the crowd until he came upon a bridge stretching across a river. The footings of the bridge were made of stone, but upon the bridge itself, running along both sides of its entire length, were a series of small wooden shacks enclosing vendors selling their goods from open tables.

"I think I know this bridge," Prester said aloud to himself as he slowed his pace. The hubbub around him was such now that no one could hear him, nor was anyone paying attention. It was, he realized, the Ponte Vecchio. He had never been to Florence, but he had seen pictures of the famous bridge many times, and even recalled having once read an article about its construction. Florence, he knew, had changed very little from the time of the Renaissance. Still, the bridge was not quite as he recalled having seen it in photographs. The bridge was supposed to have a covered walkway running its entire length above the shops. And then he remembered. The walkway would not be built until 1565, designed by Giorgio Vasari so that the Medici family could walk from their residential palace to the town hall without having to mingle with the common people. As Prester approached the Ponte Veccchio, the Vasari Corridor was not yet in existence.

Walking onto the bridge, he saw young people, old people, women carrying infants, men on crutches, everyone moving toward the far side. In the distance, he heard a church bell chime, one, two, three, four, five, six. He counted eleven in all.

Walking faster now to keep up with the ever quickening pace of those around him, he hurried by table after table of butchers selling their beef, poultry, pork and fowl. All of the merchants on the bridge were butchers, he realized, each with different meats for sale. As he neared the far side of the Ponte Vecchio, he noticed a woman yelling down to a man in a rowboat.

"*Savonarola e' in piazza,*" she shouted.

"*E' lui un prigionero?*" the young man hollered back. Prester had no idea what they were saying.

"*Egli e' legato ad un palo,*" the woman called out.

Just then he was jostled by a group of playful children running by. Sidestepping to let them pass, he bumped squarely into a young man holding a satchel under his arm, knocking the satchel to the ground.

"Oh, excuse me," Prester exclaimed.

The young man did not respond, but instead stooped to retreive the hammer and chisels that had fallen from his bag. As he rose again, the young man looked into Prester's face, sizing him up with an eye that suggested an almost scientific curiosity. Prester in turn noticed that the man had a crooked nose and angular features. The man stared at him for another moment, and then turned and continued on his way.

Prester moved with the flow of the crowd across the bridge and through several more streets, emerging from the shadows of the buildings and out into a large open air square. Mobs of people were milling about, and Prester sensed an odd mix of anger and jubilation in their behavior.

On the far side of the square stood a massive red brick fortress capped by a tall battlement-style tower, a structure designed to draw the eye of all spectators. On this day, however, all eyes were directed toward a crude wooden platform that had been erected in the middle of the open square. Rising up through the center of the raised platform was a tall wooden post standing perhaps 10 feet above the platform elevation. Tied to the post was a holy man in black robes and white collar.

Although he was a priest, no reverence was being paid to him. Indeed, quite the opposite. The priest was tied with his hands behind his back, facing outward toward the jeering crowd. He looked sullen and stern, but Prester saw that he was not afraid. The crowd was shouting invectives at him, spitting at him, and throwing tomatoes in his direction. On occasion, the priest would shout back at one or another of the rabble.

People ran and shouted like wild animals around the raised platform. Prester saw a woman stoop and pick up a stone, and then throw it at the tethered priest striking him just above the left eye. This was quickly followed by a hoard of imitators, all hurling stones. Those who could not find stones grabbed sticks or handfuls of sand with which to pelt the forsaken cleric.

Just then, stepping out onto the center balcony of the red brick fortress, came a young man regally dressed in fine clothes. He wore a purple robe tied at the waist and a yellow cape over one shoulder, and his clothes were more elegant than those of anyone in the assemblage below. Indeed, upon seeing him, the crowd grew quiet and stepped back from the wooden platform as if awaiting further instructions.

The man appeared to be perhaps 22 years old, and Prester quickly sensed that there was something familiar about him. People in the square below began to bow as the man raised up a hand to greet them. Then, turning his attention to the priest tied up on the platform, the young man spoke to the crowd.

"Morte o non morte?" he shouted over the crowd. Prester again felt a sense of recognition upon hearing the voice of the young man.

"Morte!" someone in the crowd yelled back.

"Morte o non morte?" the young man shouted again.

"Morte, morte," came another voice, followed by a third, a fourth and a fifth all shouting the same thing. Prester saw that the crowd was hesitant to act without the approval of this royal young man. As Prester stared up at the man's face, he noticed a familiar smirk curl around his lips.

"Kirkrenzo," someone shouted from the crowd.

"Kirkrenzo, Kirkrenzo," everyone began chanting.

Kirk. It was definitely him, Prester could see that now. He was older, no longer the gangly teenager he had last seen on Block Island. He had filled out, had grown three or four inches, and was now a strapping young man. Prester tried to step forward to get his attention, but was pushed back by the jostling throng.

"Morte, morte," the crowd shouted again. In response, Kirk shrugged his shoulders. He was leaving the decision to the people. Immediately they began piling straw and sticks around the feet of the defrocked friar. Within three minutes, the horde had put a torch to the straw, setting it ablaze.

Prester sank back in horror as the growing flames began to lick at the priest. Within moments, fire was shooting up above the length of the pole, and the priest's robe began to burn. The smoke became thick, and Prester's eyes began to sting. Looking through the smoke and flames, he could still see the priest. Despite the intense heat, the holy man was not crying out, but rather was staring stoically forward, never flinching, never blinking, as if staring into the eyes of God.

Finally, mercifully, the priest slouched over as the flames engulfed him, still tied by the hands but now unconscious. Prester felt as if he might vomit. He had to steady himself by grasping at the elbow of a stranger. Looking back up, he saw Kirk still standing on the balcony looking down upon the horrific scene without emotion.

"Kirk," Prester shouted. "Kirk."

Kirk's face flinched at the sound, and he seemed to freeze in place.

"Kirk," Prester shouted again, waving his arms in the air. Having moved through the crowd, Prester was now only about a hundred feet from the balcony.

Kirk's eyes locked onto Prester's, and burned into them with intensity. In his countenance, Prester saw surprise and recognition, but also fear and anger. There was no sense of fellowship. Prester then saw Kirk shout down in Italian from the balcony to a pair of soldiers standing on the ground near the fortress door. Although Prester could not understand Kirk's words, his tone was unmistakable. In the next instant, Prester saw that the men on the ground had each drawn their swords and were making their way through the crowd toward where he was standing.

Prester saw them coming, knocking people aside as they did so. He had no need of a translator to understand the danger. He dashed back through the crowd in the opposite direction from where he had come.

The square was packed with men and women, young and old, all shouting angry curses toward the human bonfire. Prester darted amongst and around them, changing directions first ninety degrees right, then forty-five degrees left, like a pass receiver running a play. Looking back, he saw that he had attained only a small lead on his pursuers. He would have to do better if he were to outrun them. They were carrying heavy swords. Perhaps if he could get free from this crowd, he could outpace them.

Reaching the edge of the crowd, he ran up one of the many small alleys leading away from the public square. Looking over his shoulder, he saw that he had gained some little distance on his attackers, although not enough for comfort. He slowed a bit to turn up another alley when a hand reached out from a doorway and gripped him by the arm. Spinning around, he saw the kindly face of an elderly peasant shopkeeper.

"This way, friend," the man said in English.

"Who are you?" Prester responded.

"Later," the old man said. "Come along, before the Prince's soldiers see you."

The old man opened the side door of his shop and pulled Prester in, then closed and locked the door behind them.

"Who are you?" Prester asked again as he caught his breath.

"Shhhh," the old man said, holding his finger to his lips and listening at the door for passing footfalls. After a few moments, he seemed to relax.

"There now, I think the crisis has passed," the old man said. He spoke with a British accent.

"Thank you," Prester said, "but who are you?"

The man grinned at Prester, the kind of toothy, self-satisfied grin one might expect to receive upon running into an old schoolmate.

"Call me Halifax," he said. "I saw you on the bridge, and if my guess is right, you're one of us."

Chapter 22

Michelangelo could see that the crowds were mad with excitement as he crossed into Florence via the Ponte Vecchio. The resentment against Savonarola had been building since his excommunication the previous year, and Michelangelo was shocked at the vehemence of the Florentine people. Savonarola, after all, had been revered by these same people since the death of Lorenzo the Magnificent. Savonarola's every pronouncement had been followed without question. The people had burned books, destroyed statues, slashed fine paintings and even assaulted other clergy at the behest of this Franciscan priest, all because he had convinced them that any works of art that dared to stray from the purely pious were displeasing to God. But there had been an ongoing struggle for power between the Pope in Rome and this upstart priest, and now that the Church had followed through on its long-standing threat to excommunicate him for his continued criticism of their traditions and practices. With that official and most significant act, the people had quickly turned against Savonarola. It was as if the rage of the public had been building up like steam in a boiling caldron, and had now blown open to scald the unsuspecting priest.

Shoulders bumped into shoulders as Michelangelo made his way across the bridge. Tucked under one arm was a small leather satchel containing his entire collection of worldly goods, a fact that did not bother him in the least. He had no use for material possessions, and had often lived for months on end with little more than discarded scraps of food seasoned with determination. As an artist, his impoverishment was one of his greatest strengths, for it gave him the luxury of having nothing to lose. Instead, he cared only for his art, and for his art he lived and breathed.

As Michelangelo neared the far side of the bridge, he noticed a woman shouting down to a man in a rowboat passing beneath. He turned his head to listen.

"Savonarola is in the square," the woman shouted.

"Is he a prisoner?" the man in the boat yelled back.

"Yes, he is tied to the stake," she replied and then moved on.

Turning back to the street, Michelangelo saw several children scurry by him, darting in and out against the flow of the crowd and knocking a man nearly off his feet. The man fell against him, jostling the satchel from under his arm and sending it crashing to the cobblestone road.

Michelangelo knelt to retrieve the bag and its contents. As he did so, he noticed that the other man had stopped and was trying to speak with him. The man's words were unfamiliar. He appeared to be speaking in some version of English which Michelangelo did not understand, but the man seemed apologetic. Standing erect again, Michelangelo held his ground against the surging crowd just long enough to get a good look at the man. He studied him for a long moment, as he often did with strangers, focusing on the facial structure, the nose, the eyes, the mouth. The man seemed out of place, which made him all the more interesting. Disengaging from his examination, Michelangelo pushed forward toward the Piazza Signoria.

Entering the piazza, Michelangelo saw that Savonarola had been placed on a temporary wooden platform that had been erected in the middle of the open square. The priest was secured to a pole running up through the platform, with thick rough ropes around his wrists and legs. Angry peasants were gathering stones all around the platform for the sole purpose of flinging them at the hapless victim, and fling them they did. One stone struck Savonarola just above the left eye, and he began to bleed profusely. Others followed suit, and soon Savonarola was being pelted with stones, sand and gravel.

Then, off to one side of the piazza, a man stepped out onto a balcony of the Signoria. It was the new prince that Michelangelo had heard so much about. The crowd quieted as the Prince surveyed the scene below him.

"Death or no death?" the Prince shouted to the crowd.

"Death," the man standing next to Michelangelo yelled up to the balcony.

"Death or no death?" the Prince asked again.

"Death, death," another man standing nearby shouted. Soon a cacophony of shouts could be heard, all the people asking for the ultimate punishment to be exacted upon their former spiritual leader.

From his balcony, the Prince sneered down at the mass of people below him, Michelangelo among them.

"Kirkrenzo," came a shout from within a group of people standing beneath the balcony.

"Kirkrenzo, Kirkrenzo," came other voices mingled with shouts of "death, death." The Prince looked over the crowd and shrugged his shoulders, which the crowd took as a sign of assent. Within a few minutes, the mob had piled brush and dried twigs at the feet of Savonarola, and had commenced to setting it on fire. Michelangelo stared at the priest as the flames engulfed him. Rarely did one get an opportunity to observe human anguish in all its direct, vivid truth. Michelangelo was at once repulsed and fascinated by the sight, not for its gruesomeness but for its revelation. Savonarola did not flinch nor cry out as Michelangelo would have expected any man to do. But then, Michelangelo knew that Savonarola was not just any man. He had been a giant.

In short order, it was all over. Michelangelo turned away and looked back up at the balcony. Prince Kirkrenzo was still there, watching Savonarola's charred body in the flame.

"Kirk," someone in the crowd shouted up to the Prince in what Michelangelo thought was a too familiar and rather insulting manner. "Kirk," came the shout again. This time, Michelangelo thought he saw the Prince look at someone in particular among the crowd. Michelangelo watched as the Prince began to shout directions to a pair of soldiers on the ground. In the next instant, a scuffle broke out. People were being pushed to one side as the Prince's men, swords drawn, began running through the assemblage. Michelangelo could not quite see who it was they were chasing.

Chapter 23

"Halifax?" Prester asked, trying to confirm what he thought the man had told him.

"Yes, but I'm not particular," the man said. "Call me anything you like."

Halifax looked to be in his mid-sixties, but the radiance that beamed from his face bespoke a more youthful spirit. There was a nimbleness too in his gestures that suggested he may at any moment break out into a jig.

"You're not English, are you?" the man asked eagerly. "You don't sound English."

"No," Prester said. "I'm American."

"Ah, American," Halifax repeated. "Imagine that. I haven't heard anyone speak of America in 20 years. You might just as well tell people around here that you're from the dark side of the moon. Say, would you care for some tea?"

Halifax did not wait for an answer, but instead lifted a pot of boiling water from a hook that had been swung into the fireplace over the flame. He then poured the steaming water into a clay jar, swirled it around, and poured it out again. Next he lifted from a shelf a small leather box which he placed upon a wooden table and carefully opened.

"This is the finest black tea from Ceylon," he said. "I got it from a ship captain who was passing through on his way to Genoa."

Taking two pinches of the contents, he placed the loose tea leaves into the clay jar, and then filled the jar with fresh boiling water before covering it with a lid.

"We mustn't let it over-steep," he said as he placed a small cloth over the makeshift teapot to insulate the warmth. "Two to five minutes is best, I find, to avoid a bitter stew. Trouble is, of course, in the timing. No bloody clocks. Also, I'm afraid I have no milk or sugar to offer you. There's not a damned thing convenient about this place," Halifax said as he worked. "Still, one must make do, mustn't one."

Using a perforated wooden spoon as a strainer, he poured out first one and then a second cup of tea into two handleless metal mugs.

"I've always believed that even in the most uncivilized of circumstances, a proper degree of decorum is required," Halifax said as he placed the two mugs on the table. "Even during the Great War, while living in the trenches, we always insisted upon keeping up tradition."

Halifax sipped from his mug, and then looked at Prester.

"How rude of me. Here I am going on about the Great War and tea and this and that, and I don't even know anything about you. Tell me, when are you from?"

Prester looked at him quizzically.

"As I said, I'm from America."

"No, no, you misunderstand me. I'm not asking 'where' are you from. We've already established that. What I want to know is, 'when' are you from?"

"When?"

"Yes," Halifax continued. "What era? What time frame?"

Prester hesitated. He had just met this man, and didn't know much about him. Perhaps silence would be the best course for the moment.

"I do apologize," Halifax said. "Doubtless this is a lot for you to take in, and you're quite right to be cautious. So let me start by telling you a bit more about me."

Prester nodded, but remained mute.

"I am from the middle years of the twentieth century. The twenty-eighth day of May in the year of our Lord nineteen hundred and forty, to be precise. That was my last day at home – a fine spring day as I recall, blue sky, wispy white clouds, a lovely warm English breeze, um, yes, and the grass, it seems to me that the grass was very green that day. I remember it, you see, because I sat down on the grass under a great old tree to do a bit of reading. It had been a frightfully busy week for all of us. I dozed off. Foolish of me really. Suddenly, I was here, what? Well, at any rate, are you at all familiar with the twentieth century?"

Prester nodded again.

"Oh, splendid. Splendid indeed. Now, have you ever heard of a chap by the name of Winston Churchill? He had just been appointed interim Prime Minister when I left home, although I don't suppose he lasted long. That is to say, things were on fairly shaky ground politically for him just then, you understand."

"Of course I've heard of Winston Churchill," Prester said.

"Oh, have you?"

"Everyone has heard of Winston Churchill," Prester confirmed.

"You don't say," Halifax said. "That surprises me, I must tell you. He was not a terribly popular fellow in many quarters when I knew him."

"You knew Winston Churchill?"

"Well, certainly I knew him. You see, before I came here, I was the personal valet to his Lordship, Viscount Halifax, the Foreign Secretary. Actually, it is after Lord Halifax that I have taken the name I now use, the reason being that since my arrival here I have not been able to remember my own. Curious, but there it is. You've heard of Lord Halifax, of course."

"No."

"Lord Halifax, I say."

"No."

"Perhaps I'm not making myself clear. I'm talking now about Lord Edward Frederick Lindley Wood, 1st Earl of Halifax. You've heard of him, no doubt?"

"No."

"No? No? How do you mean, no?"

"I mean, no. I've never heard of him."

Halifax swooned into the nearest chair.

"I mean to say, absolutely," he said. "Never heard of him?"

"Sorry. Should I have?"

"Oh my. Quite extraordinary. I'll have you know that when I left home, to come here I mean, Lord Halifax was one of the most important men in all Britain. He was about to be named Prime Minister himself. The great bulk of the Conservative party was already supporting him, as was the royal family. Even Labour found him acceptable."

"Sorry, I don't know who he is," Prester persisted.

"Indeed! You are definitely American, aren't you? Well then, let me ask you about another man. He was the leader of Germany at the time."

"You mean, Hitler?"

"Yes, Herr Hitler. You're familiar with him, are you?"

"Good God, Halifax. Every schoolboy knows who Hitler was," Prester said.

"Well, I suppose that makes sense," Halifax said. "Another Napoleon, really. He literally swept across the face of northern France in under a month. Indeed, just as I was leaving, he had our boys pinned down at a place called Dunkirk. I've often wondered how those poor boys made out. You see, when I left home it appeared to us, that is to Lord Halifax and Mr. Churchill, that Herr Hitler was pretty fairly poised to leap across the channel to England. The last thing I remember before sitting down by the tree was that we were about to go into a meeting of the War Cabinet where Mr. Churchill was scheduled to give some species of speech or another, although it seemed pretty certain that he was going to be forced from office. Chamberlain had been done in by then, you see, and quite frankly, we were groping for what to do next. Lord Halifax, for his part, was of the opinion that the best course under the circumstances would be to strike a separate peace with Hitler, to safeguard our independence and all that, and to prevent an invasion. Lots of people felt that way. But Mr. Churchill would hear none of it. He insisted that we fight on, although none of us could quite see at the time how it could be managed. That's the last thing I remember, except for sitting under the tree. I do recall that I was reading an original edition of Machiavelli's History of Florence at the time, a gift from his Lordship. I believe I was holding it when I drifted off to sleep. When I awoke, the book was gone."

"And you ended up here," Prester said.

"Yes, exactly that. Strangest thing, what? That was 20 years ago."

"You've been here for 20 years?" Prester asked with a start.

"Quite. It's not so bad, really. You'll get used to it. I've learned to speak the local lingo fairly well, and I've gotten to know a few interesting people. Still, it will be nice to have the company of a fellow W*ayfromer*."

"A fellow what?" Prester asked.

"*Wayfromer*. We are all Wayfromers, you see. That's the name I made up for people like us. It's something to call ourselves, those of us who have traveled through time I mean. After all, we can't very well go around calling ourselves time travelers, can we? They would lock us up, or worse. So I concocted the acronym 'W-A-Y,' plus the word 'From,' which of course stands for 'When Are You From' or 'Wayfrom.' It flows nicely in conversation without really being noticed if overheard. After all, the one thing we time travelers want to know about each other is when are you from, what? And so, you see, we are all Wayfromers. Brilliant, don't you think?"

"Oh yes, brilliant," Prester half-heartedly agreed.

"I thought so."

"There are others like us then?" Prester asked.

"Indeed there are. Hard to say how many. I've met exactly three, not counting you of course. Two were long 'wayfromers,' that is to say they had come more than two hundred years from when they started. One was a nice young watchmaker from Germany, Nuremberg I think, by the name of Peter Henlein. Bumped his head while hunting in the woods one day in 1725, and woke up here. The other man worked in a paper mill in my native England, Herfordshire to be exact. His name was John Tate, so he said. I think he came here from 1802, or was it 1803. At any rate, they both made their way back to their respective countries as soon as they were able. What became of them, I can't say. Unfortunately for you, it won't be quite as easy to make your way back to America, what?"

"You didn't go back to England. Why not?"

"Why not? Why not indeed. Well, it's hard to say really. I've made friends here, of course. And besides, I don't suppose I'd recognize the old place anymore. No, no, in the end, I suppose I never mustered up the courage to go back. That's it really."

"You said there was a third '*wayfromer?*'"

"Ah, yes. A young woman. She was a short 'wayfromer,' having traveled back only five years or so from when she started, just far enough to avoid the mistake of marrying a particularly brutish man. Ran off with the man's younger brother, I believe. Rather risqué, what?" Halifax laughed. "So tell me, when are you from?"

Prester could not focus on the question. His head was reeling from the avalanche of information. Halifax, however, patiently waited for him to reply, as if he'd seen this sort of delayed reaction before.

"I'm from the second decade of the 21st Century," Prester finally said. "So is your Prince Kirkrenzo."

Now Halifax seemed stunned. Prester could see that he was calculating things in his mind.

"That's some 70 years into the future," he said.

"Into your future, you mean," Prester corrected him.

"Yes, yes, of course," Halifax said, deep in thought. "Tell me," he said with a serious tone. "Old England. Old Britannia." Suddenly, he broke into song.

> "Rule Britannia!
> Britannia rule the waves
> Britons never, never, never
> Shall be slaves."

"Tell me," Halifax said, having concluded his lyric, "how did it all turn out?"

"What? You mean the Second World War?"

"Oh my, was it as bad as all that? Then yes, the second great war. How did England fair?"

"Well, the boys got out of Dunkirk thanks to the heroic efforts of lots of regular folks in small boats. And Hitler never took England," Prester assured him. "He tried. London and lots of other English towns suffered tremendous damage from Luftwaffe bombing during what they called the Blitz. But Hitler lost the Battle of Britain. Then the Americans got involved in December '41 after the Japanese attacked us at a place called Pearl Harbor, Hawaii. And Hitler made the mistake of taking on the Russians, which opened up an eastern front. Then in

June of 1944, the allies launched an invasion of Nazi occupied France. They called it D-Day. By winter, things were beginning to fall apart for Hitler, and by the spring of '45, it was all over in Europe. Hitler was dead, and Germany had surrendered."

"So England came out all right then?"

"It did."

"And what of this Japanese war you speak of?"

"The Japanese surrendered in August of that same year when we dropped a new kind of bomb on them, an Atom Bomb, that killed hundreds of thousands of people at one time."

"Such bombs exist?"

"Bombs and missiles even more powerful than that exist in my time," Prester said.

Halifax shook his head in dismay. "Such a world," he said, and shook his head again.

"In the end, millions of people were killed. The war, the Second World War I mean, changed a lot of things. It was a real mess."

"But England survived, you say," Halifax repeated for confirmation.

"Yes."

Halifax's eyes moistened. "Good old England," he sniffled, dabbing his cheeks with his sleeve. "Jolly good."

Chapter 24

Over a dinner of bean soup and saltless bread, Halifax told Prester all about his life. He had met many people since arriving in Renaissance Florence twenty years before. He had even formed an acquaintance, if not quite a friendship, with the great Michelangelo, although he described him as being rather standoffish.

Prester, in turn, tried his best to tell Halifax about the Ponnuru theory of trans-temporal equilibrium shift. He explained that, according to Ponnuru, it could only occur if no one observed it. He repeated the things Ponnuru had told him about time being like a river. He described how Ponnuru said there were multiple universes existing side by side like separate sheets in a stack of paper. He explained that he had come from the 21st Century to find Kirk Renzo, and to bring him home. He repeated what Ponnuru had said point by point. In order to get home, he and Kirk would have to make their way to his transfer point at a precise day and time. He had arrived at a particular olive tree near a rose garden archway just beyond the city walls. That is where he and Kirk had to be at exactly 2:04 PM on the next summer solstice, June 21st.

"That gives you just twenty-nine days," Halifax said, holding in his hands a cylindrical device with seven wheels that could be adjusted independently around a central axis. On the wheels where numbers, letters and symbols, and Halifax moved them with the dexterity of a Rubic's Cube master.

"You see here," he showed Prester, "by lining up the wheels properly, you can calculate whatever date and year you wish, including the day of the week, the correct sign of the zodiac, and the proper phases of the moon. Currently, for example, it is May the 23rd in the year 1498, and it is a Wednesday."

Prester held the mechanical device and turned it over in his hand. "Fascinating," he said. "Did you make this?"

"I'm proud to say that I did, well, in a manner of speaking. It's actually based on a device I learned about when I was just a lad in school, don't you know, something designed by Sir Issac Newton, you see, or should I say something he will design in a couple of hundred years. I find that I quite enjoy tinkering with it on occasion," Halifax said.

1498, Prester thought. He was struck by the seeming randomness of his descent into the past. According to Ponnuru's theory, there would be a slight margin of error in regard to where and when Prester would land upon being projected through time. For his return trip, however, Ponnuru explained that there could be no margin of error. Precision was essential. He had to be at the transfer point at the prescribed time on the day of the summer solstice. If that rendezvous were missed, then, according to Ponnuru's calculations, return would be impossible.

"I need to find a way to get to Kirk, Prince Kirkrenzo," Prester said, "without him trying to kill me, that is?"

"What we need is an ally," Halifax said, "someone who holds the favor of the Prince, and can get us safely into the Signoria. I think I have just the man."

The next morning, the two 'wayfromers' set forth upon the streets of Florence in search of the ally whom Halifax had mentioned. Halifax had described this ally only as his "friend," and it never occurred to Prester to inquire as to his name.

The cobblestone streets of the city were damp with morning dew as the pair wound their way towards an outdoor marketplace near the Ponte Vecchio. Butchers held the exclusive use of the bridge itself, but vendors of every description touted their wares in the adjacent streets.

"I often find my friend here at this time of the day," Halifax said as they strolled passed a series of tables selling apples and blood oranges.

"Is he a fruit seller?" Prester asked?

"No," Halifax laughed.

"What does he do?"

"He thinks."

Turning a corner, they came upon a group of men congregating on the steps of a church. The men, young and old alike, were being entertained by a raconteur who was the focal point of their gaze.

"Ah, there he is now," Halifax said upon seeing him.

The man in the center of the group was perhaps 45 years old. He was taller than most of the other men, and Prester could see even from the side that he wore a long grayish white beard that draped down to his chest. His shoulder length wavy hair and large red felt cap offset his fine silk purple cloak, fringed with animal fur. As he spoke, the men around him howled with laughter and shook their heads in amazement.

"Good morning, Leonardo," Halifax shouted as he and Prester approached the perimeter of the group.

Turning around, the man smiled and waved at Halifax before turning back to continue with his storytelling.

Prester saw the man's face only for a moment, but even in that brief space of time a sudden realization came over him. He looked at Halifax.

"Leonardo?" Prester asked. "Is that Leonardo da Vinci?"

"Yes, certainly," Halifax said. "I told you about my friend, didn't I?"

"You said you had a friend. You didn't say he was Leonardo da Vinci."

"Didn't I?" Halifax said, grinning, and then lifted a finger to his lips, signaling Prester to be quiet. "I want to hear this," he said, engrossed now in whatever it was Leonardo da Vinci was saying to the group.

Prester stood and listened for several minutes. While he did not understand the words, there could be no doubt that Leonardo was a man of captivating talents. Here was a true genius, perhaps the greatest genius who ever lived. He was a consummate painter, sculptor, architect, scientist, mathematician, engineer, inventor, anatomist, geologist, cartographer, botanist, writer and, it would now appear, stand-up comic. His understanding of the world was unparalleled for his time. Many of the things he conjectured, invented and conceived of – the helicopter, the military tank, concentrated solar power, the double hull ship and the theory of plate tectonics – would not become accepted ideas for hundreds of years after his death.

"Does he know about you?" Prester whispered to Halifax. "I mean, about people like us?"

"*Wayfromers*, you mean? Oh yes, we've discussed it many times."

Prester thought a moment longer.

"Is he one of us?" Prester asked.

Halifax smiled. "Oh, no, no, no. At least not that he's ever admitted to me."

Upon concluding his remarks and excusing himself from the chuckling group, Da Vinci made his way over to where Halifax and Prester were standing.

"Listen, listen, my gooda friend," Da Vinci said in excited English as he extended a hand toward Halifax. "I justa made up a new joke this morning."

"I'm all eagerness," Halifax replied.

"A painter was asked, why, if you paint such beautiful figures, are your own children so ugly? To which the painter replies, I make my paintings by day, but my children by night."

"Oh, jolly good, old man, jolly good," Halifax laughed. "So, Leonardo, how have you been keeping yourself?"

"Very, very busy," Da Vinci said. "I havea lately been working on an idea for an underwater breathing device."

"The old bean bustling along nicely, eh? So glad to hear it. Now, Leonardo, I would like you to meet a new friend of mine. This is Mr. Prester John. He is a long 'wayfrom' home, if you catch my meaning, and he needs your help."

Da Vinci looked around at Prester with a knowing eye.

"Another one, eh? Excellente. We shall have to sit together, you and I, to discuss things. I am, how do you say, curious to know more about your situation," Da Vinci said.

"That's all well and good, Leonardo old man, but what we need at the moment is an entrée to Prince Kirkrenzo. Prester needs to speak with him on a matter of some urgency."

"My friend, don'ta worry. I ama sure it can be arranged," Da Vinci said. "Let us meet this evening at the usual place."

"Brilliant," Halifax said. "We'll be there with bells on."

Just then, several men from the nearby group began to shout towards Da Vinci, causing him to turn back toward them. Another man, much younger than Da Vinci, had joined the group.

"Oh, goodness, it's young Michelangelo," Halifax said, "back from Rome."

Prester looked over at Michelangelo and recognizing him as the man he had bumped into when he first crossed the Ponte Vecchio to enter Florence. Da Vinci excused himself, and rejoined the congregation.

The men gathered around Da Vinci and Michelangelo, giving deference to them both. Yet they seemed at the same time to be taunting the two artists toward a confrontation. Even from a distance, Prester could see that Michelangelo was beginning to get angry.

"What's happening?" Prester asked.

Halifax listened carefully, and began to translate.

"The men are comparing the artistic abilities of Da Vinci to those of Michelangelo."

Stepping a bit closer, Halifax began to translate a running commentary on the proceedings.

"They are discussing the nature of beauty," Halifax said. "Da Vinci is saying that great beauty is best understood by philosophers and poets."

"And Michelangelo?" Prester asked.

"He thinks Da Vinci is being pompous," Halifax said. "Michelangelo says that life itself contains beauty, and that beauty is just as accessible to the common man as to the poet."

Da Vinci appeared to listen to the sculptor's perspective, and then made a comment to the crowd that drew laughter. Suddenly, Michelangelo lashed out at Da Vinci with loud shouts and waiving arms.

"What happened?" Prester asked.

"The men were inquiring as to Da Vinci's opinion of Michelangelo's work, and Da Vinci said that Michelangelo is a working man's artist, which Leonardo probably meant as a compliment. Michelangelo, however, appears to have taken the comment as an insult, and is now accusing Da Vinci of being a failed artist."

"What are they saying?" Prester prompted him again.

"Michelangelo is saying, 'You, the great Leonardo, complete none of your works. The giant horse,' ah, yes, 'horse, that you were sculpting for the something or other family,' I didn't quite catch it, 'was nothing but a clay model,' and, um, 'and then you abandoned it,' he says. 'Your,' er, 'your commission for the painting of St. Jerome has been left undone for 15 years,' he says. 'And,' just a minute, I'm not sure, uh, yes, 'And for the Last Supper in Milan,' he says, 'you did not prepare your paints properly and the fresco is already falling into ruin.' My, my, I think he's laying it on a bit thick, what?"

Prester could see by the grimace on Da Vinci's face that the criticism was hitting home.

"Leonardo is now mocking Michelangelo for being afraid to accept a commission being offered by the City of Florence to carve a giant sculpture out of a single large block of marble," Halifax continued.

"And what is Michelangelo saying?" Prester asked.

"He says that everyone knows that this particular piece of marble is flawed. He says it has a crack running through the length of it. But Da Vinci is calling him a coward for not being willing to try. I say, Leonardo can be a bit of a temperamental pip at times."

As Prester looked on, Michelangelo shouted out one last volley of insults, and then stomped away from the group. Da Vinci, equally indignant, shouted a responding salvo, and then stomped away in the opposite direction.

"Oh my," Halifax said. "I hope this won't put our boy off his game."

Chapter 25

That evening, Halifax took Prester to "the usual place." It was a dark, secluded cellar below a local inn with shallow arched ceilings built of brick. The cellar was quite sufficient for storing wine, but not high enough to allow a man to pass underneath without hunching over. Da Vinci was already seated at a table in the back corner, sketching madly by candlelight with a piece of charcoal upon parchment. Prester sat down across from him and watched as Da Vinci, setting down the charcoal, next applied black and red chalks to the sketch, followed by a pen with brown ink. The artist worked quickly and fluidly, holding the paper with his right hand as he raced across the page with his left. His pen darted from one corner to the next, striking the paper here and there with straight lines and circular strokes. Occasionally he rubbed his thumb across an area to soften an edge, or pressed firmly with the base of his palm to create a blurring effect. Within three minutes, Da Vinci had completed the head of a woman in three-quarter view facing right. Looking down upon his own work, Da Vinci sighed and then swept the paper to the floor with his sleeve.

"*Spazzatura*," he spat in his native tongue. "It is no good. It is never good. Michelangelo is right. I cannot finish anything."

Prester picked up the sketch from the floor and looked at it.

"I think it's terrific."

"It is trash," Da Vinci said with a discouraged look in his eyes. "It disgusts me."

"I think you're being too hard on yourself, old boy," added Halifax. "I rather fancy it."

"Why?" Da Vinci said. "Because I drew it? It is a simple picture of a woman." As he said this, Da Vinci glanced across the room to where a barmaid was washing glasses, and Prester realized that she was the unsuspecting model for his sketch.

"This would be worth a fortune at home," Prester said.

Da Vinci looked up at him, his eyes sparkling again with curiosity. Looking around the room to avoid inquisitive ears, he leaned in and gestured for Prester and Halifax to do the same.

"We are alone now," Da Vinci said, looking at Prester. "And I am anxious to know."

"Anxious to know what?" Prester asked.

Da Vinci laughed heartily at Prester's response.

"About you, of course. You must tell me everything."

"I am anxious to know more about you as well," Prester said.

"It is quite natural that you should say this," Da Vinci said, "and I will answer all of your questions. But first, you must tell me. When are you from?"

"The 21st Century," Prester said.

Da Vinci sat back, astonished.

"No."

"Yes," Prester smiled, almost embarrassed to have claimed such a faraway date.

"*Stupefacente,*" Da Vinci said.

"What?" Prester said, and then looked at Halifax for explanation.

"Leonardo is astonished that you are such a long '*wayfrom*' home."

"Tell me all," Da Vinci said.

"All right, but I'm not sure where to begin. The world has changed tremendously. For example, we have machines that can fly in the air and carry people across oceans."

"Ah, yes, I myself have studied the workings of flight," Da Vinci said. "Indeed, I believe I may yet be able to design a wing that will operate justa like that of a bird."

"The wings of our flying machines, which we call airplanes, do not flap up and down. They are straight and solid."

"Yes, that is true even in my time," Halifax said.

"And we have rockets, long cylindrical aircraft without wings at all, by which we have sent men to the moon."

Da Vinci and Halifax both stared at him.

"Did you say the moon?" Halifax asked for clarification.

"And what of medicine?" Da Vinci interrupted. "I have been mapping the organs of the body through, shall we say, surreptitious analysis conducted under the cover of night."

"We can now take out someone's diseased heart and replace it with a healthy heart from someone else, someone who was perhaps killed in an accident," Prester explained.

"Ah, the heart," Da Vinci commented, "a vessel made of dense muscle vivified and nourished by an artery and a vein. I have studied this, and have concluded that the heart is of such density that fire can scarcely damage it."

"I don't think that's really true, although I'm not a doctor," Prester said. "I just know that it circulates the blood."

"Circulates the blood?" Da Vinci gasped.

"Sure, you know, the blood runs down into your feet, then back up again to your brain, and then down again to your feet. You know, it circulates."

"Circulates. What a fantastic idea. It had not occurred to me that the blood within the body moves. I thought it just existed beneath the skin."

"That's just the beginning. We have carriages we call cars that move without horses. We have lanterns that light up without the need for oil, and that we can turn on and off by flipping a switch. We have devices that can transmit and receive sound and moving images, and can send these images across the world in the blink of an eye. We have buildings that are more than a hundred stories high, and special rooms that move up and down inside those buildings carrying people to where they want to go. We have boats without sails that can speed across the surface of the ocean, and other boats that travel beneath the waves. We have . . ."

"Stop," Da Vinci said, gesturing with his hand. "It is too much. I cannot comprehend it. Perhaps if you could explain how and why these things work, then I could understand them."

"I'm afraid that would take more time than we have," Prester said, "and even then I'm not sure I can explain them all."

"That's what I've been telling you all these years, Leonardo," Halifax interjected, "Too much has changed. It's hard to explain it all in plain words."

Da Vinci's face grew sullen, but after a moment his eyes brightened again. He scooted his wooden chair forward a bit more and leaned in even closer.

"Then tell me this," he said. "In your time of the 21st Century, do people still know of me?"

"Know of you? Why Mr. Da Vinci, in the future, you are considered to be perhaps the greatest genius who ever lived."

Da Vinci smiled.

"The greatest?" he repeated the words. "No doubt I am to be remembered for my many great works of art. Is it not so?"

"Well . . . ," Prester hesitated, looking at Halifax for help.

"I was never a great fan of the arts," Halifax said, being no help at all, "although I do recall once having a terrific crush on a young vaudeville actress by the name of Topsy Duncan."

Leaning back in his chair, Da Vinci looked up at the ceiling as if staring into some distant tomorrow.

"I imagine that I will create many great paintings," he said. "Tell me, how many paintings will I create?"

"What do numbers really matter in the scheme of things?" Prester laughed.

"I know that it will not be in the thousands," Da Vinci said modestly, "I am already too old for that. It will perhaps not even be one thousand. It may just be several hundred. But as you say, I will be long remembered, even in your world of the 21st Century. So tell me, how many paintings will I create in my lifetime?"

"Uh, well, do you mean finished paintings?" Prester asked.

"Yes, certainly, finished paintings.

"Uh, um, yes, well, there has been some dispute about that, you see, as to whether certain paintings were actually done by your hand."

"All right," Da Vinci said. "Tell me only of the undisputed works. How many paintings will I finish in my lifetime?"

"Undisputed works only?"

"Yes."

"Finished paintings?"

"Yes, yes, finished paintings only. How many will there be?"

"Sure, well, uh, that would be," Prester began to count to himself, touching each finger in turn as he did so. Da Vinci watched as his counting stopped at one hand.

"Four."

"Four hundred. Certainly not as many as I might have hoped, but one must consider that I have many other interests," Da Vinci said.

"Four. Four paintings. I can name them if you'd like. I actually wrote a paper about this in college. Let's see, there was the 'Annunciation,' which I believe by now you would have already painted about 25 years ago. Then there was the 'Virgin of the Rocks,' which again if I'm not mistaken, you already completed maybe 15 years ago. Coming up, though, you'll be painting something called the 'Mona Lisa,' which is going to be very popular. They'll hang that one in the Louvre in Paris. Then you'll do one more entitled the 'Virgin and Child with St. Anne.' And, well, that's about it in the line of paintings."

Da Vinci sat stunned and silent.

"Four?" Da Vinci finally asked.

"Yes, but if you add in the paintings that are generally though not universally accepted as yours, the total is easily twice that number."

"Twice the number four?" Da Vinci asked.

"Sure, sure. Maybe even nine or ten, counting some of the really disputed ones," Prester laughed in an attempt to lighten the mood, but Da Vinci was crestfallen.

"Michelangelo is right," the artist said. "I am a complete failure."

"Now that's simply not true, Leonardo old man," Halifax spoke up. "I've seen you play cards. He's very good at One and Thirty," he said to Prester as if the point were critical and needed clarification.

"It's not the number of paintings that will make you famous," Prester said. "It's the quality. Your 'Mona Lisa' will become the most famous painting in the world."

"Four paintings," Da Vinci said. "Where is there greatness in four paintings?"

"There are several unfinished works as well," Prester assured him. "And the frescos. You know everybody loves your Last Supper, or what's left of it anyway."

Da Vinci sank his head into his hands.

"There is no greatness in four paintings," he said again, this time with an air of inquiry. "And yet you say that I am, that I will be, well remembered."

"Oh yes, absolutely," Prester said.

"Why?"

"Why?" Prester repeated.

"Why?"

"Why?" Halifax spoke up. "Why indeed. Well, I mean to say, you are Leonardo da Vinci after all."

"But why will I be remembered? What will I do?"

"Well, it's really very simple, old man. You will, um, you will, over the course of your lifetime that is, um, well, I mean to say. Prester, tell him why he will be remembered. I seem to have forgotten."

Da Vinci and Halifax both focused their attention on Prester. Looking at the two of them, Prester considered the matter. How was one to describe the greatness of Leonardo da Vinci? Not knowing where he was headed, he looked at Da Vinci and launched into his explanation.

"Why will you be remembered? Because you will touch the future with your dreams," Prester said. "You will conceive of things that no one else will think of for another half millennium. You will invent new ways of doing things, and new ways of looking at life. You will show the world the meaning of logic and science, and the value of study. You will master every discipline of art and science and design available for your time, and you will set a standard for the world to emulate. Although you may complete fewer paintings than some others, or carve fewer sculptures, or design fewer buildings than other artists, you will outthink them all. Nothing will ever be the same after you."

Da Vinci just stared at Prester for a long time before speaking again.

"It is true that I have thought of many clever things," he said, "but I have not actually created anything. I have only written about them in my notebooks."

"Yes, your notebooks," Prester said. "Your notebooks will make you famous."

"My notebooks? I will be famous for my notebooks? They are just random scribblings. While Michelangelo is remembered for his fine marble sculptures, the world will remember me for my jottings? *Lo non ci credo,*" Da Vinci spat.

"I believe you've finally got it, old man," Halifax said, ignoring the sighs of frustration emanating from the genius. "Now to the task at hand, Leonardo," he continued. "We need your help in getting us in to see Prince Kirkrenzo."

Da Vinci, still shaking his head and mulling over his failed life, muttered a mumbled reply.

"Sorry, old man," Halifax said, leaning in to hear better. "I didn't quite catch that?"

"I said I cannot do it," Da Vinci repeated himself.

Halifax laughed out loud.

"Come now, old boy. Of course you can. All you need to do is pop over to the palace and tell the man in the steel jackets that you'd like a word with his nibs. We'll tag along with you dressed up as monks or something, and before you know it, Bob's your uncle."

"The Prince will not see me," Da Vinci said. "He only sees men of importance, such as scholars and artists. I am nothing more than a clerk."

"A clerk?" Halifax laughed again.

"A bookkeeper then. A copyist. A recorder of thoughts, not even as dignified as a notary," Da Vinci said. "I am no artist."

"Of course you are," Halfax assured him.

"No, I am not. Get Michelangelo. He is a true artist. Go to him for help, and leave me to my jottings."

Halifax peered at Da Vinci, and then nodded for Prester to step aside with him. The two men moved away from Da Vinci to a far corner of the wine cellar.

"Did I mention that he can be a bit temperamental?"

"He won't help us?" Prester asked.

"Don't worry. He'll come 'round. Give it a bit. In a month or two, I'm sure he'll be his old self."

"I don't have a month or two. You said it yourself, I have 29 days from yesterday."

"Ah, right ho. I'd forgotten that part. Well, there's only one thing to do then."

"What's that?"

"Get you a place to live. Sounds like you'll be here awhile."

"No, no, I'm not staying here. There must be some way to get him to help us," Prester said, his voice tending toward panic tones.

"Well, I don't see how, now that he's in such a tizzy about this Michelangelo business."

Prester thought a moment.

"Wait a minute," he said. "This morning, in the marketplace when he and Michelangelo were arguing, didn't he mention something about a large block of marble with a crack running through it?"

"The Carrara Giant," Halifax said. "It's owned by the Arte della Lana."

"The what?"

"Oh, sorry. The woolen cloth guild. The giant marble block, so I am told, was commissioned to an artist named Agostino di Duccio some 40 years ago to carve a statue of David. You know the chap. David? Little fellow? Took on a giant named Goliath?"

"Sure, of course, David," Prester said.

"Right. Well, no sooner had old Duccio hauled the big bloody chunk into his studio than he noticed there was a large crack running right through the middle of it. Well, I mean to say, what's a fellow to do? He threw in the towel on the spot, and near as anyone can remember got into another line of work. The block has been sitting around ever since. They can't seem to find an artist who thinks he can do anything with it. Even Leonardo rejected it as unusable."

"Where is it now?"

"In Michelangelo's workshop, last I heard. But he's making no better progress with it than were the others."

"How well do you know him?"

"Michelangelo? Gawd, I taught him to play draughts."

"Play what?"

"Checkers, old man. The old boy has a nasty disposition, there's no getting around that. But he seems to enjoy the game. We play every Saturday when he's in town."

"Take me to see him," Prester commanded.

"Take you to see who?"

"Michelangelo."

"You want me to take you to see Michelangelo?"

"Yes. Right now. As soon as possible."

"I refuse. I absolutely refuse. Well, I mean to say. He is the most disagreeable, uncouth, unfriendly and all around black-hearted man I have ever had the displeasure to triple jump for a crown."

"Tomorrow then. Please, Halifax. I can't do this without you, and I'm running out of time."

Chapter 26

"To free the human form trapped inside the block," Michelangelo had said to the Arte della Lana committee when asked about his plan for the giant marble slab. But he had been contemplating the block for weeks now, viewing it from all sides, trying in vain to solve the puzzle.

Michelangelo ran his palm across the front of the marble facing. There, almost imperceptible to the eye, but noticeable to the artist's touch, was the crack. It ran vertically like an inverted 'S' throughout the length of the massive block, and Michelangelo's instinct told him that it ran perhaps two feet deep in places. It was a magnificent and mammoth piece of marble. It stood seventeen feet tall by six feet wide and eight feet deep. Hewn from the White Mountains of Carrara in the north of Tuscany, it was transported down the mountain slopes by ox cart south to Pisa. From there the giant block was then carted along the grassy banks of the Arno River to Florence. Stones of even half this size were exceedingly expensive to obtain, and thus a great rarity. This stone was a monster, a marvel, a dream, a temptress and a disappointment.

Michelangelo stared at the behemoth white slab. Turning, he transferred his gaze to a wooden table upon which were strewn numerous charcoal sketches of his concept, and a small clay model of his planned statue of David.

He moved to the table and ran his dexterous fingers across the three foot high red clay depiction. David stood in the traditional pose made famous by Donatello's bronze masterpiece of 75 years before, the young boy standing upright in triumph, his downward pointing sword in his hand, and the head of the giant at his feet. Michelangelo's David would be more muscular than the David immortalized by Donatello, and would be depicted without a helmet, but otherwise the concept would remain the same. That was Michelangelo's intent.

But it would not work. Michelangelo could see that the crack in the marble would prevent him from positioning the left arm in the protruding position required for the concept. Moreover, the left foot standing upon the head of Goliath would cross directly over the deepest part of the crack. No, no, it simply could not be managed, and yet he could see no alternative. This design, the traditional design, seemed to be the human form crying to break free of the beautiful but unforgiving marble, and yet it appeared it would forever remain a prisoner to nature. Michelangelo picked up his hammer, and swung it at the clay model.

"Lumpish pottle," he shouted as he lopped off the left arm of the clay statue. "Dankish pox-marked swag," he yelled again as his hammer removed the clay head from David's shoulders. "Cursed figure," he spat as he threw his hammer with all his might toward the studio door.

Just at that moment, as the door swung inward on its prescient arc, the hurtling hammer crashed upon its wooden planks.

"Hallo!" Halifax exclaimed as he poked in his inquisitive head. "Having a bad day, are we old boy?"

"What do you want?" Michelangelo yelled in his native tongue. "It is only Friday. We do not play your silly game until tomorrow."

"A pleasure to see you too," Halifax responded, switching to Italian. "I hate to disturb your throwing of hammers and the like, but I have someone here who wants to meet you."

"I'm busy."

"Too busy to say hello?"

"Yes."

"It's rather important," Halifax continued to speak in Italian.

"I'm working," Michelangelo barked.

"Won't take but a minute."

"I don't want to see anyone."

"Then we'll make it quick."

"I said no."

"Oh, shut up."

Prester listened to their colloquy, but could not grasp their meaning.

"What's he saying?" Prester asked.

"He'd love to see you. Go right in," Halifax said, stepping aside to allow Prester through the door. Prester stepped into the studio and approached the great sculptor. He extended his hand in greeting.

"Hello, Mr. Michelangelo sir. I'm sure you don't remember me, but we bumped into each other the other day on the Ponte Vecchio," Prester said, smiling.

Michelangelo did not respond, but instead just glared at him.

"I think he likes you," Halifax said.

"Could you translate for me?" Prester asked, looking at the Englishman. "I'd like to speak to him."

"I can, although there's no guarantee he'll respond."

Prester looked again at Michelangelo. The artist was young, in his early twenties, medium height, slender and muscular. His forearms were massive, and his large cupped hands looked as if they could crush stone.

"Listen," Prester said, "I'm wondering, that is I'm hoping that perhaps you can help me."

Halifax translated, but Michelangelo simply glowered at them.

"The thing is," Prester continued, "I need Leonardo da Vinci to get me an audience with Prince Kirkrenzo."

Michelangelo continued to stare apathetically.

"He was going to help me, but then you and he had that argument in the marketplace yesterday morning, and now he's too upset to do anything."

"*Da Vinci e' spazzatura*," Michelangelo said as he spat on the ground.

"He says that Da Vinci is . . ." Halifax began his reverse translation.

"I think I got it," Prester said. "Look, Da Vinci said some things, you said some things. I know he feels bad about it. Halifax, are you translating?"

"When you say something worth translating, I'll translate."

"All right, all right, just tell him that I need his help. Use your own words."

"I'll bloody well have to," Halifax said as he rolled his eyes, and took Michelangelo aside.

"Listen here, old man," Halifax said, holding the sculptor by the shoulder and speaking quietly in Italian. "We are friends, aren't we?"

"No."

"That hurts me, Michelangelo. It hurts me that you would say that after all I've done for you. Who showed you how to play draughts? Huh? And who has been teaching you about manners and how to be a gentleman in polite society? Mmmm? Who does more for you than I do?"

"You interrupt my work, that's what you do," Michelangelo said.

"Oh yes," Halifax said, looking around. "I can see that you're making great progress with the David."

"It is a difficult piece, but David is in there somewhere, and I will find him."

"I'm sure you will, old boy. But in the meantime, I need you to speak with Da Vinci for us. I need you to patch things up between the two of you. He thinks you don't respect his work."

"He is right," Michelangelo said.

"You see, now that is the very kind of thing that one mustn't say. It just isn't done. Have you forgotten everything I've taught you?"

"I will do as I please," Michelangelo said, "and Da Vinci can rot in hell," he added, spitting on the ground again.

"You're being entirely unreasonable about this," Halifax said. "Entirely unreasonable."

"I don't care," Michelangelo said.

"Well then, you're nothing but an arse," Halifax retorted.

"And you're a droning doghearted bum-bailey."

"A droning, doghearted whatever it is you said, am I?" Halifax shot back. "I don't like the sound of that. Good day to you, sir."

Halifax turned on his heels and headed for the door.

"What? What's going on?" Prester asked.

"We're leaving," Halifax said.

"He won't help us?"

"Decidedly not. Michelangelo is a downright pig-headed bugger who cares more about his marble statutes than about his friends, and I want nothing more to do with him."

Prester for the first time looked at the mammoth marble block sitting in the room. On the floor, he saw the remains of the now broken clay model of the David in classic pose. Glancing at the table, he saw the charcoal sketches of the design Michelangelo had been working on.

"Wait," he shouted.

"What?" Halifax looked back at him as he reached the door.

"Tell him that I can solve his problem with the David."

"I will not," Halifax said.

Looking at Michelangelo, Prester tried himself to convey his meaning.

"The positioning is all wrong," he said, pointing to the clay model. "This isn't how it should be."

"He doesn't understand you," Halifax said.

"Then help me. Tell him for me. Translate."

Halifax sighed, and turned back to Michelangelo.

"Go ahead," he said to Prester. "You speak. I'll translate."

Prester looked again at the marble block, and then at the clay model.

"This is all wrong," he said to Michelangelo. "Forget this design. You must start all over."

Halifax translated Prester's words, and Michelangelo listened.

"Your sketches here show David after the battle, after he has already won the fight. But that's wrong. Your sculpture will show David before the fight, before he has cut off the head of Goliath. You will show David not with a sword, but with only a slingshot, thrown up over his left shoulder like this. He should be looking up at the giant as he anticipates the battle, relaxed but ready. The figure's weight, you see, should be resting on his right leg, with the slingshot held in his left hand." Prester struck a pose to demonstrate his meaning. "If you pose David like that, you will be able to work around the crack in the marble, and you will make a statue that will be remembered for centuries to come."

Michelangelo listened to the translation, looking first at Halifax and then at Prester. He then turned to the marble, and examined it again for the thousandth time, running his hands across the surface, and imagining the figure inside. Slowly, he turned to look at Prester.

"You are a sculptor?" he asked, with Halifax translating.

"No," said Prester. "But I know that I am right about this. You see it now too, don't you?"

Again Michelangelo looked at the marble block looming over them all.

"Yes," he said. "Yes, I see it. I had not understood the marble in that way. It was trying to tell me what to do, but I was too stubborn to listen. Now I see it, I see it perfectly."

Michelangelo grasped a bit of charcoal from the table and began to sketch out a fresh drawing on a large piece of new parchment. It was a rough depiction, but quickly began to resemble the David figure in Prester's memory.

"What do you want of me?" Michelangelo said as he continued sketching.

Halifax looked surprised, and then translated the question to Prester.

"Please, come and speak with Da Vinci," Prester said. "You are both great artists, and you need to make your peace with each other," Prester said.

Michelangelo's hand moved across the paper, his mind working faster than his fingers.

"When?" the sculpter asked.

Prester looked at Halifax, who shrugged.

"Today," Prester said, "if that would be all right."

"I will go to see him at noon," Michelangelo said, still working on his sketch. "Da Vinci does not wake earlier than that," he added with a disbelieving shake of the head.

"Thank you," Prester said.

Without another word passing between them, Prester and Halifax backed their way toward the door and out of the studio, leaving the artist to his work.

Chapter 27

The Palazzo Vecchio in the L-shaped piazza della Signoria had for centuries been the heart of Florentine government. Here lived the nine randomly selected members of the governing body known as the Priori. These men were chosen from the guilds of the city. Six were from the major guilds, which included lawyers, judges, bankers, physicians, wool and silk merchants, and furriers. Two more were from the minor guilds, which counted tailors, leather workers, shoemakers and bakers among their ranks. The ninth member, selected at random from the whole, was known as the Gonfaloniere of Justice. While his voting rights were the same as his colleagues, he was provided with a distinguished crimson coat lined with ermine and embroidered with golden stars. He was charged with enforcing the internal security of the city, and with maintaining public order.

Elections for the Priori were held every two months. The names of all guild members over thirty years old and who were not in debt were placed in a leather bag called a borse. This bag was then taken to the Santa Croce church where nine names were then ceremoniously drawn out at random. Those selected would rule over Florence until the following election two months hence. It was a perfect system, for it created a sense of democracy among the business class of the city. But it was perfect too for the city's elite. With terms of office being limited to just two months, the Priori had little actual ability to shape the course of the city's political destiny.

The real power in Florence had always been held by the Medici. Upon the death of Lorenzo the Magnificent, however, the silver-tongued priest Savonarola had held sway as the city's most popular and politically potent power. But Savonarola was not alone in the public's affections.

A new young and mysterious Prince Kirkrenzo had joined the papal court just months prior to Lorenzo de' Medici's death. Under the tutelage of Pope Alexander VI, the young prince had taken up residence in the Vatican Palace in Rome. Through demonstrations of wisdom far beyond his tender years, he had gained the fickle trust and support of the Italian people. Following the excommunication of Savonarola in 1497, the Pope had sent the young prince to Florence.

"What exactly did Kirk do that was so special?" Prester asked Leonardo da Vinci, who was relating the history of the city to the group as they sat in the vestibule of the Signoria awaiting the arrival of Prince Kirkrenzo.

"It was ingenious," Da Vinci said. "Some years ago, I had proposed a similar idea. Through the use of interior pipes and water flow, a system for the indoor disposal of bodily waste coulda be achieved. Unfortunately, I could never solve the vexing problem of noxious fumes coming up from the underground water system into the living quarters. But Prince Kirkrenzo, he suggested a modification to my design. A pipe curved in a downward half circle was placed directly beneath where the waste was to be flushed. The water traps the fumes from coming back up the pipe. Smart, eh?"

"A toilet? He designed a toilet?" Prester asked.

"A toilet, yes," repeated Da Vinci. "That isa what he called it. A French word, I think. Noxious things always seema more agreeable by cloaking them in Gallic finery, don'ta you agree?"

Michelangelo shook his head.

"Your pomposity astounds me, Da Vinci," he said.

"I maya be pompous, but I believe that I am also correct."

"Now, now, boys," Halifax interjected. "No bickering. Remember our plan. Let's not spoil things with petty disagreements."

"I doubt that the Prince will give his consent," Michelangelo said.

"Why should he not?" Da Vinci asked. "You and I are offering to engage in a public competition to determine which of us isa the greater artist. It will be a spectacular affair, and will undoubtedly draw great acclaim for Florence. Why should Prince Kirkrenzo not agree to sponsor such an event?"

"I do not know the man," Michelangelo said. "Perhaps he has no taste for art. Perhaps he dislikes public competitions. Perhaps he will demand that I first finish the David before I engage in any other endeavor."

"If he asks you about your progress on the David, simply explain your new design. That should satisfy him," Da Vinci said.

"Why should I explain my art to him? What does it matter what he thinks?" Michelangelo snarled. "I know my art, and that is enough."

"Oh, my dear young dreamer," Da Vinci replied, "have you already forgotten what we spoke of together just days ago? Have you forgotten what you said to me, what you in fact taught me? You were quite right in your criticism of my penchant for leaving things unfinished, you know. Watching you, listening to you, seeing your work, suddenly I have become impressed with the urgency of doing. Knowing is not enough; we must apply. Being willing is not enough; we must do. And so you must tell the Prince of your design. To leave him with the thought that you might fail risks losing the stone to a lesser artist, and that cannot be. You must carve that stone. You must make your David. And so you must play politics to assure yourself the chance."

"Hrumph!" Michelangelo grunted.

"Ah, here comes someone now," Halifax said.

The vestibule of the palace was a spacious and ornate hall. Frescos of clouds and angels covered the ceiling. The walls were adorned with intricate landscapes. Chandeliers of Murano glass and gold leaf hung in abundance. Through a door at the far end of the hall, two soldiers in metal armor entered, followed by a rotund man in a cape.

"Gentlemen, welcome," the stout man shouted as he waddled his way toward the foursome seated on a bench at the far side of the room. As he drew nearer, Da Vinci began to stir.

"Piero? Is that you?" Da Vinci asked.

"Eh, Leonardo, how are you, my friend," the large man said as he engulfed Leonardo in a bear hug.

"This is Piero Soderini, the butcher," Da Vinci explained to the others, first in Italian, and then in English. "What are you doing here, Piero?"

"I am the new Gonfaloniere of Justice," he said with a sheepish grin.

"No," Da Vinci smiled.

"Yes, since last Tuesday."

"You don't say."

"Yes, yes, look at my robe. Nice, eh?"

"Oh, yes, Piero. Wonderful. But who is watching your shop while you are playing in the palace?" Da Vinci asked.

"My nephew, Torrigiano. You know, Chino's boy?"

"Ah, yes. But I thought he was a bit . . ."

"He is slow, but he can cut meat. And while I'm here, no one will dare to take advantage of him. I am in charge of security, you know."

"Yes, I can see that. Gonfaloniere of Justice! Very nice."

"So I have to ask you all some questions, official business, you understand. It is my job," Piero said.

"Sure, sure. Ask whatever you need to," Da Vinci said as he resumed his seat.

"First, what are your names? Wait just a minute." He signaled for one of the soldiers to take notes. The first soldier handed his sword to his fellow man-at-arms, and then reached deep inside the recesses of his own armor breasted plate. After a struggle reminiscent of someone trying to scratch an unreachable itch, the soldier withdrew a quill pen. A bit of parchment was also produced, along with a small corked bottle of black ink. He then motioned for the second soldier to bend over, which he did. Thus, still holding his fellow's sword, the second soldier exposed his iron sheathed back as a makeshift writing surface. After a moment of clumsy positioning, the first soldier was ready with pen in hand.

"All right," Piero began again, "now what are your names?"

"I am Leonardo da Vinci," the artist said in a formal tone. "And these are my associates, Mr. Halifax . . ."

"Hallo-allo-allo," Halifax offered.

"Prester John."

Prester nodded.

"And of course, Michelangelo Buonarroti."

"Are you getting all this?" Piero asked his soldiers, both of whom nodded.

"Good. Now, my next question. What is your purpose in coming to the palace?"

"We have come to propose a contest," Da Vinci responded. "Ita is a matter concerning art."

"Art. I see," Piero said, rubbing his ample chins. "Write that down," he instructed his soldiers. "And this matter of art you speak of, does it entail the use of muskets, explosives, swords, daggers, knives, poison, clubs, rope, black magic or witchcraft?"

The foursome looked at each other.

"No," Da Vinci assured him.

"All right then," Piero said, suddenly all smiles. "I think I have what I need. Gentlemen, please follow me."

Piero and the two soldiers led the group back across the expansive vestibule and through a series of interior doors. They emerged into a large room, covered along its four walls with tapestries depicting maps of the great cities of Europe. In the center of the room, a portrait artist was at work on a small canvas which sat upon a wooden easel. Posing opposite him in a seated position was his subject, Prince Kirkrenzo.

Prester was amazed at the change in Kirk's appearance. Dressed in a black collar and red fur-trimmed tunic, he looked older now, no longer the thin teenage boy he remembered from Block Island. Kirk had filled out and grown into a robust young man. His chin was held aloft, and his hair was parted to one side. He was the very portrait of a young man of confidence despite the slight crookedness of his nose. Next to him, lingering over his shoulder, was a short and stout older man. The man held up various papers for the Prince to see, and whispered constantly in his ear.

"Your visitors have arrived," Gonfaloniere Piero Soderini said, nodding toward the Prince. Kirk returned the nod, and so Piero turned back toward Da Vinci and the others. "Gentlemen, I give you Prince Kirkrenzo, and his adviser, Nicolo Machiavelli."

"Hey, Leonardo, what's up?" Kirk said as he glanced away momentarily from his pose.

"Please, my Lord, you must hold your position," the painter pleaded.

"I see you brought some friends with you," Kirk said, ignoring the painter with a wave of his hand.

"Yes, my Prince. May I introduce to you the young sculptor, Michelangelo Buonarroti. This is the man working on the Carrara Giant," Da Vinci said.

"The statue of David," Kirk responded.

"Exactly, my Lord," Da Vinci said. "Clearly you are well informed."

"I try to stay up on the important stuff," Kirk said.

"And this gentleman," Da Vinci continued, "this is Mr. Halifax, hailing all way from England."

"Oh yeah? I was in England once," Kirk said.

"How nice," Halifax responded. "When was that, my Lord?"

"Just after they built the London Eye."

"I'm sorry, my Lord, the London what?"

Prester tapped Halifax on the shoulder. "I'll explain it later," he said. "And finally . . ."

"Mr. John," Kirk said, still holding his pose for the artist. "I thought that was you I saw in the square. I wasn't sure. It's been a long time."

"Hello Kirk," Prester said.

"It's Prince Kirkrenzo now," he said. "I really must insist that you call me by my proper and official title."

"That will take some getting used to."

"Well get used to it because that's the way it is from now on."

"All right, Kirk . . . Prince Kirkrenzo, I mean."

"It's for appearances sake, you understand."

"Sure, I understand."

"Ah, my Lord, can it be that you and this gentle stranger have a prior acquaintance?" Machiavelli asked suspiciously.

"An amazing coincidence, if it is true," Da Vinci said as he winked at Halifax.

"Yeah, we know each other," Kirk said. "We go way back, isn't that right, Mr. John?"

"Absolutely," Prester said. "You've grown. I hardly recognized you."

"Well, what did you expect after six years?"

"Six years?" Prester asked, genuinely astonished at the concept. "Has it been that long for you? From my perspective, it seems you've only been gone a year."

"A year? Are you kidding? I was only 16 when I arrived."

"You were 16 just last year, at least that's the way I see it," Prester commented.

"Well, I don't really get what happened to me," Kirk said. "Some sort of magic, I guess. I'll tell you this though, I never thought I'd see anyone from home again."

"I think I can explain a little bit about how and why this happened," Prester said. "Can we speak privately?"

Machiavelli, listening intently to the colloquy, rested a hand upon Kirk's shoulder.

"Anything you've got to say to me," Kirk said, "you can say in front of my adviser."

"If I may, your highness," Machiavelli said, stepping forward. "It is my understanding that these gentlemen have come here today for the sole purpose of proposing a contest of sorts between Leonardo and Michelangelo."

"A contest? What kind of contest?" Kirk asked, turning to look at Da Vinci.

"A public spectacle. A test of our individual artistic skills," Da Vinci said.

"Da Vinci is not much of a sculptor," Michelangelo chimed in, "so perhaps a painting competition would be more fitting."

"My good friend Michelangelo has a high opinion of himself, and a rather low one of me," Da Vinci said. "Nevertheless, perhaps a painting competition would be the easiest way to determine which of us is the most talented."

"An excellent idea," Machiavelli said to Prince Kirkrenzo, "although if I might suggest, perhaps a fresco competition would be more appropriate. Fresco must be completed within a very limited space of time, for the paint must be applied while the plaster of the wall is still wet.

It is necessary to have well thought out designs prepared prior to their actual application to the wall. Thus, a competition could easily be had as to the competing designs. Each artist could create their own cartoons in color and exhibit them in a public forum side by side."

"Yeah, yeah, all right. I can get into that. Where do you suppose we should do this thing?" Kirk asked.

"If I might suggest further," Machiavelli replied. "The Hall of Five Hundred here in the Palazzo Vecchio has just undergone a reconstruction. It would be a perfect venue for such a contest. The proceeds should add substantially to our treasury."

"Set it up, Nicolo. You have my approval," Kirk proclaimed, still maintaining his pose for the portrait artist.

"I will see to the details," Machiavelli said with a slight bow to his Prince.

Looking at his portrait artist, Kirk raised a regal palm. "Enough for today," he said. "I'm tired. Come back tomorrow."

"Certainly, my Lord," the portrait artist said. Gathering his brushes and pallets, the painter departed.

"I too should go, my Lord," Da Vinci said after the painter had left. "If you will excuse me."

"Yeah, yeah, see you later," Kirk said. Da Vinci bowed and retreated from the room in the direction he had come. As he did so, he grabbed Michelangelo by the sleeve and pulled him along. Halifax, seeing that the end of their visit was upon them, also bowed to the Prince and followed Da Vinci and Michelangelo toward the exit.

"Prester," Halifax said as he approached the exit, "shall I wait for you outside?"

"No," Prester answered. "Go home. I'll be along soon."

Halifax nodded and slipped out of the room.

With the others now gone, Prester looked at Kirk and his adviser, Machiavelli.

"We have to talk," Prester said. "There are some things I need to tell you if we're going to get home from here."

"Ah, Mr. John, you still don't get it, do you? Why would I want to go home? I've got everything I want right here."

"Kirk, you have to listen to me."

"No, I don't. See, that's the thing about this place. I don't have to listen to you. In fact, I don't have to listen to anyone. From now on, you have to listen to me."

"But your father . . ."

"Stop!" Kirk shouted, jumping up from his chair. "Don't mention my father to me. I don't want to hear it. Do you understand me? My father may be a big man back home, but I'm the big man here whether he likes it or not. So do not talk to me about my father. Ever!"

Chapter 28

Manhattan Island, New York

Annie stepped quickly across the crowded gallery to where the two small children were wrestling.

"Children, children," she whispered as she pulled them apart. "None of that now."

"He pulled my hair," the little girl whined.

"She said I have big ears," the little boy retorted.

"Did not."

"Did so."

"Did not."

"I heard you."

"That's cause your ears are so big," the little girl said.

"See, I told you she said it," the boy exclaimed.

"Well, they are," the girl repeated.

With that, the little boy grabbed another fist full of his sister's hair and gave it a twist.

"Stop it, stop it," Annie said, trying again to untangle them. "You must be quiet, children. Please, shhh, shhh."

"I knew you'd get us in trouble," the little girl said.

"It's your fault," the boy insisted.

"Where are your parents?" Annie asked them.

The children suddenly stopped fighting and looked around. Not seeing a parent, they simultaneously burst into tears and began wailing.

"Mommy, mommy," they both cried.

"Shhh, children, please, shhh, shhh, you must be quiet," Annie whispered in vain. "It will be all right. Your mother couldn't have gotten far, no matter how hard she might try."

Just then, a woman turned the corner from the neighboring gallery and spotted the children. Looking like a vulture disturbed at finding her prey very much alive, she marched over to them. Grabbing each by the wrist, she dragged them away without a word. As they left her area, Annie took a deep breath and flashed a smile at the numerous patrons who had stopped to observe the disturbance.

"Kids," she sighed, and strolled away.

Resuming her normal rounds, Annie passed by Edouard Manet's 'Boy With a Sword,' wondering what carnage might ensue if modern children were so well equipped. As she walked, she came to the spot on the wall where the 'Portrait of a Young Man' had hung just a few days before. The spot was empty, a conspicuous blank space where the painting should have been.

Standing in front of the vacant spot, Annie turned and looked up at the new and improved security system that had been installed. The new hi-definition digital cameras, with built-in infrared illumination and high-resolution image capture capability, could record images even in low light conditions. They had been put in place since the discovery of the fake Da Vinci drawing, and they ran with remote monitoring access twenty-four hours a day. If someone is stealing paintings, Annie thought, how in the world did they get past this?

Chapter 29

Florence, Italy

Kirk continued to stare at his former teacher as Machiavelli approached from behind.

"Shall I ring for tea, my Lord?" Machiavelli asked, trying to break the tension.

"I don't want tea," Kirk snapped. "I don't drink tea. I don't like tea. I've told you that. Haven't I told you that?"

"Pardon me, my Lord. No tea."

"I hate tea," Kirk added.

"I shall make note of it."

"See that you do," Kirk barked.

Machiavelli bowed his head in submission. He then looked up again and locked eyes with Prester as if to say, good luck. Prester turned his attention again to Kirk.

"Kirk," Prester said, "I mean, Prince Kirkrenzo, I wonder whether we might perhaps speak alone." Prester glanced back into Machiavelli's black eyes.

"Would you prefer that I depart, my Lord?" Machiavelli asked.

"No," Kirk said. "Stick around."

"Yes, my Lord," Machiavelli said. "I shall stick all around," he added, misusing the unfamiliar colloquialism.

Kirk crossed the room and took a seat at a large wooden table covered with maps. Machiavelli and Prester followed suit. The three men sat for a long moment.

"They drink a lot of tea here," Kirk said, having regained his composure. "I can't stand the stuff myself. My father liked tea, but not me. You know what I miss? Coca Cola, and ginger ale. Oh, and Dr. Pepper. I really miss Dr. Pepper."

"This Dr. Pepper," Machiavelli said, "he is an acquaintance from your home? Perhaps we can send for him."

"I don't think so, Nicolo," Kirk said, laughing. "Where we're from is too far away. Isn't that right, Mr. John?"

"It's not as far as you might think," Prester said. "I know how to get us home."

"I told you, I don't want to go home," Kirk said. "I'm through with home. This is my home now. These are my people now," Kirk said.

"Kirk, your father . . ." Prester stopped himself, hoping to avoid another outburst.

Kirk shook his head.

"All right, Mr. John, what about my father?"

"He's been searching for you since the day you disappeared. He sent me here to find you. He misses you terribly, and wants me to bring you back with me."

"My father," Kirk snickered. "You know, I think dear old dad would appreciate seeing me here, seeing the kind of power I have now. He always respected power if nothing else."

"You mean like the power to burn priests at the stake?" Prester chided.

"That was not my choice. That was the choice of the people. That was democracy at work," Kirk responded. "Savonarola wouldn't stop preaching even though he was excommunicated a year ago, and the people had simply had enough. Don't blame me. I had nothing to do with what happened."

"You could have stopped it."

"Maybe," Kirk said, "but it's what the people wanted."

"It was a mob, Kirk, not democracy. There's a difference."

"Enough of the civics lesson, Mr. J. I'm not your student anymore."

"Look, Kirk. This, all this, it isn't real. It's all an illusion, or a dream of some sort. I don't know the science of it, but I know it isn't your home. We need to go back to our lives, back to Block Island."

"My Lord," Machiavelli interrupted, his hands and eyes scanning the maps on the table. "Where exactly is this Block Island? Shall I send for additional charts?"

"You won't find it on those maps," Kirk said. "It won't show up for quite a few years yet."

"You have some power here now, Kirk, but do you think you can hold on to it forever?" Prester asked. "You know the history of Renaissance Florence. Or at least you should. I tried to teach it to you."

"Ah, Mr. John," Machiavelli interrupted again, "you may be interested to know that I myself have written an extensive history of our Florentine Republic."

"I'm not talking about the past," Prester said, continuing to address his comments to his former student. "I'm talking about the future. Listen to me, Kirk, you can't stay here. There will be invasions and power grabs. There will be plots and murders. If I remember correctly, King Louis of France will soon be amassing his forces for an invasion of this place."

"Where did you get this information?" Machiavelli insisted as he rose to his feet. "We have a treaty with King Louis. He is our ally. Why do you think he will invade us?"

Prester realized that he had allowed his emotions to get the better of him.

"It's just conjecture, of course. I don't know anything," he said. "How could I know?"

"My Lord, I regret to advise you that, in my opinion, your friend is a spy."

Prester laughed out loud.

"He's not a spy," Kirk said. "He's just a history teacher."

"Listen to what I'm telling you, Kirk?" Prester said. "Come home with me now. It's not safe here. Bad things will happen here."

"Who's to say what will happen, Mr. J?" Kirk said. "I'm not supposed to be here, right? I'm not in any of your history books, am I? Maybe it will all be different now, because of me, because I'm here. In fact, I think I can make things a lot better."

"Kirk, think carefully. You don't know what may happen here. But you've got a life back home, a good long life for you to live. Come back with me and live it."

Kirk grinned and shook his head.

"No," he said, "I think I'll hang here."

"That's just exactly what I'm afraid might happen," Prester said.

Kirk laughed.

"Touché, Mr. John," he said. "But the fact is, I'm sort of enjoying things just as they are."

"You're making a mistake, Kirk," Prester said.

"Maybe. I've made them before."

"I'll have to go back without you. What should I tell your father?"

Kirk smiled again. "Don't worry. You won't have to tell him anything."

With these words, the doors to the room burst open as several soldiers rushed in.

"Take this man into custody," Machiavelli orded as the soldiers grabbed Prester by the arms.

"Kirk, what are you doing? What's going on?"

"Niccolo is of the opinion that I really shouldn't let you go," Kirk said. "And I think he's right. You're my insurance policy."

"But, Kirk . . ."

"ENOUGH!" Kirk shouted, pounding his fist on the table. "You will address me as Prince Kirkrenzo."

Chapter 30

Leonard da Vinci and Michelangelo each mounted their large paper drawings about twenty feet apart on one wall of the Hall of Five Hundred. A month had passed since Prince Kirkrenzo had commissioned the competition. Now all the major dignitaries of Florence, led by the Prince and the Gonfaloniere of Justice, crowded into the hall. They were there to see which of the two renowned Florentine artists would receive the majority vote of the Priori as the greatest artist. In the middle of the crowd was Halifax, but there was no sign of Prester. Indeed, Halifax had not seen Prester since their visit to the palace a full month before.

Da Vinci's drawing was on the right, draped in a black cloth. The artist stood before it preparing to reveal his work to the judging committee.

"I present for your consideration," Da Vinci said, "the Battle of Anghiari." He pulled off the black drape.

"Ah, yes, very nice, very nice," said Piero Soderini, the Gonfaloniere of Justice, to his genius friend.

"So what's it all about?" Kirk asked as he stared at the jumble of horses, men and swords.

"The Battle of Anghiari," Piero laughed. "Everyone knows about the Battle of Anghiari." Looking around, he saw that Prince Kirkrenzo was still staring at the cartoon with a perplexed gaze. "Of course, it was a long time ago. I'm not sure whether I remember it very well myself."

Machiavelli, standing next to the Prince, stepped forward to offer an explanation.

"If I may, my Lord."

"Sure," Kirk said. "Go ahead."

"It is a battle quite famous to all Florentines," Machiavelli said. "Florence and Milan fought the battle over 50 years ago. Niccolo Piccinino, fighting for the Duke of Milan, led his forces against the Florentines encamped near the town of Anghiari. Niccolo had arrived within two miles of the encampment when Micheletto Attendulo . . ."

"That was the leader of our glorious Florentine troops," a grinning Piero interrupted, and then fell silent again.

"As I was saying, Niccolo had come to within two miles of the encampment when Micheletto observed great clouds of dust. He conjectured at once that it must be occasioned by the enemy's approach. Micheletto with his troops hastened to the bridge which crossed the river a short distance from Anghiari. Micheletto bravely withstood the enemy's charge upon the bridge, but the enemy attacked so vigorously that he was compelled to give way. Regrouping, the Florentines attacked again, and in turn repulsed the enemy and drove them over the bridge. The battle continued for two hours. Each side had frequent possession of the bridge, and their attempts upon it were attended with equal success."

"But the Florentines had the advantage," Piero interrupted again. "Well, they did, didn't they?"

"They did," Machiavelli said. "And this is how it happened. Prior to the battle, the Florentines filled up the ditches on either side of the road, leveling the ground between Anghiari and the bridge. Across the bridge, in contrast, the road remained flanked by deep ditches on either side. Thus, the disadvantage of Niccolo was manifest, for when his people crossed the bridge they found the Florentines unbroken and able to maneuver without difficulty. But when the Florentines crossed, Niccolo could not relieve those that were harassed on account of the hindrance interposed by the ditches and embankments on either side of the road. Thus, whenever his troops got possession of the bridge, they were soon repulsed by the refreshed forces of the Florentines. Soon, Niccolo's rear-guard became mingled with his vanguard, and the Milanese were forced to flee."

"It was the greatest of victories," Piero shouted triumphantly. "The Duke of Milan was thoroughly trounced."

"In truth, the victory was much more advantageous to the Florentines than injurious to the Duke. Never was there an instance in war with less injury to the assailants than at this. In the battle which continued for four hours, only one man died. And he died not from wounds inflicted by hostile weapons, or any honorable means, but, having fallen from his horse, was trampled to death."

"Only one guy got killed?" Kirk asked, now even more perplexed as he looked at Leonardo's cartoon. "But look at the picture. There's all kinds of fighting going on."

"I agree completely," Piero said. "Leonardo has depicted a furious battle of horses and men."

"I do not deny that it is a magnificent cartoon, and will make an equally magnificent fresco," Machiavelli said. "But the fact remains that combatants at that time engaged with little danger, being nearly all mounted, covered with armor, and preserved from death whenever they chose to surrender. There was no necessity for risking their lives. While fighting, their armor defended them, and when they could resist no longer, they yielded and were safe."

Kirk looked at the drawing again and nodded his head. "It's a good picture, I'll give you that," he said.

"A good picture?" Leonardo mocked.

"Yeah, good, you know, lots of details and, you know, realistic looking. I mean, this picture makes you think that lots of guys must have bought it, been killed I mean. But you say just the one guy bit the dust, huh?"

"Just one was killed, yes, my Lord," Machiavelli assured him.

"All the same, I like it. It's, uh, it's neat," Kirk said.

Leonardo furled his brow. "I am so pleased that the Prince thinks I have drawn neatly."

"So what do you say, boys?" Kirk said, turning to the members of the Priori standing behind him. "Let's get a look at the other picture." Kirk turned and walked several paces to his left. The crowd and the Priori followed on his heels.

Standing in front of Michelangelo's draped work, the assemblage waited for the artist to step forward, but Michelangelo was no where to be seen.

"He was just here," Piero said. "I'm sure I saw him just a moment ago."

Everyone looked around, but Michelangelo was gone.

"We don't need him," Kirk said. "Let's have a look."

The drape was pulled off. Underneath was a magnificent depiction of nearly twenty naked or half naked men. They appeared to be climbing up out of a river in a mad rush to get dressed.

"What the hell is this?" Kirk shouted. "I thought the rule was that they had to draw a battle scene. This is a bunch of naked guys swimming."

"A most shameful depiction," Piero Soderini said, feigning indignation.

"My Lord," Machiavelli interjected. "The artist has indeed depicted a battle scene with his cartoon."

"Battle? Where? I don't see any battle. Where's the battle?"

"If I may explain," Machiavelli said.

"Somebody better explain," Kirk said, rolling his eyes and smirking at the Priori members behind him.

"It is the Battle of Cascina. The battle took place on the 28th day of July in the year 1364 between our Florentine troops and those of Pisa," Machiavelli began. "It was, they say, an unbearably hot summer day. The heat was such that the metal armor of the soldiers was a torture under the heat of the sun."

"I can certainly understand that," Piero said, trying to be helpful.

"The road to Pisa was clear of enemy troops, and our soldiers were encamped near the Arno. Feeling secure in their position, many of the Florentines removed their clothing to swim in the river. This left the road unguarded for a time. What they did not know was that spies had been sent by the English mercenary, John Hawkwood, to watch the Florentine camp. These English troops were in the employ of Pisa. Hawkwood was a cunning tactician. Upon learning that the

Florentines had let down their defenses, he immediately ordered all the troops under his command to attack."

"But as always, our glorious Florentine troops prevailed," Piero proclaimed.

"Indeed, Florence did prevail, for Hawkwood made two fatal errors in judgment. First, being from England and therefore unfamiliar with the terrain, he misjudged the distance of the road between the two armies. Thus, even before the English and Italian troops under his command had reached the Florentine camp, Florentine trumpets had sounded the alarm. Second, being from England, he misjudged the heat of the Italian summer. He did not count on the fatigue that his soldiers would face while fighting in heavy armor. The Florentines, although caught by surprise, were fresh and rested next to Pisa's fatigued mercenary troops. Hawkwood quickly realized that his surprise attack had failed. And so, not wanting to lose his company, he withdrew his English troops up a nearby hill. There they took refuge behind the stone walls of the Abbey of San Savino. This left the regular Pisan infantrymen to continue the fight on their own. The Pisans, without their English mercenaries, were feckless, and the Florentines cut through them like quicksilver. The next day, dead Pisans were scattered across the countryside, along the ditches, upon the vineyards, and in the fields. For more than a week, bodies were seen floating with the current down the Arno towards Pisa. In all, more than 1000 Pisan's died that day, and 2000 more were taken prisoner."

"As I said, my Lord," Piero jumped in again. "A great victory."

"A thousand dead? Now that's a battle," Kirk said.

"Yes, my Lord," Machiavelli agreed. "It was indeed a great battle. But we are today concerned with art, not warfare, are we not?"

"Sure, sure, you're right. So let's get this over with," Kirk said as he turned to the members of the Priori standing behind him. "Well boys, what do you say? You've got the Da Vinci over there. It looks like a lot of action, swords, horses, all kinds of stuff going on, but which in the end nothin' much really happened. Over here you've got the Michelangelo. This one looks at first like just a bunch of guys taking a swim. It turns out it was a pretty big battle, with lots of guys getting killed. So what do you think?" Kirk continued. "Michelangelo, or Da Vinci? Which of them is the greatest artist?"

The Priori members stared at each other, no one wishing to cast the first vote for fear of displeasing the Prince.

"Which do you prefer, my Lord?" a member of the Priori shouted out.

"Me?" Kirk asked. "What do I know? I don't vote. No, no, you guys pick."

The members of the Priori remained silent, shuffling in place, but not raising their hands or voices in support of one or the other cartoon.

"Perhaps the best approach, my Lord," Machiavelli suggested, "would be for each member to simply walk over and stand next to the cartoon which they most favor. In this way, we can determine the outcome of the contest."

"Yeah, that sounds good. Let's do that. You heard him, boys. Everybody go stand next to the picture you like best. Go ahead. Just wander over to one or the other of the drawings. Come on, now, move it along," Kirk said as he shooed the reluctant Priori members away from the center of the room. It was impossible to remain uncommitted. Slowly, the Priori members moved toward one or the other cartoon. After a minute or two, the vote of the Priori was clear. Four members stood next to the cartoon by Da Vinci. Four stood astride the Michelangelo drawing. Piero Soderini, the Gonfaloniere of Justice, remained in the middle, a member of the Priori, but uncommitted as to his vote.

"Well, Piero," Kirk said. "It looks like it comes down to you. What's your choice?"

Piero gulped, and then looked again at both drawings before turning toward the Prince.

"My Lord," he said meekly, "I cannot vote."

"Sure you can," Kirk said. "Just pick one."

"My Lord, I am but a poor butcher. What I know about art can fit into half a thimble. To me, I see two drawings of the same size. Both are hung properly and straightly on the wall. The frames on each are very nice, yes, quite nice indeed. I greatly admire the frames. But as to the merit of the art contained within them, my Lord, I am not the man to ask."

"But Piero, you have to vote," Kirk said. "If you don't vote, it'll be a tie."

"Perhaps you should cast the deciding vote, my Lord," Machiavelli suggested, much to Piero's relief.

"Me?" Kirk asked.

"Yes, yes, you should vote," the Gonfaloniere of Justice said. "It was you, after all, who decided to hold the contest. Definitely, you should decide who wins. I defer to you."

Kirk turned again toward the cartoons, looking at them now more carefully than he had before.

"Well," he said, "I don't know if I really can say which is best."

"Look at them with your heart, my Lord, not your eyes," Machiavelli said. "Tell us what you feel about them."

Kirk moved in front of the Da Vinci cartoon and looked up at it for a long moment while the crowd waited. Da Vinci himself stood off to one side, hoping that the power of his art would see its way through to the inner core of the Prince. Then, like the brightening of a new day, a smile began to form on Krik's face.

"Wait a minute," Kirk said. "I think I see now. Sure, sure, look at it. Can't you see it? It's fantastic. Just look at the depth he has created through his use of light and dark shading, and the detail and variety in the soldier's uniforms. Look at the crests of the helmets and the intricate ornaments on the shields and breastplates. And do you see how perfectly drawn the horses are? You can actually see their muscles tensing as though they're really moving. It's like you can feel the intensity of the moment. Look at how graceful and strong they are. Do you see it now? Leonardo has drawn boldness and bravery in action. That's the only way to describe it. I didn't know you could draw a feeling, but that's what he's done. Leonardo, let me tell you something. This is a very great work of art."

"Thank you, my Lord," Leonardo said, bowing to the Prince. "You are too kind."

Kirk then moved to his left and positioned himself in front of the Michelangelo cartoon. Again, he stared up at the drawing for a long time, letting his eyes drift across the canvas, and letting the lines and shadings of the work touch his mind. At last, a knowing smile washed across his face, and he began to nod.

"Oh, okay, sure, I see what Michelangelo has done here. This is really very clever. He's showing the very beginning of the battle. See that? The Florentine soldiers have been taken by surprise, and the trumpets are just sounding the alarm. Look, you can see that the troops have been cooling off in the river, but they suddenly realize they're under attack. See how the soldiers are dressing as quickly as they can, buckling on their armor? That soldier there is pointing off to the left toward where the attack is coming from. In fact, you can see that they're already under fire. This soldier at the bottom has already been hit and is falling back into the river. This other soldier is reaching out to help him. Can you see the confusion? You can't look at this picture without feeling the panic that the soldiers are feeling. I didn't see it at first, but this is definitely a battle scene, and a very great one too."

"My Lord," Machiavelli said with surprise. "You seem to have suddenly found your artistic temperament."

"Yeah," Kirk said. "I had a teacher once who taught me a lot about art, although I'm only just now realizing it."

"So?" Machiavelli asked. "Who shall it be? Who is the greatest artist of all?"

The Priori waited anxiously for the answer, as did the assembled crowd. Off to one side, Leonardo da Vinci leaned against a wall as he awaited the verdict. On the far side of the room, having now reappeared, Michelangelo chewed on a knuckle. Piero Soderini looked on, and Machiavelli stood by as Prince Kirkrenzo contemplated his decision.

"I think..," the Prince began, "I think..."

Suddenly a commotion arose near the entrance of the great hall, and an armored soldier on horseback burst in, ducking his head as he rode through the door.

"What is the meaning of this?" shouted Machiavelli as the crowd parted for the horseman.

"I have a message for Prince Kirkrenzo," the rider said.

"What message?" Machiavelli asked.

"King Louis of France, with troops numbering twenty-five hundred strong, has taken Pisa in a surprise attack."

The crowd gasped at the news, and various shouts and rumblings began to emanate from the now cacophonous gathering.

"Louis' troops are at this moment descending upon Florence from the west," the rider continued, shouting to be heard above the clamor of the crowd. "They are but a two hour ride from the city gates."

"But King Louis has no designs on Florence," Machiavelli said, his voice betraying surprise.

"Louis is accompanied by Piero Medici, son of our late Lorenzo the Magnificent. They are intent on retaking Florence for the Medici. They are demanding that Prince Kirkrenzo be surrendered to them or they will decimate the city."

"Surrender?" Kirk gasped. "So they can hang me? Are you kidding?"

"They will not hang you, my Prince," Machiavelli assured him.

"No? Even though we took over the Medici banks?" Kirk asked.

"Certainly not, my Lord. No, I should think they are more likely to draw and quarter you," Machiavelli added.

The horseman turned his steed a quarter turn to the left and looked down upon the Prince.

"What are your orders, my Lord?" he asked.

Kirk looked up at the rider, but was speechless.

Machiavelli gave the Prince a momentary chance to respond, and then grabbed hold of the horse's bit.

"Rider, go quickly to the gates of the city and secure them if it is not already too late. Then assemble your troops near the Santa Croce to await further instructions. Ride directly there. Speak to no one on the way."

"Yes, sir," the rider said. Rearing his horse back, he galloped out the door, the tip of his scabbard striking upon the solid oak jamb as he went.

"My Lord," Machiavelli said, turning to Kirk, "we must move quickly. I have seen this sort of thing before. Word of the impending invasion will spread from house to house, from street to street, throughout every corner of the city in a matter of hours. The people will demand action. We haven't much time."

"What should we do?" Kirk asked with a frightened voice.

Machiavelli looked around, drawing in closer to the Prince.

"Not here, my Lord," he said in almost a whisper. "Let us retire to the tower where we may discuss the matter at hand."

Chapter 31

A sliver of sunlight pierced the darkness, striking high on the damp wall of Prester's cell. Each day, the thin ray of light would make its first appearance at a height of about 10 feet, and then creep downward as the hours progressed until it vanished in the ambient light of the late morning. Each day, Prester gauged the sun's progress with a flint stone by scratching a mark upon the wall where it first appeared. And each day the mark moved by degrees to the right of where it had been the day before. Twenty-nine scratches now scored the stone wall to mark the spinning of the earth, the movement of the calendar, and the passing days of his confinement. Twenty-nine mornings of frustration, but none so frustrating as those leading up to the flint mark of nine days previous. That was the score that marked the summer solstice, and the passing of his opportunity to go home.

Little changed in Prester's tiny cell from one day to the next, so that even the most subtle variance became a welcome event. Indirect sunlight filtered in through a small venting window some twenty feet up, near to where the ceiling met the upper wall. The window was perhaps a foot wide and eight inches high. Prester thought that it must have been covered by some sort of overhang on the outside, for he could not catch even the slightest glimpse of blue sky through its bars. And yet, on occasion, life would make its way in through the opening. Welcome rainwater would splash in if accompanied by a strong wind. Squirrels and birds would peak in curiously at him, but then decide to leave well enough alone. Insects and rodents on the other hand, having no sense of discretion, would climb or drop in through the vent without hesitation.

Prester had to sit along the opposite wall to avoid them tumbling down upon his head. These, save for the pot of warmish stew that was slipped into his cell once each day, were his only connections to the outside world.

The door to the cell was a mere four feet high, and was constructed of solid oak boards secured by heavy iron hinges. Near the bottom was a second smaller door through which the food and chamber pots were both passed, the two being identical. Prester suspected that little care was given to keeping them separate and apart. For the first week of his confinement, Prester refused to eat anything, and had demanded with each opening of the small door that he be released. But hunger is a persistent drummer, and he eventually succumbed to its calling.

On the thirtieth day of his confinement, Prester sat crouching before the small door awaiting his meager daily victuals. He was surprised to hear the unlatching of the large, rather than the small door. When the large door swung open, he was surprised again to see Kirk and the jailer standing just outside his cell.

"Good God," Kirk said with a shock, looking down upon his squatting bedraggled teacher. "What have they done to you?"

"My orders were that the prisoner be locked up, my Lord," the jailer said.

"Not like this, not in these conditions. Look at him. He's half dead."

"This is where the prisoners are kept," the jailer explained, surprised at the Prince's indignation.

"Well, release him immediately. And get him some real food."

"Yes, my Lord. Right away."

The jailer stepped forward and, hoisting a large iron ring with several hefty keys attached, unlocked Prester's ankle chains. Then, uncertain as to his next move, he handed the key ring to the Prince before vanishing up a winding stairwell.

Kirk slammed the keys to the ground, and reached down to help Prester to his feet.

"I'm sorry, Mr. John," Kirk said. "I had no idea you were being kept like this."

Prester coughed as he nodded his reply. "I'm glad to see you, Kirk," he choked out with a parched throat. "I'm glad to see anybody."

"I'm sorry, I'm sorry," Kirk said again as Prester's legs stretched to their full length. "I shouldn't have had them arrest you. I didn't realize. I didn't know they'd put you down here. I let Nicolo talk me into it. I shouldn't have listened to him. Are you all right?"

"I'm all right, Kirk, I'm all right," Prester said, gathering himself together and standing upright. Looking to his left, he noticed Machiavelli hovering nearby. Prester shot him an angry glance.

"My Lord," Machiavelli said, "I really must protest. Why are we wasting valuable time here, with this prisoner?"

"I told you," Kirk said, "I need his advice."

"But you already have my full counsel, my Lord," Machiavelli replied, his voice revealing his frustration.

"You don't know what he knows," Kirk said.

Just then, Prester's knees began to buckle. Kirk held him up.

"You must be starving. Can you walk?" Kirk asked Prester.

"I think so," Prester said, trying to regain his footing.

"Then come with me," Kirk said. "Niccolo," he added, glancing at Machiavelli, "arrange for food and clean clothes to be brought up immediately."

"Of course, my Lord," Machiavelli said as Kirk and Prester hobbled off up the tower stairs.

Forty minutes later, Prester was seated at a large wooden table in the tower counsel room. He was pressing another mutton chop to his lips and ripping at the meat with his teeth. Behind him, Kirk and Machiavelli stood arguing over strategy.

"Call out the army," Kirk shouted. "Call out the marines. Call out the navy. Do we have a navy? Call out everybody."

"I am afraid, my Lord, it is no use," Machiavelli responded. "King Louis' troops will almost certainly be successful in crossing into the city before nightfall."

"Not if we blow up the Ponte Vecchio," Kirk said, his eyes wild at the idea.

"The Ponte Vecchio is only one bridge, my Lord," Machiavelli pointed out, "and it is essential to the commerce of the city. The people would never tolerate its destruction."

"Well then, we'll place soldiers at all the bridges."

"The enemy numbers twenty-five hundred. We have but a thousand men at arms, and it would be foolish to split our force," Machiavelli explained. "We might slow their progress temporarily, but Louis' troops will cross the Arno and enter the city."

"This is unbelievable," Kirk said as he began pacing back and forth across the room. "What about Siena? Aren't they our allies? Can't we send for their army?"

"I am afraid the Sienese will be of little comfort to you, my Lord. They are not true friends of Florence. Indeed, they would almost certainly arrest you and turn you over to the invaders to curry favor with King Louis."

"Are you kidding? What kind of an ally does that?"

Kirk stopped in mid-stride, turning his head to listen to a building hum from outside.

"What's that?" he asked.

A restless crowd was gathering in the Piazza de Signoria, the murmur of their activity growing louder. Kirk moved toward the noise.

"Listen, listen to that. Can you hear that?" Kirk asked. "That's the sound of the people. The people! That's the sound of our salvation, Niccolo. The people are the answer. They'll never stand for this. They are proud Florentines. They are our citizen soldiers. The people will rise up against King Louis, won't they? The people will protect their city, their beloved Florence, right Niccolo?"

Machiavelli, with a heavy sigh, sat upon a chair.

"Alas, my Lord, the Florentine people will do as they have always done. They are of a practical nature."

"A practical nature? What does that mean?" Kirk shouted. "Don't they love Florence?"

"Indeed they do," Machiavelli said. "They love Florence too much to see it burned by Louis' army. You will recall that the people embraced

Savonarola in lieu of the deceased Lorenzo, and they embraced you upon Savonarola's downfall. In similar fashion, the people will undoubtedly flock to King Louis if he appears to gain the upper hand. The people will always rise first to the defense of their self-preservation."

"I don't understand. What are you saying?" Kirk shouted.

Prester, finishing his chop, now wiped the corners of his mouth with a white cloth napkin.

"What he's saying, Kirk," Prester said, "is that the fine people of Florence are about to throw you over like yesterday's news."

"Throw me over?" Kirk gasped, his voice betraying something very near to panic. "Nicolo, they wouldn't do that. The people love me. I gave them their freedom. Have they forgotten how Savonarola bullied them, always telling them that they'd go to hell just for having fun? I let them live, Nicolo. Didn't I? I let them do as they please. They wouldn't throw me over, would they?"

"My Prince," Machiavelli began, "certainly many among the people do feel a genuine affection towards you, for they believe that God has favored you with the gift of prophecy. Moreover, you have granted to them the freedom to do as they please for the most part. It was a great change from Savonarola's stringent rule. The people are undoubtedly imbued with a sense of loyalty towards you, as am I. But as I have often warned you, in granting liberty to the people, you inevitably incur their wrath. It is not easy to hold people to your will once they become accustomed to freedom."

"What are you saying? Should I have been a tyrant? Should I have made the people fear me instead of love me?"

"In truth, one ought to be both feared and loved. But as it is difficult for the two to go together, it is much safer to be feared. It may be said of men in general that they are ungrateful, voluble, dissemblers, anxious to avoid danger, and covetous of gain. As long as you benefit them, they are entirely yours. They will offer you their blood, their property, their lives and their children when danger is far distant. But when it approaches, they turn against you. The prince who has relied solely upon the love of the people will be lost, for men have less scruple in offending one who makes himself loved than one who makes himself feared. Love is preserved by the link of obligation which, owing to the baseness of men, is broken at every opportunity for their advantage. But fear is maintained by a dread of punishment which never fails."

Kirk listened, waiting for Machiavelli to complete his soliloquy.

"So I should have been cruel?"

"That may have been a reasonable strategy prior to today, my Lord. Indeed, if you will recall, many is the time that I advocated a harsher tone with the people. But as it is, the people currently fear Louis and his troops more than they love you. Thus, once it becomes known that King Louis will destroy the city unless you are turned over to him as his prisoner, the people will throw you aside to preserve their own lives."

Kirk listened to Machiavelli's analysis in stunned silence. Moving again to the window, he looked out once more upon the people in the square below. The crowd had increased noticeably even in the last five minutes. Groups of men now huddled in conspiratorial packs while others stood alone looking up at the tower as if waiting for an answer to some unasked question. Kirk turned back into the room and strode to where Prester was sitting.

"Can we go back?" he asked.

"Back?"

"To Block Island. I can't stay here any more. These people are nuts. You said you had a way to get us home again. So let's go, right now."

"Kirk," Prester said, "I did have a way to get us home, sure. But that was before you threw me in your dungeon for a month. It's too late now, Kirk. The time for going home has past."

Kirk seemed stunned by the news.

"You mean, for good?"

"I'm afraid so," Prester said with resignation.

"You can't mean forever. There must be a way to get home."

"No," Prester said, "there isn't. I'm sorry, but I tried to tell you."

Kirk looked at him with a combination of perplexity and astonishment.

"So what do I do now?"

"You're the Prince. Why are you asking me?" Prester said.

"Because you're my teacher, and I'm your student. Debemus invicem adiuvent. We must help one another, isn't that our school motto?"

"You remember," Prester smiled.

"Sure, I remember," Kirk said.

Prester smiled.

"You're right," he said. "We should help one another. Mr. Machiavelli, it would seem that our young Prince wants to know what he should do next? Shall I tell him, or would you like to?"

"There is but one honorable avenue of action left open to you, my Prince," Machiavelli said.

"What's that?" Kirk asked.

"Capitulate, of course. Give yourself up for the sake of the people. It is only a matter of time before they will take you by force in any case. Thus, you gain nothing by waiting. Conversely, by willingly offering yourself up, the people will respect you all the more for your courage. They will love you all the more for your self-sacrifice. And they will honor you all the more in their memory. Indeed, I should not be surprised if poems are written about you, and statues erected in your likeness."

Kirk's shoulders seemed to wilt at the realization of his imminent demise. With a dejected air, he slunk down upon a nearby stool and stared into the middle distance.

"Think it through," Prester said. "Think it through."

Kirk sat staring straight ahead for a long moment as the noise from the restless crowd outside grew louder and more insistent. Inhaling and sitting upright, Kirk suddenly took on a new look. His countenance relaxed, his shoulders squared, his chest seemed to extend outward, and his chin tilted upward.

"There comes a time in each man's life," Machiavelli continued, observing the change in Kirk's demeanor, "when boyhood is at an end."

Kirk stood up.

"Mr. John, I don't suppose you would by any chance consider coming with me? It's not that I'm afraid, you understand. But a bit of company might be nice along the way to wherever it is they plan to take me."

Prester wiped his lips once more with the cloth and, as he rose from his chair, returned Kirk's smile.

"Well, there's certainly nothing for me here," Prester said. "Besides, as you so aptly pointed out, I am still your teacher, and you are still my student."

"*Debemus invicem adiuvent*," Kirk said.

"Always," Prester responded.

Chapter 32

Prester and Kirk emerged from the tower surrounded by a dozen armed guards, swords drawn at the ready. The Florentine mob jeered at the Prince as he and Prester moved forward. Insults and invectives were hurled at every step. But as they passed through the streets, making their way toward the Ponte Vecchio, word began to spread as to the true nature of their foray. The crowd began to realize that it was Prince Kirkrenzo's intention to submit himself to the authority of King Louis in order to save the city from destruction. What had been jeers turned to shouts of gratitude and admiration. By the time they reached the bridge, the throng was cheering them wildly.

As they began to walk up onto the Ponte Vecchio, a man broke free of the cheering crowd.

"Prester, old man," came a familiar voice as the man ran up to them. Prester smiled at the sight of him.

"Halifax, how are you?" Prester asked.

"Tolerably well. The question is, how are you?"

"In for an adventure, I assume."

"So I understand. The whole city is abuzz about it." Halifax turned to Kirk. "You should say something to them, you know. You are their Prince. They want to hear from you."

"What should I say?" Kirk asked.

"Tell them what's in your heart," Halifax offered.

Kirk looked at Prester and Halifax, and then at the mass of people surrounding them. Then, climbing up onto the railing of the bridge and taking hold of a stanchion for support, he looked out over the throng.

"*Ciao,*" he shouted. "*Silenzio, per favore.*" The crowd grew quiet and respectful as they waited to hear the words of their departing Prince. Kirk continued in passable Italian, with Halifax translating for Prester.

"I came to Florence six years ago when I was just a boy," Kirk began. "I was lost. I was hungry. I knew no one, and I had no place to go. But you took me in – into your hearts and your homes. You showed me your ways and taught me your language. In time, you came to believe that I knew things you did not know, that I could foresee things that had not yet happened. You came to believe that I had a gift from God, so you sent me to live with the Pope in Rome. Then a year ago, after Savonarola's excommunication, the Pope sent me back to Florence as his emissary. You placed your trust in me, and I have tried to lead you in the best way I know how."

"You have been a fine prince," someone shouted from the middle of the crowd.

"The finest," another person yelled.

"I thank you for that. But now our beloved city is in danger, and yet I have it within my hands to save her. So that is what I will do, what I must do. I leave you now for the good of Florence."

"No, no," someone shouted from the pack of bodies pressing upon the bridge. "We will fight King Louis. If you stay, we will fight him." The shout echoed against the buildings that lined the street leading up to the Ponte Vecchio, but only a small murmur of support followed.

"King Louis' army is too strong," Kirk said, squelching the few embryonic embers of patriotic fervor. "If I stay, Florence will be destroyed. This cannot be. Florence must survive, not just for you, but for all the generations yet to come. This city, the city of Michelangelo and of Leonardo da Vinci, of Boticcelli and Dante Alighieri, of Brunelleschi, Donatello, Boccaccio, Machiavelli and Lorenzo the Magnificent, this city must live to be a beacon of light pointing the way to the future. Florence will never be forgotten. She belongs to the world."

As the crowd broke into thunderous cheers and applause, Kirk jumped back down onto the wooden planked bridge and slapped the dust of the stanchion from his hands.

"Very eloquent, my young scholar," Prester said.

Kirk smiled. "I think I finally understand what you were always trying to teach me."

"What will become of you?" Halifax asked.

Prester and Kirk looked at each other.

"We don't know," Kirk said.

"One way or another," Prester added, "I don't think we'll be coming back."

"I should come with you," Halifax suggested.

"You're a good man, Halifax," Prester said, "but there's no need for that. You have a life here."

"Isn't there something I can do for you?"

"Perhaps one thing," Prester said. "Have you seen Leonardo?"

"Not since this morning at the contest."

"Find him. Tell him what happened. Maybe he can think of something."

"I will tell him," Halifax said. "Wait." Reaching into his belt, he withdrew his mechanical calendar calculating device and tossed it to Prester.

"No," Prester protested. "You worked so hard on this."

"Take it," Halifax insisted. "Perhaps it will come in handy."

"Thank you," Prester said, taking the device and then giving his friend a bear hug. "Take care of yourself, Halifax."

"God speed, Prester John. Good luck to both of you," Halifax said.

With that, Prester and Kirk turned and started over the bridge as the roar of cheers rose behind them.

"Sounds like you're leaving a few fans behind," Prester noted.

"I guess so," Kirk responded.

As they reached the far side of the Ponte Vecchio, six men in the uniform of Swiss mercenaries came up to them on horseback.

"Which of you eez Prince Kirkrenzo?" one of the soldiers asked in a thick French accent.

Prester and Kirk looked at each other.

"I'm the one you're looking for," Kirk said.

The soldier nodded and then pointed to an elegant horse-drawn carriage that stood waiting nearby.

"If you please," the soldier said.

Kirk and Prester, following the soldier's direction, stepped up into the enclosed carriage.

"Where do you think they'll take us?" Kirk asked.

"To see the King of France, I presume," Prester answered.

The carriage lurched forward and struck a steady gait away from the Arno River. After a few minutes, they passed under the stone arch of the city wall, the outermost boundary of Florence. Prester recognized this as the path upon which he had entered the city over a month before. In due course, as the carriage moved beyond the last outcropping of buildings, Prester suddenly spotted the small rose garden where he had first arrived.

"I recognize this place," Prester said.

"Of course," Kirk agreed. "I assume you landed here too, didn't you? By the garden arch?"

"Yes, right next to the old olive tree," Prester said.

"Same with me, six years ago at that very spot," Kirk said.

"He was right," Prester said.

"Who?"

"Dr. Ponnuru."

"Oh, right, you told me about him and his timetree theory. I still don't understand it," Kirk said.

"It's a bit complicated. But according to Dr. Ponnuru, to get home, we should have been touching that olive tree at exactly 2:04 in the afternoon nine days ago."

"Um, yes, well, I'm sorry about that," Kirk said.

"Well, truth be told, things weren't working out so well for me back home anyway," Prester said, staring again out the window and falling into his private thoughts.

The coach rattled on for the better part of an hour surrounded at all times by Swiss mercenaries on horseback. The path led through a thick wood where twigs and branches scratched the sides of the coach as they rode. Eventually, upon entering a clearing, they traversed up a steep hill with switchbacks and narrow ledges. As they crested the top of a hill and began down the other side, there came into view a gleaming white palace nestled within a small valley.

As they drew nearer, Prester saw that the palace was a three-story symmetrically shaped building. Its large central square was surrounded by grand protruding loggias on each of its four sides. The roof of each loggia was embellished with three elegant Romanesque statues. Each loggia was in turn supported by six white glistening Corinthian columns that seemed to float atop shimmering marble steps. The main floor of the building rose one full story above the manicured landscape below. Atop the central square of the building was a squat circular dome that Prester recognized as being in the style of the Pantheon. Prester leaned his head out of the coach window and shouted up to the driver.

"What is this place?"

"La Villa Rotunda," the driver shouted back down in English thickly laden with a French accent. "It eez the home of Signor Francesco di Bartolomeo di Zanobi del Giocando and heez wife. Heez majesty the King eez for the moment encamped eer, at the owner's invitation of course."

"Oh, of course," Prester said, and then pulled his head back into the coach. "It's not easy to say no to the King."

The carriage rolled along a Cypress lined drive that curved toward the estate. The road ended in a gravel courtyard at the entrance to the house accented by a sprawling oak. Two servants, in formal red tunics and white gloves, attended the carriage upon its arrival. Prester and Kirk were conducted up one of the long marble staircases, and through a large brass double door. Once inside, they were shown down a short wood-paneled entry hallway and into the building's central two-story rotunda. Ornate ceramic-tiles adorned every wall and surface of the rotunda, and the sky could be seen through its central Oculus.

"Beautiful," Prester observed while looking up at the ceiling.

"Yes, she is," Kirk said, his gaze having been directed elsewhere.

Prester lowered his head and followed Kirk's line of vision. Watching from the far side of the rotunda was a young woman standing with hands folded in front of her. She wore a flowing black gown that plunged to just above the bosom exposing the radiant olive skin of her neck and upper chest. Her curly brown hair, carefully parted in the middle, flowed down to shoulders that were covered by the sheerest of black veils. She said nothing, but smiled a furtive smile upon seeing them look her way.

"Who is she?" Kirk asked.

"The lady of the house, I imagine."

"I know it's crazy, but she looks somehow familiar, don't you think?"

"Actually, I had the same thought," Prester acknowledged.

"*Par ici, s'il vous plait*," a servant interrupted, gesturing for Kirk and Prester to enter one of several anterooms.

Dark carved wooden bookshelves, red velvet furnishings and the smell of potpourri greeted them as they stepped into the small anteroom.

"*Asseyez-vous ici*," the servant said, pointing to a pair of straight-backed chairs. Prester and Kirk understood that he wanted them to sit down, and they did so.

Turning, the servant stepped back out of the room, closing and audibly locking the door behind him. The moment he was gone, Kirk was up and scanning the walls for an exit.

"What are you doing?" Prester asked.

"I'm looking for some way out of here, what else?"

"You mean like some sort of hidden passageway? You've seen too many movies, Kirk."

"Do you have a better idea?"

"Not at the moment," Prester admitted.

"Then leave me alone," Kirk said as he continued his frantic search. After fifteen minutes, his hopes began to ebb and he plopped himself down into a chair.

"Everyone here is French," Kirk observed.

"So it would seem," Prester said.

"Then I guess it'll be the guillotine for us."

"I highly doubt it," Prester responded.

"Really? Why?"

"Because they won't invent the guillotine for another 300 years."

"Oh," Kirk said. "Well, I'm sure they'll think of something equally horrible."

"Maybe, maybe not. Maybe they'll just ship us back to France. Maybe they'll let us go. Don't assume the worst."

As Prester spoke, he glanced around the room and chanced to gaze upon a large wood-panel painting hanging on the wall. The painting showed people seated at two long white banquet tables under a sequence of arches. Prester stared at it with interest.

"I think I've seen that before," Prester said.

"What?"

"That painting. I've definitely seen that somewhere."

"It's just another painting. There are probably a million others just like it."

"New York," Prester said.

"What?" Kirk asked, now looking over at the painting in question.

"I think I saw that painting in New York," Prester repeated.

"Oh my God, that's my father's painting," Kirk added, now staring at the artwork. "He owns it. It's hanging in his New York apartment, in his den."

"Right, I remember now," Prester confirmed.

"It's called *The Story of Nastagio degli Onesti* by Botticelli, painted around 1480 I think," Kirk said. "My father paid a fortune for it at Sotheby's."

Kirk moved closer to the painting and examined it carefully.

"It's egg tempera on wood – pigment mixed with egg yolk. You see there," he said, pointing to a particular spot on the panel, "how the arches get smaller as they go back? And here how the long tables get more narrow as they recede into the painting? That's what you call linear perspective. It's a technique that was invented by the same guy who built the dome of the cathedral in Florence."

"Brunelleschi," Prester added.

"Yeah, that's him. I remember when you were teaching us about Brunelleschi. I always thought he was just a builder, you know, an architect. But it turns out, he was a real genius. He invented new types of cranes and all kinds of machines. He also worked out the mathematics of painting, like linear perspective. He even built ships. Anyway, the fellow who painted this, Botticelli, was among the first artists ever to use linear perspective in their paintings."

Prester smiled as he looked upon his pupil.

"Kirk, you've been holding out on me," he said. "I didn't realize you knew so much about Renaissance art?"

"I actually learned a lot about it from my father."

"So why did you always play like you didn't know anything? It would have made your father very happy to know you understood his passion."

Kirk thought for a moment before answering.

"I didn't want to make him happy," he said.

Prester nodded.

"You know, Kirk," Prester said, "I think I understand about fathers and sons. You were just a kid then."

"I wish I could tell him I'm sorry," Kirk said.

Prester's eyes flashed.

"You did."

"What do you mean?"

"You did tell him. I can't believe I didn't remember this right away," Prester said.

"What are you talking about?" Kirk asked.

"The painting, when I saw it in your father's apartment in New York, there was something written on the back. He didn't know how it got there."

"I don't remember ever seeing anything written on the back of that painting."

"That's just it, neither had your father. That's why he was so astounded when he first discovered it. But he knew that it was some-how connected to your disappearance."

"How did he know that?"

"Because of what it said. When he showed it to me, I was shocked too. But now I think I understand."

Kirk looked at Prester and raised one eyebrow. He then walked to where the painting hung on the wall and lifted it off its mooring. Looking again at Prester, Kirk turned the painting over, exposing the back of the plank. He stared at the back, holding it high up to the window for more light and straining to see what might be there. Lowering the painting again, he looked back at Prester.

"There's nothing there," he said. "Nothing is written on the back."

"No, not yet," Prester pointed out. "You're going to write it now."

Looking around the room again, Prester spied a quill pen and ink well on a table top. He rose from his chair, picked up the quill, dipped its tip in the ink, and handed it to Kirk.

Kirk took the pen in his hand and looked down again at the blank back of the wood-panel painting.

"I don't understand. What should I write?"

"Look, your father will own that painting one day, so whatever you write will be seen by him."

"So I should write something like, 'Hey Dad, it's me, Kirk, from 500 years ago? Sorry about being such a jerk?'"

"That's too modern. If you wrote that, no one would ever believe it was from the Renaissance," Prester pointed out. "The painting would become worthless, and chances are your father would never bother to buy it."

"So what should I write?" Kirk asked. Suddenly a flash passed over his face as he held the painting in his hands. "Hey, wait a minute," he said. "You already know what was written on it. Tell me. What's it say?"

Just then, the door burst open, and in walked a tall, thin man dressed in black knee-high riding boots, a white tunic with purple riding vest and a black felt hat. Rushing in behind him was his valet.

Chapter 33

"Your majesty," the valet shouted. "Please wait for your military guard."

Ignoring the plea, the tall man threw his gloves on a chair and gave Prester and Kirk the once over.

"*Et alors,* which 'ave you eez the English Prince of Florence?" the man said, his English infused with a thick French accent.

Kirk and Prester looked around as if perhaps a random Englishman had been lurking in the vicinity all along. Seeing no one of that description, Kirk spoke up.

"I'm guessing you must mean me," he said with a grin. "But just so the records straight, I'm not English. I'm a red, white and blue blooded American." The King looked confused and glared at his valet for an explanation. The valet just shrugged. "And who might you be?" Kirk asked.

"Sacre bleu!" the valet gasped.

"Who am I?" the tall man bellowed. "Who am I?"

"If you don't know, we're both in trouble," Kirk said.

"You are in the presence of his majesty, King Louis XII, King of all France," the valet sputtered.

"Is that right?" Kirk said.

The King, still holding his riding crop and slapping it forgetfully against his leg, noticed that Kirk was holding a painting.

"What a' you doing with that painting?" the King barked.

"This?" Kirk replied. "This painting belongs to my father."

"Put it down," the King commanded.

Just then, three colorfully dressed Swiss guards entered the room behind the King, withdrew their long swords, and pointed them at Kirk's throat.

"I could be mistaken," Kirk said, leaning the painting gently up against a chair.

The King began to pace back and forth across the small room as his guards sheathed their swords.

"They say you are a clever young man," the King said.

"Really? Well, you know, I mean, I don't know," Kirk grinned as he kicked at the floor with his toe.

"I don't like clever young men," the King added while his three Swiss guards, still glaring at Kirk, rested their hands upon the hilts of their weapons.

"Cleverness is overrated, wouldn't you say?" Kirk offered.

"It is said that you possess the gift of prophecy," the King continued, "though much good it has done you. The people of Florence 'ave abandoned you now, eh?"

"Well, yes, yes, that is true. But to be fair, you do have a much bigger army than they do, and the people of Florence aren't stupid. They may be bloodthirsty, money hungry and fickle, but they aren't stupid."

"You a' wrong. They a' stupid as well," the King smirked. "They think that by giving you up I will not attack them."

The sarcastic grin left Kirk's face as he stared at King Louis.

"Now wait a minute. That was our agreement," Kirk said.

"They think," the King laughed, "that by giving you up I will not set fire to their city."

"Well, sure, that was our deal. You said you wouldn't attack Florence if I turned myself over to you," Kirk raised his voice. "So here I am. A deal's a deal."

"What do I care of deals?" the King said. "Tomorrow morning, I will ride in with my army and burn Florence to the ground. I will destroy her churches, and her statues, and her paintings. I will lay waste to it all, and wipe it from the map of Europe. Let them sleep well tonight in their ignorance, for tomorrow their city will be no more."

As the King was speaking, two figures entered the room from behind. One was the young dark-haired beauty, the lady of the house, who had observed them from across the rotunda. With her was a tall man wearing a purple cape looking both perplexed and disturbed at what he had just overheard.

"Your majesty," the tall man interrupted, "did I hear you correctly? Perhaps I misunderstood."

The King swung around.

"Lord Medici," the King said. "Lady Lisa. You should not be here."

Prester realized that the man was Piero Medici, son of the late Lorenzo the Magnificent. Seizing his opportunity, Prester stepped forward.

"He plans to set fire to Florence in the morning," Prester stated loudly to be sure Piero was clear as to the topic under discussion.

"Surely not," Piero said, and then began to laugh. "It is merely a misunderstanding, no doubt. Why, the very idea. Burn Florence? Preposterous."

"No misunderstanding," a new voice said as yet another man entered the room. It was Machiavelli, out of breath from having just arrived on horseback. "His majesty is quite serious. You see, the people of Florence have too long been of the impression that they are in control of their own destiny. The King understands that this is a very dangerous thing. By burning the Duomo and the other churches, by destroying the artwork, the statues, the paintings, and the frescos, the King will decisively demonstrate that he, and not they, are in charge. Only by this means, my dear Piero, will the Medici name again be respected and feared. It is not a pleasant task, I agree, but it is an essential one."

The tall, thin frame of Piero Medici stiffened as he listened to Machiavelli's words.

"Your majesty," Piero said, "do not listen to this man, this Satan, this Philistine. I remember him from when he would give counsel to my father. Even then, even as a child, I knew he could not be trusted."

"All the same, he eez now my adviser," the King said.

"Your adviser?" Kirk spouted.

"That is correct, Prince Kirkrenzo," Machiavelli said. "You see, like the Florentines themselves, I am a practical man."

"And is it your advice to the King that burning Florence to the ground is the practical thing to do?" Piero shouted. "Your majesty, do not be tricked by his clever words. You yourself will recall that Savonarola tried burning the art of Florence, but in the end the people turned against him. They will turn against you too, if you cause such destruction."

"Savonarola's failing," Machiavelli responded, "was that he did not go far enough. What is needed, what the people of Florence will respond to most assuredly, is fear. This is what I have advised his majesty, King Louis. But then, I am merely an adviser. Perhaps his majesty would prefer to listen to you, Piero."

Piero looked at the King for any sign of empathy or understanding, but the King's jaw was locked in place, and his chin pointed vaguely in the direction of the North Star.

"Your majesty," Piero pleaded, "you must reconsider. The Medici have been leaders in Florence for generations. Yes, the people on occasion have looked elsewhere for guidance. They have here and there taken on other leaders, temporarily. But they have always come back to the Medici, and they will do so again, and willingly. There is no need to burn the treasures of their city, treasures that belong not only to Florence but to the world."

"Enough," the King shouted. "It eez decided, and I will have no more talk about it. You, Piero, and the Medici, will again control Florence. That is what you wanted. That is why you sought my help. But I will control the Medici. Never forget that. And as for you two," the King added, pointing toward Prester and Kirk, "you will both be hanged from the courtyard oak at dawn. You, my young Prince, because we have no more need of princes just now. And you," he said, pointing at Prester, "who are you?"

"I'm nobody. I'm just a high school history teacher," Prester gulped.

The King again looked perplexed, and once more turned to his valet for guidance. The valet, having no insight to offer, again shrugged his shoulders.

"We are full up with those too," the King said. "Lady Lisa," he bowed to the lady of the house, "please excuse me. Guards, lock them in for the night, and watch the door well."

"*Oui*, your majesty," one of the guards responded as the King strode from the room, followed by a smirking Machiavelli.

"Your majesty," Piero Medici shouted after them, "I beg you to reconsider." He too stepped from the room.

Standing to one side, the Lady Lisa observed the scene.

"You 'ad better leave," the French guard said to her in broken English.

"*Monsieur*," the Lady Lisa said in reply, speaking for the first time in a soft but firm voice that bespoke control even in the midst of chaos. "*Parli Italiano?*" she said in Italian.

"*Italien?*" the French guard responded in his native French. "*Non, je ne parle pas Italien.*"

"*Loquerisne Latine?*" she tried again, this time in Latin.

The French guard just stared at her.

"I speak but little French," the Lady Lisa now continued in hesitant English, "and you no Italian, no Latin. Then for English we must use."

"*Oui*, Madame?"

"Understand please a fact. This house, it is mine. It is not for a French soldier to tell me when I may come and when I must leave its rooms."

"Of course, my Lady," the guard said, taken aback. "I am, how do you say, following orders, Madame. Perhaps, for your own safety . . . ," he motioned toward the door.

Lady Lisa remained aloof for a few more moments.

"Very well," she said, "I shall leave because I choose to leave."

"*Oui*, Madame," the guard said.

"Lady Lisa," Kirk interjected. "Just a moment, if you please."

Picking up the quill pen again, he scratched out a quick note on the back of the wood-panel painting. "I think this is yours," he said, holding out the painting for her to take.

She turned and looked at him with a frown, but made no move to take the piece.

"Have you eaten?" she asked.

"I'm not hungry, ma'am, thank you," Kirk replied.

"Still, I shall have food sent."

She turned to leave again.

"Lady Lisa," Kirk continued, still holding out the painting, "won't you please take this?"

Hesitating for a moment, the Lady Lisa took hold of the painting as she departed. A moment later, the heavy oak door to the small den was slammed shut, and the room was locked from the outside.

"Well?" Prester asked.

"What?"

"You wrote something?"

"Yes."

"What?"

"I don't think she speaks English very well. So I wrote down the only thing I could think of that I knew she'd understand and that might also help us out of this mess. You know what I wrote."

"I think I do, but I want to hear it from you," Prester said.

Kirk shrugged.

"I wrote something in Latin. I told her that we need to help each other," Kirk grinned. "You know, our school motto: Debemus invicem adiuvent."

"Yes," Prester said. "That was it."

Chapter 34

"It's Marcel Moreau calling from Paris, sir," Mrs. Trumbull said over the intercom.

Director Brennan lifted his head from his paperwork.

"Marcel?" the Director said with a worried tone.

"Yes, sir. He wants to speak with you."

"Does he say why?"

"No, sir."

"How does he sound? Do you think he's heard anything?" the Director asked.

"I'm sure I don't know, Mr. Brennan."

The Director hesitated.

"What line?"

"Line one, sir," Mrs. Trumbull said, and then clicked off, leaving the call on hold.

The Director took a deep breath, rose from his chair, picked up the receiver, and clicked the button for line one.

"Marcel," Brennan said in as pleasant a voice as he could muster, "it's late in Paris, my friend."

"Yes, mon ami," Marcel Moreau's voice sounded clear but tired.

"How is everything at the Louvre?"

"My job occupies me constantly, as I yam cer-tin yours does for you."

"We each must bear our burdens," Brennan said.

"Joseph, are you alone?"

Brennan could hear the tension in his voice.

"Actually, I have someone waiting to see me," Brennan lied. "What's on your mind?" There was a pause. "Marcel? Are you there?"

"Ah oui, Joseph, I yam eer."

"What is it, my friend?"

"I yam calling you on a mat-tear of great seriousness."

"It sounds ominous," Brennan said with a forced chuckle, hoping that his voice did not betray his fear.

"I 'ave 'eard of your troubles," Marcel said.

Now it was Brennan's turn to hesitate. After a moment, he forced himself to speak.

"Troubles?" he said. "What troubles are those, Marcel?"

"I was 'oping to avoid this discussion, but what 'as been 'appening at the Metropolitan 'as also been 'appening eer at the Louvre."

"What do you mean, exactly?" Brennan said, refusing to be drawn in without clear evidence that the secret had become known, at least within the literary and artistic circles in which Marcel Moreau traveled.

"Joseph, my friend, we 'ave no time for games. It 'as become too serious. I yam talking about the changes, the changes to the paintings."

"How do you know about that?" the Director demanded.

"I know," Marcel said. "It 'as been 'appening eer as well, and also I yam told at the Uffizi in Florence."

"My God, Marcel, I don't understand this," the Director said, slumping back down into his cushioned leather chair. "How could this be? It's unimaginable. Is it more than one person, do you think? Is it a gang of some sort doing this?"

"I don't know," Marcel said. "We 'ave no answers either."

"This could ruin us, you know," the Director said. "If this gets out, it could ruin us all."

"Joseph, listen to me. Are you listening?"

"I'm listening, Marcel, of course I'm listening."

"Tomorrow at 4:00 o'clock in the afternoon Paris time – 10:00 o'clock for you – I will be 'olding a press conference eer at the Louvre. I will be explaining . . . no, no, that is impossible. I cannot explain this. What I mean to say is that I will be advising the press of what 'as been 'appening. I yam going to tell them that the paintings are changing."

The Director almost dropped the phone.

"Marcel," he pleaded, "that is not what you should do. Don't you understand, my friend? This will destroy us, destroy our reputations and those of our museums. No one will want to come to see our paintings if they think they are not real."

"I yam calling you, Joseph, because I think that you should also make a public announcement. You should speak tomorrow at 10:00 o'clock in the morning your time, simultaneous with my statement eer in Paris."

"Marcel, listen to me. There must be another way. Just give this thing some time, time for us to figure out what is happening, and what to do about it. We need time, Marcel."

"Time is what we do not 'ave, Joseph. We are out of time."

"What do you mean? Why do you say that?" the Director asked in a near panic. "What has happened?"

"It is the Mona Lisa," Marcel said.

"No, no, no, don't tell me," Brennan gasped.

"The Mona Lisa is not smiling."

Chapter 35

La Villa Rotunda near Florence

"Ah," Prester said, pushing away the empty bowl and leaning back with a satiated expression. "That was one fine stew."

"You seem awfully content for a man who's about to be hanged," Kirk said as he stood staring out the only window in the room.

"Content?" Prester replied. "No, not content. But if they mean to hang us, I don't suppose there's very much we can do about it."

"I'm sorry I got you into this mess," Kirk said.

"It wasn't your fault. You didn't mean to disappear. But when you did, my life pretty much disappeared too. So you see, trying to bring you back was the only thing I really could do. The way I see it, we're in this thing together. Say, is that guard still out there?"

"Yes, just beyond the window. Actually, I think there are two of them now. It's kind of hard to see in the dark."

"Well then, we're not going anywhere. Try some stew. It's really quite good."

"I'm not hungry," Kirk said, turning away from the window and looking toward the center of the room.

"Too bad. You're missing out. If I live, I may even compliment the chef."

"Do you think she'll try to help us?" Kirk asked hopefully.

"The Lady Lisa you mean? Who knows? Even if she wanted to, even if she saw your message and understood it, how could she help? Guards are at the window. Guards are at the door. What could she do?"

Kirk shook his head. "I kept thinking that maybe there'd be some sort of secret passage out of this place. You know, a revolving door or hidden tunnel or something? But I've pushed and pulled on everything that's not nailed down in this room. Nothing."

"Worth a try, I suppose," Prester said.

Kirk picked up a small chunk of stewed meat from a bowl on the table and nibbled at it as he wandered back toward the window to resume his staring vigil.

"Hey," Kirk said, staring out the window. "What do you suppose that is?"

"What do I suppose what is?"

"That flashing light. I keep seeing it way out there across the field. It keeps flashing on and off, on and off."

Prester looked up at Kirk with interest.

"Flashing light? They won't have flashlights for another 450 years."

"Well, I don't know. It's kind of like a flashlight. Or maybe some kind of a torch with something moving in front of it."

Prester rose and went to the window.

"Where?" he said.

"Wait for it," Kirk replied, pointing toward the woods at the far side of a flat meadow where he had seen the light. Suddenly, from the blackness of the far distance, four flashes could be seen in succession, the first three being short and the last being longer.

"It's been doing that over and over, every few minutes," Kirk said.

"For how long?"

"I don't know. Maybe a couple of hours. It always starts out the same, three short flashes and then a long flash. Then there's some other stuff I can't make out. I mean, I can't see any pattern to it. Then nothing for a couple of minutes. Then it starts all over again."

"It can't be," Prester said. "Can it?"

"You know what that looks like?" Kirk asked rhetorically. "My grandfather worked at the old Brooklyn Navy Yard as a scraper, you know, tearing apart the old World War Two ships. I remember once he showed me this big round spotlight kind of a thing with a handle on the side. You could open and close these shutters that ran across the front. I forget what he called it."

"A Navy signal lamp?" Prester suggested.

"Yeah, that's it. A signal lamp. They used them to signal from one ship to another."

Prester and Kirk continued to stare across the darkness, waiting for the lights to flash again. Finally, the sequence began anew. Three short flashes followed by one long flash, and then a series of additional flashes.

"You don't figure the U.S. Navy is out there somewhere, do you?" Kirk said, only half joking.

"No, I'm afraid not," Prester said. "But I'll tell you one thing. That flashing looks an awful lot like Morse code."

Just then, a bookcase behind them lurched twelve inches forward, causing Prester and Kirk to spin around on their heels. Watching with awed disbelief, the bookcase proceeded to slide smoothly to the left, revealing a secret passageway leading through the wall and down the stone steps of a hidden stairwell.

"I knew it," Kirk gasped.

The telltale sound of footsteps climbing upwards could be heard from the depths of the dark subterranean space. A few seconds later, light flickered into the room and a figure carrying a flaming torch emerged from the darkness.

"Lady Lisa," Prester uttered with astonishment.

"Shhh," she whispered. "The ears of French soldiers are just beyond the door."

Prester nodded his understanding.

"I have with me someone who can help," the Lady Lisa continued.

As she said this, Leonardo da Vinci stepped up out of the darkness and into the light of the room.

"Mya good friends," Da Vinci said in a quiet yet cheerful tone.

"Leonardo," Kirk said. "Where'd you come from?"

"From the town of Vinci, of course, in the Tuscan hills very near to where we are now, actually. But I suspect that is not what you really meant to ask, is it?"

"What are you doing here?" Prester clarified.

"Ah, yes, well, thata is also easily explained. Halifax told me thata you 'ad been taken by French soldiers. And now I have found you. You see, I know this place well. I have been coming here as often as I can for several months to see the Lady Lisa. Her husband has commissioned me to paint her portrait, and I have been working diligently upon the project."

Prester and Kirk looked at each other with mutual realization.

"Mona Lisa!" they said in unison.

"Pardon?" the Lady Lisa asked.

"Sorry, nothing," Kirk responded.

"Unfortunately," Da Vinci continued, "I fear the project is nota turning out as I 'ad hoped. I ama not satisfied with it, and although the Lady Lisa believes it to be a fine painting . . ."

"I do, most earnestly," the Lady Lisa said.

"I ama not a sure that I shall finish it," Da Vinci completed his sentence.

Prester and Kirk looked at each other again, and then both looked at Leonardo.

"Finish it," they said in unison.

"Do you thinka so? Well, I shall give it somea more consideration. Meanwhile, to more urgent matters," Da Vinci said, changing the subject. "What isa this I hear about King Louis planning to burn Florence?"

"He's double crossed us," Prester said.

"Ah, most unfortunate, but it is the nature of politicians," Da Vinci said. "Perhaps in the future, things will nota be this way."

"Don't count on it," Kirk added.

"The King said he'd spare the city if Kirk stepped down," Prester said. "But now he says he will destroy it anyway."

"I have never trusted Louis," Da Vinci said. "You shoulda not 'ave attempted to strike a bargain with him. Moreover, he has designs ona hanging the two of you as well, so I understand. Well, this is a treacherous business. How can I help?"

Da Vinci stared at Prester, expecting the answer if there was one to come from him. Kirk too shot Prester a pleading stare.

"The King will be leaving here at dawn to march on Florence," Prester said. "If there were only some way to warn Florence, some way to tell them to send their soldiers here, tonight, perhaps they could surround Louis' men and take them by surprise.

"Yes, I was thinking exactly that," Da Vinci said with a grin.

"But is there enough time?" Kirk asked.

"I don't think so," Prester answered. "A rider would have to be dispatched to Florence with instructions to bring the army at once. There's no way he could get to Florence and get the army back here in time to surprise Louis' troops."

"You are quite right," Da Vinci said. "Which is why I senta word to Florence three hours ago."

Prester looked at Da Vinci with amazement, and then looked at the window.

"You," he said. "The flashes. It is Morse code."

"Not exactly," Da Vinci said. "Halifax told me of this Morse code, but this is a signal language of my own a design. I combined the ideas of this man Morse with those of another man, a Signore Benjamin Franklin, whom Halifax told me invented a firebox. I simply replaced one wall of the firebox with a shutter device that could be opened and closed as desired. After that, ita was simply a matter of training several of my apprentices in the details. Also, I had to set up a system of firebox signals within visible range ofa each other throughout the region, which I did some weeks ago. In any case, Florentine troops shoulda be completely surrounding Louis' army by morning. The Swiss, I think, will not fight once they see our soldiers lining every hilltop. They are only mercenaries after all, and for them fighting is simply a matter of money."

"Did you say, 'should' be surrounding Louis' army?" Kirk asked with sudden concern.

Da Vinci shrugged his shoulders and turned up both palms.

"It is a full moon," he said, "and our troops know this country very well, although it will be difficult for them to move at night. Still, there is I think a good chance of success."

"Now it's just a good chance?" Kirk asked.

"A very good chance, I would say," Da Vinci added. "But there is no need for you to take chances. You botha need to come with us now. I will show you the way out. You should not be here when they come for you ina the morning."

"Let's go," Kirk said, moving toward the secret passageway. Prester, however, remained still. "What?" Kirk said, stopping short. "What's the matter?"

"We can't go," Prester said.

"Sure we can," Kirk responded, "right through this hole in the wall. Come on."

"If we're not here when they come for us, they'll know something is up," Prester pointed out. "They'll assume we have escaped and have headed back to Florence to warn them."

"So what?" Kirk asked.

"We'll lose the element of surprise. Don't you see? Our only chance of stopping them, of stopping Florence from being burned to the ground, is if Louis is taken completely by surprise. We have to stay."

Da Vinci looked down as if in deep thought.

"Stay?" Kirk balked. "To get hanged?"

"He isa right," Da Vinci said. "If you are nota both here in the morning when they come for you, alla hope for Florence is lost."

"Now wait a minute," Kirk said. "They wanted to throw me to the wolves. They tried to buy their lives with mine, and I agreed to it. But it didn't work out. Is that my fault?"

"Your fault?" Prester asked. "No, certainly not. But it is your opportunity. If we leave now, Florence and all her treasures, art, statuary, architecture, will be lost to the world forever. But if we stay, we just may be able to save her."

"And we may get our necks stretched in the process," Kirk replied.

"We may," Prester agreed.

Kirk and Prester looked at each other for what seemed like an eternity. Finally, Kirk sat down.

"A good chance, you think?" he said to Leonardo.

"A very gooda chance, I do believe," Da Vinci said.

"Well then, get out of here before they bust in on us," Kirk said.

Da Vinci looked at the young man and smiled.

"I believe I should one day like to paint you," Da Vinci said.

"Yeah, well, I'm pretty well already painted into a corner as it is," Kirk replied.

"God bless you both," the Lady Lisa said, and then kissed each of them on the cheek. A moment later, she and Da Vinci were gone, disappearing once again behind the moving bookcase.

Chapter 36

The tops of the hills that surrounded La Villa Rotunda had yet to catch the first glimpse of the approaching dawn when Prester, looking through the window, saw the King enter the still darkened courtyard.

"Kirk," Prester said without looking around.

The young man, slumped across an armchair, rolled clumsily over and buried his face in a cushion.

"Five more minutes," Kirk mumbled. "Just five more minutes."

"Get up."

Outside, several soldiers bearing torches entered the courtyard. A horse whinnied, and Kirk stirred.

"Kirk," Prester said again.

Just then, three sharp and loud raps at the door shook them both.

"Okay, okay," Kirk exclaimed. "I'm up."

The door opened, and in walked four Swiss mercenaries in full battle gear. Behind them was the Lady Lisa. She looked pale and tired, as if she had not slept, yet full of nervous energy.

"The King has left it to me to inform you," she said, her voice cracking with emotion, "to please come at once to the courtyard."

Prester and Kirk looked at her for any clue that the plan of the previous night had borne fruit, but their pleading eyes were met only with a worried gaze of uncertainty.

"*Allez, allez,*" one of the guards said, motioning with his sword for them to go.

"Is everything all right, Lady Lisa?" Prester inquired.

The Lady Lisa met his eyes, but said nothing.

"*Allez*," the soldier insisted again.

Lady Lisa left the room. Prester and Kirk followed after her, and were directed toward the main entrance. They emerged from the house just as King Louis was mounting his white steed.

"*Ah oui, bonjour*," he called to them as he threw over his right leg and took hold of the pommel of the saddle. "Good av' you to join us at such an early a'ware. With your pear-mission, we would like to get sta'ted right away. My men and I, you see, a' in a great hurry this morning to set off for Florencia. It should be, I think, a glorious day."

Armed Swiss soldiers were now streaming into the still dark courtyard, the light of multiple torches reflecting yellow and orange off their silver armor. Just beyond where the King sat astride his horse, two men were tossing a pair of thick ropes over a large branch of the courtyard oak tree. One end of each rope was tied to the trunk. Each was then looped up over the thick branch so that the ropes ended in two perfectly formed hangman's nooses that swung some ten feet off the ground.

"The prisoners," the King shouted, "make them ready." Several soldiers grabbed Prester and Kirk by the arms, pinning them behind their backs, and tied them by their wrists. Two horses were then brought forward, and each man was hoisted up onto their respective saddles. To avoid a sudden leap from their mounts, soldiers remained on either side of the horses. The two condemned men were led to the tree and the hangman's nooses.

"It is a shem'," the King added, "that you will not be eer to see what appends to your precious city."

"You don't have to do this," Prester said as one of the nooses was placed around his neck and cinched up tight.

"You a' quite right," the King agreed. "But you see, I want to do it."

"Why?" Kirk shouted, trying to twist his neck away from the persistent efforts of the would-be hangmen. "Why kill us? And why destroy Florence? They said they would surrender to you. What more do you want?"

"*Ah, oui*, a good que-shion. What more do I want? The an'ser eez, I want them to suf-air. I want them to fear me. I want all of Italy to fear me. That is the shur-east way to pow-wear, no?"

"Those are Machiavelli's words," Kirk barked. "But he's wrong, do you hear me? Dead wrong! Sure, you can kill us. We don't count for much. But Florence, my God, you can't do it. Florence is a special place. If you burn her, you gain nothing, nothing but the lasting hatred of everyone throughout history. People will hate you now and for the next 500 years. The name of Louis will be spit on and cursed like the Roman Emperor, Nero, who burned down Rome, or like Judas Iscariot himself. And your ancestors will live in shame forever. You will lose your place in history. Is that what you want?"

When Kirk was finished, King Louis sat for a few moments weighing the words in his mind.

"You speak well, young Prince, an' maybe there eez truth in what you say. But in the end, I think, we must leeve for our own time, for that eez all that we can do. History, I suppose, must be left for the few-chair."

As the King's words left his lips, the sun at last crested above the surrounding hills and streamed brightly into the valley.

"Proceed," the King ordered. Two Swiss mercenaries took hold of the horses upon which Prester and Kirk sat. They began to pull them forward, tightening the hanging ropes. Then abruptly they stopped.

"Continue," the King ordered. "What a' you doing? Continue, I say."

Despite the direct order, the Swiss soldiers remained still.

"What eez the mat-air with all of you," the King shouted. "Ave you seen a ghost?"

"Not a ghost, your majesty," Prester said from atop his horse.

"Then what eez eet?" the King shouted as he turned his head to follow the collective upward gaze of his soldiers.

Standing shoulder to shoulder on every crest, brow and summit of the hills surrounding the valley, were the armed men of the Florentine citizen militia. In stark black silhouette set off against the bright rising sun, their horses, swords and spears were sharply outlined against the new day. They numbered a thousand strong. They held the upper ground and had the upper hand, and all who observed them knew it.

"Sacre bleu!" the King's valet wheezed, and then lit out toward the cover of the nearby woods. In similar fashion, the two Swiss mercenaries dropped the reins of the horses they were pulling and began waving their arms as if to call off any further proceedings.

"*Non, non. Nous avons termine,*" they shouted at the King while continuing to wave their arms. "*Termine, termine.*"

All around the courtyard, Swiss soldiers one by one began to disarm. They unbuckled their corsalets of leather, detached their armor, removed their iron helmets, and dropped their swords, spears and muskets to the ground. Across the open field, where the bulk of the Swiss mercenary force had bivouacked, the sound of clanking metal being thrown off began to build. The sound made Prester think of popcorn kernels over an open flame. Then, *en masse,* and with a suddenness of purpose, the mercenary soldiers of the army of King Louis of France began to walk away. They walked out of the dale in all directions at once, dispersing from the would-be field of battle. They would have had to defend the low ground against the onslaught of a downhill attack on all sides at once. Their strategic position had been completely and foolishly compromised by a false sense of security. They would have been given no advantage while giving their opponents every advantage. It was a battle they were bound to lose, and so they left. They headed for their homes, every last man jack of them. They were, after all, soldiers of fortune. They were in the employ of King Louis merely for personal profit, and the scales of profit and loss now tilted against them. So they dropped their weapons, and walked away.

King Louis was arrested, along with Machiavelli, and it was decided by Leonardo Bruni, Captain of the Florentine citizen military contingent, that they should be returned to Florence to face charges. Bruni was not the most experienced Florentine soldier on the field. He had, however, drafted the plan for the reintroduction of a citizen militia after the mercenary system had fallen into disfavor in Florence upon the death of

Lorenzo the Magnificent. Upon the adoption of his plan, he had been named commander of the regiment.

Also arrested was Piero de Medici, son of Il Magnifico. Piero had taken no part in the planned destruction of Florence, yet it was upon the strength of his financial backing that King Louis had set forth on his adventure of conquest. It would now be for the Florentine people to decide the fate of these misguided men.

The prisoners were placed on horseback for the return journey to Florence. Each horse and horseman were secured together by a rope that ran from the bit and bridle of the lead horse, through the tied hands of the rider, and back to the next horse and rider in line. No rider could attempt to break free from the others so long as the rope remained secure.

Following behind the three prisoners, Prester and Kirk rode together in the same carriage that had originally carried them to the Villa Rotunda. Riding in the coach with them, having decided to return to his studio to complete work on his latest portrait, were Leonardo da Vinci and the Lady Lisa.

As the carriage rolled through the countryside, its occupants, relieved and exhausted, rode in silence. Kirk and Prester had closed their eyes to snatch a bit of rest if they could, while Da Vinci was busy scribbling out a new thought on saddle design.

The Lady Lisa, meanwhile, stared out the window. She was dressed in a gown of green and white silk, and carried a macramé fan with which she attempted to cool herself from the dry heat of the road.

"Is there not an annual fair to be soon commenced in Florence?" she asked dreamily, breaking the silence. "It is a hardship to live so long in the country. I do not often chance to attend such events, but should very much like to."

"Ah, witha regret, signora," Da Vinci said from below his velvet red cap replete with ostrich feather, "you refer to the festival of the Fochi di San Giovanni which isa held every June 24th. I am afraid that we have missed it by a week."

"Truly?" the Lady Lisa asked.

"Regrettably, yes my lady," Da Vinci said as soothingly as he could.

"I am sorry to hear this. I would have liked to purchase silks if they were available."

"Fear not, my lady," Da Vinci said. "Florence isa rich with silk vendors. There are many shops where you will find the finest silks spun from the purest thread cultivated from the most excellent worms of the best mulberry trees in all Tuscany."

Da Vinci leaned his head out of the carriage window and shouted up to the driver.

"Gregory."

"Si, Senor Da Vinci," the driver shouted back.

"Dove e il miglior negozio di seta a Firenze?" Da Vinci shouted. "I am asking him for the best silk shop in all Florence," he repeated to the passengers inside.

"L'Antico Setificio sul Via de' Tessitori," the driver shouted back without hesitation.

"Yes, yes, I believe Gregory is correct," Da Vinci said, pulling his head back in. "The Old Silk Factory on the street of weavers has a very good reputation. Gregory isa seldom wrong about sucha things."

"Thank you," the Lady Lisa said. "I shall to this shop go to see for myself their silks."

"What is this festival you mentioned, the Fochi di San Giovanni?" Prester asked after another bumpy silence.

"The Feast of Saint John the Baptist," Kirk said. "They hold it every year."

"Every June 24th," Da Vinci added. "There is a granda parade through the center of the city, followed by a Calcio Storico match in front of the Basilica of Santa Croce."

"Calcio Storico?" Prester asked.

"It is a game played by the aristocratic young noblemen of the city," Da Vinci explained. "The players, they come from all the different districts of the city. Each district dresses up ina different colored costumes. There isa blue for the Santa Croce team, and red for the boys of Santa Maria Novella, and white for Santa Spirito . . ."

"And green for Santa Giovanni," Kirk completed the list.

"What are the rules?" Prester asked.

Kirk and Leonardo da Vinci looked at each other.

"I don't think there are any rules," Kirk said.

"There musta be rules," Da Vinci countered. "It is played thusly. Sand is laid upon the entire square, and the players, they run with a red and white ball in their hands. They pass the ball to their fellow players asa they go, while the opposing team tries to pin them down."

"Sure, sure, but what is the point of it all?" Kirk asked. "I've never understood how a team actually wins."

Da Vinci looked puzzled. "There must be some method by which success is determined," he said. "I can tella you this. At the end of eacha match, the standard bearer of the winning squad, he runs around the square waving his team's flag. The losing team, meanwhile, sits downcast upon the dirt. This much I know. But how they counta the score, I cannot say as I have never been temperate enough at the end of the festivities to have taken notice."

Prester smiled and returned his gaze to the road. As they approached Florence, the olive tree and rose garden archway came into sight. Swiveling his head inward, Prester looked at Da Vinci.

"When did you say that festival is held?"

"Annually," Da Vinci responded.

"But when? What day of the year?"

"As I say, it is held on June the 24th of each year."

"Always on the 24th of June?"

"Certainly, without fail."

Prester stared at him a moment as if calculating some equation in his head.

"But didn't you say, that is, I thought you said the festival was held a week ago."

"Seven days exactly," Da Vinci confirmed.

Again Prester stared at Leonardo as if seeing him for the first time.

"What's up, Mr. John?" Kirk asked.

"You seema troubled, my friend," Da Vinci observed.

Reaching into his waistcoat, Prester withdrew the cylindrical mechanical calculating device that Halifax had given him to determine and keep track of the days, months and years. Twisting the dials that surrounded the central cylinder, and lining them up as required, he confirmed his calculation.

"July the first. Today is July the first," Prester repeated. "Can that be right?"

"Gregory," Da Vinci shouted up to the driver again. *"Qual e la data?"*

"E' il primo giorno di Luglio."

"Gregory tells me that it is indeed the first day of July," Da Vinci confirmed.

"Gregory," Prester muttered to himself. "Good God, of course," he shouted. "Gregory, stop the carriage, stop the carriage."

"What is it?" Kirk asked.

"We have to hurry," Prester said. "I think we're going home."

Chapter 37

"What has happened?" the Lady Lisa asked, not accustomed to shouting.

"Pope Gregory XIII, that's what happened, don't you see?" Prester shouted again. "No, of course not. It hasn't happened yet. But it will, it will. Pope Gregory XIII will set it all straight."

"My friend, please, you shoulda calm down. Have a drink of water. You are delirious," Da Vinci cautioned as the carriage pulled to a stop. "There is no Pope Gregory XIII. The last Gregory was the Venetian Pope Gregory XII during the time of the Great Schism nearly a hundred years ago."

"No, no, I'm fine, Leonardo. I'm fine. Listen to me. The Church uses the Julian calendar, isn't that right? The calendar created by Julius Caesar in 46 B.C.?"

"Yes, sure, what other calendar shoulda it use?" Da Vinci answered.

"The Julian calendar has 365 days in the year, plus an extra day every fourth year, right? So on average one year of the Julian calendar is 365 and one quarter days long."

"Yes, that is exactly correct," Da Vinci responded with increasing interest in what Prester was saying.

"And they've been using that calendar for, what, almost 1500 years now."

"Justa so," Da Vinci said.

"You of all people, Leonardo, must be aware of the problem," Prester said.

Da Vinci nodded his understanding.

"Yes, you are quitea right," he said. "I have done my own calculations on this subject. I have compared the Julian calendar with the
observable seasons of the solar cycle."

"And there is a problem, isn't there?" Prester asked.

"Most certainly there is," Da Vinci concurred.

"What problem?" Kirk asked. "What are you talking about?"

"The length of one actual solar year," Prester continued, "is not
really 365 and one quarter days, is it?"

"It is not," Da Vinci responded. "The precise measurement is 365
days, 5 hours and 49 minutes. Thus, the true solar year is approximately
11 minutes shorter than that ascribed to the Julian calendar."

"Eleven minutes?" the Lady Lisa interjected. "This is not so much
a problem."

"It's not a problem if you're only talking about one year," Prester
pointed out, "but over 1500 years, it starts to add up."

"It isa true," Leonardo said. "By mya calculations, this extra eleven
minutes eacha year gives the calendar two and a halfa more days every
four hundred years. The calendar hasa now lost its intended relationship
to solar events. Did you know, for example, that Easter wasa fixed by the
First Council at Nicaea in the year 325 to occur on the 21st day of March.
But now, the vernal equinox by which Easter isa determined occurs nearer
to the 11th or the 12th of March. Many ina the Church see this as a problem."

"Couldn't they just come up with a more accurate calendar?" Kirk
spoke up.

"They did," Prester said. "That is, they will. Pope Gregory XIII will
commission the creation of a more accurate calendar in the year 1582."

"That's, what, 87 years from now?" Kirk asked.

"Exactly. It will be called the Gregorian calendar, and it will fix the
problems of the Julian sliding days. But to make up for the extra time
accumulated over 1500 years, the Pope will make a simple but dramatic
alteration to the calendar for the year 1582. He will cut out ten days and
throw them away."

"Throw away days?" the Lady Lisa asked. "This is, I think, not a
good thing. We have so little time as it is."

"Of course! A simple adjustment," Da Vinci said. "I should have thought of it myself."

"Right. In that year, Pope Gregory XIII will ordain that when people go to sleep on October 4th, they will wake up on October 15th."

"He can do that?" Kirk asked.

"He did do that, or I should say he will."

Da Vinci began to laugh. "This will, I suspect, cause many difficulties. The people will object to having their lives shortened by papal decree. Servants will no doubt demand their monthly pay while their masters will refuse to compensate them for ten days nota worked. Oh, I should like to live to see it."

"How does this all affect us?" Kirk asked.

"We've been using the Julian calendar, don't you see?" Prester explained. "That was our mistake, my mistake. I should have realized it sooner. By the Julian calendar, it is July the 1st, a full ten days past the summer solstice, ten days too late for us to return home. You see, I thought we had missed it."

"But by this Gregorian calendar you speak of," Da Vinci interrupted, "this more accurate calendar that you say will not exist for another 87 years, it is nota the 1st day of July at all, is it? It isa ten days earlier."

"Exactly," Prester said. "Today is June 21st, the actual June 21st, the day of the summer solstice. Today is the day we can go home to our own time. We haven't missed it. It's not too late."

The Lady Lisa, having listened as carefully as she could manage, now arched her eyebrows to new heights and grasped Da Vinci's hand.

"Leonardo," she said. "It is, I think, too late. He has gone mad."

"No, my dear," Da Vinci reassured her. "He is not mad at all. He is quite sane." Da Vinci smiled and looked at Prester for permission to speak the truth.

"Go ahead," Prester said. "Tell her who we are."

"Do we not already know this?" the Lady Lisa asked.

"I shall explain it all once we reacha my studio," Da Vinci said, "but you musta promise to keepa the secret."

"Oh, a secret," the Lady Lisa said. "I enjoy secrets. Nothing shall pass my lips. If anyone asks me about it, I shall simply smile and say nothing."

"We don't have much time," Prester said, recalculating the dates and times on the Halifax device. "Kirk, are you ready?"

Kirk stared first at Prester, and then at Leonardo da Vinci and the Lady Lisa. He reached out and shook hands with each of them.

"Lady Lisa, it's been a pleasure to meet you. I just wish I had a camera. And Leonardo, it has been a genuine honor."

"Thank you, my Prince," Da Vinci said. "But the honor has been mine."

"Be sure to finish that portrait," Prester interjected. "It'll be a real hit."

"You are too kind," Da Vinci said. "Wait just a moment. I have something for you."

Pulling a large piece of parchment from his portfolio, Da Vinci laid it across his lap. On the paper, Da Vinci had drawn in charcoal a rough yet elegant sketch of Prester staring out the carriage window. Taking up his charcoal again, he now signed his name in the bottom right corner, writing backwards with his left hand, *"odranoeL."* He handed the drawing to Prester.

"I shall treasure it," Prester said, rolling the paper and tucking it into his belt.

Prester and Kirk got out of the carriage and closed the door behind them.

"Gregory," Da Vinci shouted up to the driver, *"a Firenze."*

The coach started up again, lurching forward as the driver snapped his whip above the backs of the horses. A few moments later, Leonard da Vinci, the woman whom the world would come to know as the Mona Lisa, Nicolo Machiavelli, King Louis XII of France, Piero de Medici and the soldiers accompanying them all, moved beyond a turn in the road and were out of sight. Prester and Kirk, now alone, walked toward the garden archway and the olive tree that they hoped would convey them home.

"I don't understand something," Kirk said as they made their way along.

"What's that?"

"You told me that Halifax built his calculating device based on the ideas of Sir Isaac Newton?"

"That's how he explained it to me."

"But Newton lived in the 1600's, didn't he?"

"Yes. He died in 1727 at the age of 85."

"So Gregory had already been Pope, right?"

"That's right," Prester confirmed.

"Then why does the Halifax device give you Julian time and not Gregorian time?"

"Ah, I was wondering whether you'd notice that little paradox. It shows you're thinking like an historian."

Prester smiled as he and Kirk followed a brick walkway down a slope toward the rose garden. They took up positions next to the olive tree.

"Rest one hand on the trunk," Prester said. "We should only have a few minutes until the solstice."

Each man laid an open palm upon the trunk of the ancient olive tree.

"Now, very importantly," Prester instructed, "we must close our eyes. Remember, no one may observe the phenomena of trans-temporal equilibrium if it is to work. Do you understand?"

"Sure."

"This is critical, Kirk, absolutely critical."

"Yeah, yeah, I get it. I'm not an idiot."

"I never thought you were," Prester assured him.

With one hand each upon the tree, the two stood facing away from each other and waited.

"So?" Kirk asked.

"Hum?"

"So why does the Halifax calculator give you Julian time rather than Gregorian time?"

"Politics," Prester said.

"Politics?"

"Newton was English, right? Well, Protestant England didn't much like the Catholic Pope telling them what to do. So when Pope Gregory ordained the new Gregorian calendar in 1582, the English simply ignored it."

"You mean, England decided to stick with the Julian calendar even though it was wrong?"

"Yes, as did their American colonies at the time. That's why Newton's calculations were based on the old style calendar. Their stubbornness didn't last, of course. They finally came around."

"When?"

"A hundred and seventy years later. It wasn't until 1752 that England and its colonies caught up with the rest of the world. In fact, if you had asked George Washington in 1751 when his birthday was, he would have told you he was born on February the 11th. But if you asked him again the following year, after the Gregorian adjustment, he would have said he was born on February the 22nd."

"Maybe someday I will ask him," Kirk quipped.

"One never knows," Prester said as he looked up at the sun. "Eyes closed, Kirk. It should be any moment now."

"Ciao," came the sudden voice of a child. Prester looked around. There, watching them from the ridge overlooking the small garden was the same little boy who had pointed the way to Florence upon his arrival.

"This isn't good," Prester announced.

"Hey kid," Kirk yelled, "go away, would ya? Get outta here, scram, skedaddle."

"*Lo voglio giocare, giocare,*" the boy said.

"I think he wants to play," Kirk said.

"We've got to get rid of him. It won't work if he's watching us."

Kirk picked up a small handful of rocks and threw them in the direction of the child.

"Kid, take off, run away, go home to your mama," he shouted more loudly now, but still to no effect.

"*Giocare,*" the child shouted back.

"We're out of time, Kirk," Prester said. "We've got to get rid of him right now."

"Hey kid, beat it," Kirk shouted now as loudly as he could. "Go fly a kite or something."

Prester withdrew from his belt the rolled up parchment drawing that Da Vinci had given him. Folding the paper once, and then twice, and then three times lengthwise, he quickly fashioned a large paper airplane. With one quick stride and a forward thrust of his arm, Prester sent the winged gossamer sailing into the air.

Upward it went, catching the breeze and wafting further and further above the rose garden. The young boy watched in amazement, following each dip and swoop intently, for he had never seen a toy of this design. Around and around it went, circling back upon itself, and dancing with each puff of the gentle wind before finally crashing against the top of the stone archway. The boy ran to retrieve it. He grasped it and held it high above his head.

"*Volo, volo,*" he shouted triumphantly as he turned back toward the olive tree. But his playmates were gone.

Chapter 38

Manhattan Island, New York

Annie dressed in a simple white blouse, classic gray two-button suit jacket and matching knee-length skirt. Standing off to one side, she looked at the podium with its multiple microphones already in place, and at the press corps still assembling in the room. There would likely be questions directed at her, she had been told by the Director. After all, it was she who had discovered the most recent peculiarity. Standing to her right, looking as if she were about to cry, was Mrs. Trumbull, and to her right, Trace Gilmore, looking more amused than worried.

The members of the press looked tired, she thought. She recognized some of their faces from their occasional news spots on local television. Milling about in their rumpled overcoats, they drank steaming coffee from paper cups and waited for the press conference to begin.

"Does Brennan know it's Sunday morning?" the field reporter from Tri-State Channel 12 News quipped, but no one responded. They all appeared to be preoccupied, as if already mentally preparing for their on-air time. They probably thought they'd be reporting on some new senior staff appointment, or the opening of a new exhibit. They probably thought this would be just another routine assignment. Well, hold onto your hats, Annie thought. We're about to shock the world.

Above and behind the podium, the clock already read 10:05 AM

"They've begun in Paris," Annie whispered to Mrs. Trumbull. "Where is he?" Mrs. Trumbull offered no response, but her tired eyes began to well up with tears all the more.

Just then, Director Brennan entered through a door at the back of the room and made his way through the gaggle of reporters to the microphones. He squared himself up to the podium, eyes downcast, and waited for the noise to subside. The room grew quiet.

"I'd like to get started right away," he said, looking up.

"God bless us and save us," Mrs. Trumbull muttered from the sidelines as she made the sign of the cross.

"An event has recently occurred," Brennan began his remarks, "that is, well, unparalleled in the long history of the Metropolitan Museum of Art. As you know, we here at the Metropolitan care very deeply about the integrity of our institution, and work daily and diligently to protect that integrity. What is more, our commitment to security is unsurpassed by any artistic institution in the world. We have always prided ourselves on keeping safe the great treasures that we have been privileged to collect, all so that we may continue to share them with the public."

With these words, Mrs. Trumbull could no longer control her emotions. Breaking down into tears and sobs, she withdrew a handkerchief from her sleeve and dabbed her eyes as she stepped from the room, departing through a small door behind the podium. As she did so, Annie noticed that the press corps was suddenly listening.

"Changes have been occurring in the museum," the Director continued, "subtle changes, to be sure, but distinct, definite changes, changes that we cannot explain." With this short introduction to the topic, the Director fell silent as if unable to find the words to explain further. The reporters looked at each other, and then back at the Director.

"Look, Mr. Brennan, you got to give us something to go on here," the Channel 12 reporter said. "What are you talking about? What changes?"

"Changes to the paintings, of course," Brennan said. "Was I unclear about that? Yes, the paintings. That's what I'm referring to."

"Changes to the paintings?" a petite female reporter from WPRX jumped in. "You mean, vandalism?"

"No, no," Brennan said, "well, of a sort, but no, not vandalism per se."

"Then what?" the female reporter asked again.

"What I'm saying is that the paintings have been changing."

"I don't get it," the Channel 12 reporter spoke up again. "Paintings don't change. They're paintings. So what are you saying?"

"I realize it is difficult to grasp, and we do not fully understand the phenomenon ourselves. But nonetheless it is a fact. Our paintings are changing, and the time has come to bring all of you in on what is happening. We cannot, indeed we should not, keep this a secret any longer."

The press corps to a person began to smirk as if realizing that they had been put on.

"Okay, okay, Mr. Director," the Channel 12 reporter spoke up again. "It's Sunday morning. We're all here. Obviously you want to gin up our interest by making out like there's something mysterious going on here at the museum. We get it. So what's this really all about?"

The Director sighed, and looked over at Annie who shrugged.

"Perhaps the best way to explain this is to simply show you what I'm talking about," he said. He turned to Annie again. "Would you please bring them in?"

"Yes, sir," Annie said.

The small door behind the podium popped open, and Mrs. Trumbull darted in.

"Mr. Brennan, Mr. Brennan," she stammered.

"Ah, Mrs. Trumbull, I was just asking that the paintings be brought in."

"Mr. Brennan," she repeated herself, "Paris is calling."

"Paris?"

"Yes, sir," she said, "Marcel Moreau."

"Well, ah, tell him I'll call him back. Tell him I'm in the middle of our press conference."

"He knows that, sir. He said to tell you to stop immediately and come to the phone right away."

"Now? What does he want?"

"He said . . . oh God bless us and save us."

"He said what?"

"The Mona Lisa is smiling again."

The Director stared at her in disbelief as the press corps began to inch closer.

"What's this all about?" the reporter from Channel 12 demanded.

"What's the story here?" the petite journalist from WPRX shouted.

Brennan turned around to face them, and raised his hands in the air as if calming wild horses about to bolt.

"Give me a moment, ladies and gentlemen," he said. "I promise I'll be back with you shortly."

"What's going on?" another reporter chimed in.

"What are you hiding?" came yet another voice from the back of the herd.

As question after question from the press corps began to buffet him like the stinging mist of a sea storm, the Director stood his ground. He did not want to commit to any one course of action.

"Annie," Brennan said, looking over at her. "Go get the paintings."

Annie dashed off through the open doorway and disappeared. A few moments later, she returned. In each hand, she grasped a painting by its frame. Thrusting the 'Portrait of a Young Man' at the Director, she tried to catch her breath.

"It's the original," she gasped, "the way it was."

The Director grabbed the painting, held it up in front of him, and looked it over thoroughly. It was indeed the original 'Portrait of a Young Man,' artist unknown. The figure in the painting was in his early twenties, brown eyes, straight unbroken Roman nose, dressed in a collar with a red fur-trimmed tunic. The changes to the painting that had existed the night before were now gone.

Grabbing the second framed painting from Annie's hand, the 'Madonna and Child with Saints,' Brennan saw that it too had returned to its original condition. The paper airplane that had been evident in the hands of one of the angels was no longer there.

"They're back," Annie said. "All of them."

"Are you sure?" Brennan asked.

"I'm sure. They're all back," she said.

Turning toward the podium, the Director held up his hands to quiet the crowd. The gaggle of reporters fell silent, waiting for an explanation. Finally, the Director spoke.

"E. M. Forster once said that works of art are the only objects in the material universe to possess internal order." The Director looked at the confused expressions before him. "He was wrong. Thank you for coming."

Chapter 39

A door slammed shut.

Prester, as if awaking from a dream, looked around him. He was in a room. There was a couch and a side table with an electrical lamp. Duck hunting paintings hung on the walls. Turning to his right, he saw Kirk sitting on the floor. Kirk was a teenager again, thin and wiry, as he had been before he had vanished.

"It would appear we're back where we started," Prester said.

"Guess so," Kirk responded as he rose to his feet.

"Are you all right?" Prester asked.

Kirk touched his hands to his face, nose and lips.

"I'm still all in one piece, I guess."

The office door opened, and a man wearing a suit and tie looked in.

"One more thing," the man said. Prester and Kirk stared at a familiar face they had not seen for a very long time, Principal Beem. "Perhaps we ought not bother the senior Mr. Renzo with this," the Principal continued, "unless it is absolutely necessary. Understood? Good, good. Then I'll leave you two alone. Um, try not to let the door slam when you leave, will you? I'm getting it fixed next week. Oh, and be careful of the Queen Anne." He closed the door as he left.

Kirk and Prester stared at the closed door.

"Like nothin' ever happened," Kirk said.

"He never changes, does he," Prester observed.

"Good old Balanced Beem," Kirk said.

"So," Prester said, looking at Kirk, "what did happen?"

"I don't know," Kirk said, shaking his head. "But we're here now."

"So we are. I think maybe you and I should sit and talk about this before we do anything else."

"Let me get my feet on the ground first," Kirk said as he absent-mindedly sat on the armrest of the Queen Anne chair. Suddenly, the armrest cracked under his weight, pitching him forward hard against the coffee table.

"Aaah!" Kirk shouted.

"Ouch!" Prester reacted. "Are you all right?"

"Yeah, yeah," Kirk said as his nose began to bleed. Prester handed him a handkerchief.

"Unbelievable. After everything that's happened," Prester grinned, "to be done in by a Queen Anne chair."

Just then, the door opened again and a teenage girl peeked in.

"Oh, I'm sorry," she said. "I was told that Principal Beem wanted to see me."

"He's not here just now," Prester said.

"Oh, okay. Well, bye." Just as she left the room and closed the door, the familiar sound of the class bell rang out.

"I guess I'd better get to class," Kirk said, standing up again.

"Class, of course. But we should discuss what happened."

"Sure thing, Mr. J," Kirk said. "We'll discuss it later. But right now, I'm kinda anxious to get back, believe it or not."

"I don't know what to believe," Prester said. "Go. I'll see you in class."

Kirk crossed the room as if walking on a rolling deck, opened the door and left the room. Prester watched him go, and then turned to look at the office in which he found himself. Sitting near a table was his familiar leather valise. Crossing to it, he opened the valise and removed his father's antique mahogany box. He laid it upon the table and lifted the lid. There, displayed on red velvet cloth, were both of Lorenzo's daggers.

—⁓—

A short time later, Prester stood before his students as they shuffled toward their seats. In the back row right, Kirk sat smiling. Next to him whispering in his ear about her plans to apply for an internship at the Metropolitan Museum of Art was the redhead Annie Sage.

"HISTORY!" Prester began, causing the class to drop into silence. "What is it really?"

As anticipated, there was no response from the class. Then, subtly at first, but with an increasing intensity, Kirk began to laugh. His laughter grew louder and louder, and as it grew tears began to well up in his eyes. Annie soon became infected and began laughing along with him as did several other students. Within a few moments, the entire class was in hysterics.

"What is history?" Prester smiled and shouted again over the cacophony. Kirk wiped his tears away and looked up.

"It's us," he chuckled.

Epilogue

Saint-Rémy-de-Provence, France – 1514

"How old was he?" Suzette asked as they quietly pushed open the door to the dead man's room. She was twelve years old, and wore her hair in pigtails.

"I don't know," Michel responded. Only ten, he was determined to show that he was not afraid. "They say he was very old."

"And he died here, in this very room?" Suzette asked.

"Right there in that bed," Michel answered.

"I don't think we should be here," the girl said, hesitating near the door.

"It's all right," Michel assured her. "No one will know."

"What did he die of?" the girl asked.

"Die of?"

"Was it a disease?"

"No," Michel said. "He was just old, I think."

The boy walked closer to the deathbed and touched the curtains that still hung from the canopy.

"What did they call him? What was his name?" the little girl asked.

"They called him Halifax," the boy answered. "They say he knew Leonardo da Vinci."

"Who?"

"Have you never heard of Leonardo da Vinci?"

"I don't think so," the girl answered.

"Well, I have. He is just the most famous man in the world, that's all. He is very old now, of course. They say the dead man was his friend. That's what they say."

"What if it was contagious?"

"What?"

"Whatever it was the man died of. What if it was contagious? Aren't you afraid, Michel?"

"I'm not afraid," he said. "I'm going to be a physician when I grow up."

"Well, I don't think we should be here," the little girl said again.

"I just want to look around," the boy replied.

"We're going to get in trouble," she warned.

"No, we won't," he assured her.

Moving around the room, the boy began to pull open the drawers of a dusty vanity.

"You shouldn't be doing that, Michel. We're going to get caught."

The boy just smiled, confident that she was becoming ever more impressed with his feat of courage.

"Michel," she warned again in a staccato whisper.

"Just another minute," he said as he dropped to his knees and peeked under the bed. Spying a large box, the boy stretched out his arm under the bed as far as he could.

"Michel, I'm going. I'm leaving right now," the girl spouted.

"Just one more minute," the boy said again, stretching even further under the bed. His little fingers groping for a hold, he caught the edge of the box and pulled it towards him.

"You better not open that box, Michel. You're really going to get it from your mother if she finds out."

"She won't find out," he said as he opened the box and looked inside.

"What's in there?" the girl asked, still clinging to the doorway.

"Just papers," the boy said. "Lots of papers and notebooks. These must have belonged to the dead man."

"I think you should put them back," the girl said.

"I want to read them," Michel reacted. "Who knows what they may say?"

He picked up a few pages and gave them a quick glance.

"What's wrong?" the girl said, seeing that he was disappointed.

"This is English writing, I think," he said.

"You can't read English. So put them back."

"I'm learning it in school," he said. "So you see? These will be good to study with."

"But it is stealing," the girl said.

"Not if he's already dead."

"I'm leaving before you get us in trouble," the girl said. "I'm leaving right now."

"So leave," the boy responded, now more interested in his newly discovered paper treasures than in her fickle opinion.

"Come on, Michel. Come on."

"In a minute," he replied.

"You better come right now, or I will tell your mother on you, Michel de Nostradamus."

"In a minute," he said again. "Give me time."

THE END

CPSIA information can be obtained
at www.ICGtesting.com
Printed in the USA
LVHW092150100419
613755LV00001B/318/P

3 1270 00850 6109